*For the dreamers and the daring,
whose spirits flicker in the shadows.
Never give up.*

The Bone God's Wrath

HELEEN DAVIES

THE BONE THIEF SAGA BOOK THREE

THE UND
TARTARUS
Pandemonium
The Shadow Court
Halls of Night
The Children of Night
The River of
Vile
Shadowhold
The White Mountain
The Waves of Nowhere
Deadfort
The Woods of No Return
The Flying Dutchman
Triple Wall of Bronze
Twilight Vault
THE BLACK SEA
We are all b

RLD
Heleen Davie
The Land of Dreams
hodel
ows
The River of Wailing
The Dragon's Tread
The Oracle of the Dead
Cave Town
Ashville Grove
The Elysian Fields
Cryptic Falls
Dreadhold
The Outskirts
Nevergate
The River of Forgetfulness
Vale of Mourning
Catterville
The Blood Court
Poseidon's Labyrinth
The Realm of the Nereids
The river of pain
Abyssum
Death
The Bone Court
The Compass of Destiny
Doom
Life
Charon
Story....
Salvation

TRIGGER WARNINGS

The Bone Thief Saga is a dark fantasy romance set in a brutal, morally grey world and some elements may be triggering for you.

PLEASE BE careful and take note of the following elements: *war, blood, gore, hand-to-hand combat, death, mentioning of rape, mentioning of suicide, domestic violence, graphic language, graphic violence, explicit sexual content, alcohol usage, grief.*

REVIEWS ARE CRUCIAL FOR INDIE AUTHORS

Thank you so much for reading and taking a chance on this series. Reviews are crucial for indie authors. If you could take a moment to share your thoughts on Amazon and/or Goodreads, or just leave a rating, it would mean the world to me! Thank you immensely! Here are the links for Amazon and Goodreads!

LOVE
Heleen

The Bone God's Wrath

HELEEN DAVIES

THE BONE THIEF SAGA BOOK THREE

PROLOGUE

There are screams everywhere.

Shattered glass. Blood. Fire.

The smell of death.

Chicago is gone.

I scribble down these words and cross my fingers that someone stumbles upon them and doesn't let the horror we went through fade away. Maybe we are insignificant, just some meal for the demons that roam our world, but with these letters, everyone will know that I lived.

That we lived.

All stories contain a kernel of truth, and now these dark creatures from the pit of our nightmares claw relentlessly at the frail barriers of our sanctuary.

They will destroy everything.

They are coming for us.

And they'll eat us, like they did with everyone else.

And now—

Unknown, written in blood on a wall in 1006 Elm Street, Chicago, IL 60601, found by officer Jeremy Johnson.

CHAPTER ONE
LYNNE

I landed on the ground of Englewood cemetery and vomited right onto a tombstone while Bory screamed my name in the background.

Biting back panic, I struggled to push myself up from the ground, my arms trembling and my breath coming in ragged gasps as I tried to erase the images burned into my mind, but they lingered like a festering wound.

I blocked out that the Blood Queen had sent us to the Topworld with her damn book.

I blocked out that Rio was gone, that he was asleep now, that he wasn't with me. Again.

I blocked out that we were all thrown into the Topworld like vermin.

I blocked out that I had once loved it with all that I had.

My stomach convulsed, and bile burned my throat as I doubled over to vomit once more. Sweat beaded on my forehead and dripped down my back as I gasped for air. My heart felt like it was about to burst out of my chest. This was rock bottom. This was it. This was my downfall.

"Lynne…" Bory hopped in front of my face, whispering and searching for my gaze.

And when he found it, he sucked in a deep breath.

In the cold, my body trembled uncontrollably, and dirt streaked my tear-stained cheeks. I never thought I could feel so broken, hurt, used, and betrayed all at once.

Looking away, I curled up and these damn tears welled up in my eyes again. Why did they take Rio away from me every single time? Why? Why couldn't we just be two mundane people fighting over trifles? Why was this life so skulling hard?

Bory's eyes narrowed as he let out a heavy sigh, his jaw clenched and his furry shoulders tense with hurt.

I finally noticed Ebony standing beside him, her arms crossed tightly over her chest and my gaze shifted to the group behind her—Any next to Mal and Ash with his hands shoved deep in his pockets. The tension was palpable.

We were all catapulted into the Topworld to save the world, but we had no plan how to. A desperate laughter bubbled up in my throat as I kept on wiping away the tears. We were nothing against the mess we were in. Nothing.

A sudden creaking noise made me startle.

We jumped like deer in the woods, surprised by a forester, but there was nothing to be found.

All was dark and—gods.

As I gazed out at the rows of tombstones, I saw it.

Everything was destroyed. My beautiful Topworld was… gone.

The resting place of the tombstones was disturbed, with scattered pieces of stone littering the ground, as someone had brutally ripped them. The once magnificent branches of the giant willow hung limply, as if struck by lightning. Not a single bush or tree showed signs of life, their barren twigs reaching towards the sky like bony fingers. And the grass beneath my feet was no longer vibrant green, but a deep shade of black that reminded me of the depths of the Underworld. Even the earth beneath it seemed to have turned to tar, seeping through visible cracks in the ground. It was as if all color and vitality had been drained from this place.

I flinched. This couldn't be true. No, not my beautiful Topworld! They took everything from me! Everything!

"No!" I cried out. "No!"

"Aria," Any said, stretching out a hand for me. "Come on, we have to go…"

I glanced at him, not understanding why he wasn't shocked, why he was so calm, but I just had no energy in me to fight it. Fight him. Fight everyone. And with shaky knees, I forced myself to stand up—without taking Any's hand. "W- who did this to my Topworld?" My throat constricted as my eyes still took in every piece of the cemetery that had been my haven over the last years.

"Look," Any said, touching my arm, his sudden closeness and the intensity of his touch making me jump. "We'll make it alright again, but we need to go. We need to do something against it, or the destruction will go on. We have to find the Omphalos Stone."

I just looked at him, my lips trembling, and said nothing.

Absolutely nothing.

I already knew we didn't have time to spare, but tell that to my nerves! It was impossible. I couldn't muster a step. My nerves paralyzed me. This was a nightmare. My life was a nightmare.

As Any's fingers dug into my arm, I winced at his grip.

"We need to hurry," he urged, yanking at my arm. Anger simmered in my chest, fueled by frustration and a lack of control.

"I know, okay?" I snapped, pulling away from him. "But I

can't keep doing this. I'm sick of being told what to do and being kept in the dark. All of you skulling lied to me!"

"Aria…"

"You know what? Go back to the Blood Queen. I'll stay with Eb and Ash."

"Well, I'd rather go to…" Ash mumbled, but I ignored him.

I stormed off, not caring where I was going as long as it wasn't with Any or Mal.

I needed answers, and I was done being told what to do.

Any was with the Blood Queen, and he conspired with her and Mal behind my back.

I was just fed up with everything and wanted nothing more than to strangle all of them.

"Where are we going? Where do we start searching for it?" I heard Bory's voice as he trotted beside me.

I shrugged and brushed away a stray tear that slid down my face.

Any was right about one thing—I had to hold myself together. Crying like a little girl wouldn't bring Rio back. And yet, another tear fell and my fingers clenched.

"There's no reason for you to be angry at us, Aria," Any said, falling in step beside me.

I stopped dead in my tracks.

Turning around, I glared at him. Had he lost his mind?

"Lynne…" Bory warned, touching my knee.

"No reason?" I said, charging at him. "No reason? Are you skulling serious? You all made plans behind my back, kept me in the dark until the very end, and now you say there's no reason for me to be angry? No reason to be sad? No damn reason?" A desperate laughter bubbled up in my throat. I was on the brink of going crazy, too. I jabbed a finger at him. "Don't you dare take away my right to my own feelings! I can be angry as much as I want."

Any scoffed and shook his head, bitterness evident in his features.

Out of the corner of my eye, I saw Ebony and Ash retreat, probably embarrassed by our confrontation, but at some point, it was just enough. I would fix this, but on my own. They had to earn back their trust.

Any's fists clenched at his sides, his voice shaking with anger as he said, "You have no idea what happened and yet you're oh so quick to judge!" He took a step towards me, invading my personal space once again."We all need you to trust us. I live to protect you. When will you fucking understand?" His voice rose to a shout.

His words echoed in my ears, a painful reminder of the trust I had once put in him.

With my heart beating rapidly in my chest, I instinctively moved backwards.

"Trust you?" I spat, my voice barely above a whisper. "Why should I?" The silence that followed was deafening.

We locked eyes, standing frozen in the moment. As he gazed at me, I watched a flicker of pain cross his face, and I knew my words had cut deep.

"Because I love you," he whispered.

I gazed at the yellow in his green irises, and I saw myself in his face.

I suddenly saw us as children. Memories I never wanted flooded my mind, replaying like a movie on Earth.

I wanted to switch them off, but I couldn't. They just came. Whether I wanted them or not.

Taking advantage of my hesitation, Any grabbed me by the shoulders, and it happened.

It felt like plunging into icy water. A strong power pushed me backwards, deeper into my own mind.

Suddenly, it was all happening again in front of me, as if I were reliving the moment in real time.

As if my mind was yelling at me, screaming out everything I had forgotten during my reincarnation. The memories hit me like a powerful wave, breaking through the walls I didn't even know I had put up, flooding my senses with the damn echoes of my past. I was yanked right back to Olympia, the world where Any and I were born. The world of the Titans. Later, when they stumbled upon Earth, humans started calling them gods. But truth be told, anyone who could wield magic from within was a Titan. Even the demigods with one human parent or the divine who were born as humans but could harness mana and turn it into magic, all had some Titan blood running through their veins. But life was toughest for the divines. They were seen as mere humans—deemed worthless. And that's where my mother, Nyx, fell into the mix. She was a divine, and although our father was Erebos and my mother a powerful and enigmatic divine, controlling the night and darkness, our family wasn't the most respected.

That's why we lived on the edge of Olympia, in a stone-carved house on a cliff, far away from the hustle and bustle of the Titans. Any and I meant everything to our mother, which was why we stayed far from other Titans. She always tried to keep us away from the Pantheon, but since our father missed the old days, it was rather difficult. He was important once and couldn't handle the downgrade. And that's exactly where I found myself drawn to now. Home. And I saw Any... how he pulled me away from Mother as nightfall descended, when she conversed with the stars. I witnessed Any's comforting embrace when I was hurt and no one else was there. I saw him staunch my bleeding. I watched myself weep uncontrollably when my sister Hecate had to leave for the Olympia Academy to hone her abilities. I saw Any take our father's blows when I sneaked outside against his orders. It was Any who slept beside me, stroking my head when I couldn't sleep.

I took a deep breath as I returned to reality.

Any's grip on my shoulders tightened, and I gazed into his eyes once more, tears glistening in them now too. When I let another tear fall down my cheeks, I saw that he was crying, too. Hell, we've been more than just siblings. We've been best friends and now we were... not. And it was all my fault. He fought so hard for me to remember, to remember what we used to be.

"I love you, Aria," he repeated. "I would never work against you. Never. You are everything to me. It has always been us against the world... everything I did, I did for you. All I wanted over the last decades was to bring you back... and yes, we worked with the Blood Queen, but we never did it to work against you. She's with us. We all want to end the curse. To save the world."

I breathed in and out deeply and just stared at him. His love for me was so visible. It truly had always been the two of us, twins united against all odds, until we weren't. Until I fell hopelessly in love with the Shadow King, and everyone tried to tear us apart.

I clung to his hands with a fierce grip, as if they were the lifeline keeping me tethered to reality. Deep down, I sensed the ember of his affection for me, and in the secret corners of my heart, I knew I loved him, too. I always did. But that sentiment remained elusive, slipping through my fingers like sand. Maybe it was too much history that couldn't just be swapped out. Trusting anyone, even him, felt like a leap I wasn't ready to take yet. I did trust too quickly in the past, and I always paid the price for it. Those scars from being let down before? They weren't fading anytime soon.

"Why can you show me memories from the past?" I asked, breaking the heavy silence between us.

He swallowed back the tears, visibly glad that I was keen to change the subject. "We all can. Anyone you share memories with can draw them forth when the time is right."

"With just a touch?"

Any nodded. "With closeness, with words, with whatever triggers the memories within you. It's your mind that chooses to set your memories free."

"But when does it stop? These memories... it's draining." I didn't want to keep remembering. I hated that everyone knew more about me than I did.

He pulled the corner of his lips up into a crooked smile. "When you have all your memories back. Only then will it end."

"Any, I—" Before I could finish my sentence, a deep growl cut through the night.

"Shit," I heard Mal say, and I turned to follow his gaze. And there they were. Deadwalkers.

From the backdrop of a small belfry adorned with a bell in the serene cemetery, a dozen of them emerged and advanced directly toward us.

CHAPTER TWO
LYNNE

"Run!" Ebony screamed, charging forward alongside Ash, both of them drawing their swords and aiming them straight at the Deadwalkers. I stood there momentarily rooted in place. There were so many of them. How could this be?

"Lynne, we really should—" Bory began, but I grabbed him and hurled him backward into the bushes. He grunted, but I wanted him safe. I couldn't lose another one I loved.

Then my heart leaped with adrenaline in my chest. Just as the Deadwalkers clashed with Ebony and Ash, I caught a glint in the air and Mal shouted, "Lynne, sword!"

I lunged forward, gripping the sword he'd tossed to me, and charged at the Deadwalkers as well. I could decapitate them too. In fact, I was damn good at it. For the first time since arriving here, I could breathe freely. Fighting was easy, since killing was muscle memory. Keeping them alive was harder.

"I'll take the ones in the middle!" Ebony yelled, and as Ash rushed toward the horde approaching from the right, I took charge of the ones on the left.

In the corner of my eye, I spotted Mal and Any sprinting

toward us. But before I could even register their approach, a Deadwalker lunged at me with gnarled teeth and outstretched arms. Without hesitation, I raised my sword and sliced through its neck with precision. Its head rolled to the ground with a satisfying thud.

The wet splatter of black blood brought a grin to my face. Finally, I could channel my anger into something useful.

Another came and tried its luck and I spun in a swift pirouette, sidestepping the grasp of another Deadwalker lunging at me. My blade jabbed forward, severing the arm of the oncoming undead as it stumbled past. The scent of decay and dirt filled the air as I leaped back, the iron tang of blood mixing with the earthy stench.

A second undead emerged from the shadows, tall and lanky, with outstretched arms. I quickly swung my hair back, the white strands glittering in the moonlit sky. With a fierce kick to its legs, it crashed to the ground like a puppet with its strings cut. I followed up with a sharp blow to its stomach before swiftly decapitating it. The rush of adrenaline and power surged through me as I took down another opponent.

"Damn, this is just what I needed," I said.

"You're weird," Mal whispered, his face contorted with disgust as he stood against my back.

I shrugged. "I'm a fighter. Whatever obstacles you throw at me, I'll fight them."

A third one, bulky and relentless, swung a decaying fist my way. I ducked and weaved, narrowly avoiding the slow, heavy blow. Using the momentum of my evasion, I swung my weapon low and sliced through its ankle, causing it to crumple to the ground and Mal took off his head.

"This was mine," I snapped.

"I'm here to help you," he said.

"No thanks, I had enough of your helping. Lying traitor."

The Deadwalkers were closing in, their groans filling the air.

With a quick breath, I launched myself into action once again as Mal screamed, "I wasn't lying! It's called holding back information! And it was for your own good!"

"Still angry!" I said and my gaze zeroed in on a bulky Dead-walker, scraps of armor still clinging to its frame.

Its enormous sword swung in a wide arc, aiming to smash me into oblivion.

Mal let out a curse, but I quickly dodged the swing, feeling the rush of air graze my skin.

"Lynne! Be careful!" someone yelled, but I didn't pay attention.

With my eyes trained on my opponent, I watched with precision because, in that moment, I drove the hilt of my sword into his chest.

Seizing the opening, I thrust forward, aiming for the neck. But the Deadwalker, realizing it was too weak for a parry, threw itself backwards to avoid my strike. It fell with a thud onto its back, disoriented but far from defeated.

I exhaled deeply and brushed away the sweat from my brow.

I lunged towards it, ready to deliver the final blow, when the Deadwalker punched me in the face and suddenly the ground beneath me gave way. My heart raced as the earth shifted and crumbled. In a split second, the horizon twisted, shifting from horizontal to vertical, and I crashed to the ground, my sword flying through the air.

I heard a grunt, twisted around and the Deadwalker loomed over me, its gaping mouth wide open, black tendrils of spittle trailing between its teeth, and its yellow eyes fixated on me as it was poised to strike. Time felt like it was dwindling away rapidly, my instincts kicking in as I rolled away just in time. One bite and it would have been over. Deadwalker could turn anyone, including deities. I wasn't so sure about how it would affect me, since Rio bound my soul to his, turning me immortal, but I wasn't keen on finding out. I watched the Deadwalker tearing a gaping hole in the charred earth. And then it charged at me again. Panting, I raised my hands in protection and, in an unforeseen twist, our hands brushed against each other.

And it happened.

It collapsed. It was lifeless. Within the blink of an eye.

My body flinched involuntarily, my gaze locked onto it as if time itself had paused. The other Deadwalkers stared at us, their disbelief written on their faces, caught in that fleeting moment of incredulity. Because the Deadwalker was unraveling before us. It wasn't merely death. No, my touch was triggering a reversal, transforming it back into a human!

Backing away, my movements mirroring that of a crab retreating, I observed the metamorphosis unfold before my eyes. Its limbs contorted, shrinking, the obsidian hue fading to a ghostly white tinged with crimson. I couldn't believe my eyes. What the skull?

"What is happening?" Mal's voice, a mere whisper beside me, held the same bewilderment I felt.

"I don't know." The words escaped my lips in a rush.

As soon as they did, the suspended silence shattered around us. But amidst the chaos, a woman laid drenched in blood, a gruesome tableau that seemed to beckon them towards me. Shit, I could turn them back again.

"Freaking hell!" Mal cried, hoisting me up and tugging me toward him. A sea of Deadwalkers erupted into a chorus of enraged roars, and I knew we had to get the skull away.

"To the belfry," I said, grabbing my sword in haste as we sprinted away.

"What's the plan?" Mal's voice, strained and anxious, matched my own gasping breaths.

"I don't know. But—somehow—I have to touch them."

"What? Why?"

"Because my touch saves their soul and I want to save them."

"No freaking way."

"Watch me."

Maybe it was my gnawing guilt, since I created about three Deadwalkers myself, or maybe it was my curiosity, fueled by this newfound ability. Who knows? But I simply had to go and try to save their souls.

Casting a glance over my shoulder, I saw Ebony and Ash battling to forge a path towards us, yet the sea of Deadwalkers paid them no heed. Their sights were fixed solely on me.

And then it struck me.

A thick rope dangled from a creaky old bell hanging high up on the small belfry before us.

Mal and I used to flee from Cave Town dwellers. We could climb a belfry. I sprinted towards the bell tower, my heartbeat almost drowning out the crunch of gravel beneath my feet. Finally reaching the tower, my lungs burned from the effort and I focused on that belfry and its rope. It hung down from the bell. I had no idea why, but it seemed to make the bell make a sound.

As I was about to grip the cracks in the wall in front of me, a loud and rough scream interrupted the silence.

I twisted, just in time to catch Any aiming his crossbow at a charging Deadwalker. Ash joined the party, whacking off a Deadwalker's noggin with one well-aimed blow while Ebony sliced another in half. Okay, they didn't need me.

"Wait here. I'll cut the rope from above," I told him.

I grasped at the rough texture of the walls, my fingers digging into crevices and clinging to any bit of stability I could find. Sweat dripped down my forehead as I struggled to lift myself higher. Mal stood below me, his outstretched hand offering support as I tried to hoist myself up the steep walls of the rock face. The sharp edges of the rocks dug into my skin, but I refused to give up. The wind howled around us, threatening to knock us off balance at any moment.

Summoning the last of my strength, I hoisted myself onto the ledge. The end of the rope hung inches away from my face, a reminder of the intense climb I had just completed.

Mal's voice was filled with fear as he pointed at the rope. "What can we use this for?"

Swallowing, I spotted countless Deadwalkers closing in on us. With a lump in my throat, I unsheathed my sword and gripped onto the notches of the rope tightly. In one swift motion, I sliced through the rope with my blade, causing it to fall to the ground with a dull thud.

I leapt off the ledge, the sound of the bell fading away behind me.

With a determined resolve, I turned my gaze towards the approaching Deadwalkers and charged at them. Their decrepit faces turned, their clawed hands reaching out. I heard Mal swear, but he followed me, nevertheless. Just before I reached them, I signaled to Mal and tossed him the other end.

He gripped it like a lifeline.

"Entwine them!" I cried out.

We raced towards the Deadwalkers, and the rope looped around them, ensnaring them one by one. Once we surrounded them, I pressed my end of the rope into Mal's free hand. His eyebrows shot up as I signaled him to hold the Deadwalkers.

"You're not serious," he panted, but I was already walking away as he struggled to keep the ensnared horde at bay and before the rope could snap, I chanted a spell I knew from the Book of Silva. Thanks to the Blood Queen, I made the rope unbreakable, trapping them within its borders.

And as Mal fought valiantly to hold them all together, I

embraced my newfound power, reaching out to every Deadwalker within my grasp. Each touch was a mercy, an act of redemption. They collapsed around me, the once-ferocious pack becoming a pile of lifeless bodies thanks to my touch, a scene both haunting and strangely satisfying.

Mal's teeth clenched, his efforts relentless as Any and Ash joined to hold the rope and Deadwalkers in place.

"You're out of your mind." Ebony's voice found me.

"If their souls get a shot at redemption, we better grab it," I whispered.

I'd do a sweep of the whole graveyard later. Maybe even with their heads off, I could still save their souls. I'd forgotten that Deadwalkers could trap some good folks, too. They were just the result of one messed-up curse—just like me.

Just when I touched the last one, the surrounding ground exploded in blue flame, seething in a dust cloud. We all shot back, our eyes glued to the mess before us.

"This is sick!" Ash cried out, and we took a wide berth around the glowing Deadwalkers.

We watched them as they turned into a mound of people. Everyone was injured, a wild mess. Their hair, black, blond, red... their skin, all the colors the world offered, were intertwined. When I saw the fire crawling over their skin and slowly transforming them back, guilt pierced me. Had we done that? Rio and I? Was this the result of our love?

No. I couldn't allow this. I had to restore my Topworld to what it once was, even if it was the last thing I did. I would set everything right again. Suddenly, Any stood beside me and gently stroked my back. "Many of the souls before us will ascend to heaven. Aria, you did well."

"I wish I could have turned them while they were still alive, but once I touched them, they dropped dead."

Any tenderly caressed my shoulder. "You can only turn what's left to turn. They are already dead."

I bit my lip. "I need to find the others. I have to see if even those without heads can be saved."

I could kick myself for forgetting that all Deadwalkers were once human, that even if they emitted a current danger, deep down in their core, they were still good. I think this is often the case for many. We judge quickly. Far too quickly.

I hugged myself, running my hands over my upper arms, and walked back to where, just a few minutes ago, I had been beheading Deadwalkers as if it were a game.

CHAPTER THREE
LYNNE

"We really need to start thinking about a plan," Ebony hissed, and I noticed everyone was following me while I was scanning for Deadwalkers among gravestones, rotting trees, and broken walls. Everything here was destroyed. Everything. God damn.

I leaned in closer to Ebony and hissed back, "Well, then go and think! I need to turn them first. I won't leave them here to suffer."

I could see the frustration and anger building in her expression, but before she could respond, Mal interjected. He positioned himself between us, his gaze piercing into mine. "Aria, I appreciate your selflessness, but time is of the essence here," he said urgently. "We need to follow the queen's orders and find the Omphalos Stone that Rio has hidden. You have the best chance of finding it. We can't afford to waste any more time."

I rolled my eyes. "Fine. You're right. You can go, I'll catch up."

Why was it so difficult for them to comprehend that I had to preserve some of my power? I possessed the ability, so why shouldn't I use it? No one desired to decay within the depths of the Underworld.

"Your queen forgot to mention why we're needed," Ash grumbled as he reluctantly followed behind with Ebony in tow.

"You're skilled fighters," Any interjected.

"And him?" Ash asked, pointing his thumb at Mal.

"He's a healer," Any replied, causing Mal to hiss in frustration.

"Are you out of your mind? That's not something people should know about," Mal said as he fell back to walk with Any.

"They belong with us," Any insisted.

"But they were just serving the Bone Queen," Mal argued. "Not exactly a glowing recommendation for trustworthiness."

"But working for the Blood Queen is?" Ebony chimed in. "And we did it to earn some money, cut us some slack. Our king was gone for decades."

"At least the Blood Queen helped us solve this chaos," Mal retorted. "The Bone Queen is causing chaos."

"Yeah, but we were never under contract with her," Ash added. "We took contracts wherever we could to survive."

"Such a shame," Mal muttered.

I tried to ignore their argument as I saw another Dead-walker on the ground.

I crouched down, touched the head that had been separated from the body, and it immediately transformed back into a human head.

I pondered whether touching just its head was enough to rescue its soul or if every inch of its body was essential to rescuing the soul... Well, I better focus on searching for the body—just in case. No one could assure me that manipulating a single part would suffice. What if he was fragmented into a hundred pieces? What if he'd donated a kidney? What if—

I spotted the body a few feet away and rose from my crouched position.

There was no other deity of Rebirth but me. So, I had to figure it out on my own and give it a shot. Touching as many body parts as I could find, hoping it'd do the trick and save their souls.

I approached it and touched the skin of his tormented torso, glad it turned back immediately.

Behind me, they were still arguing, discussing where we might find the Omphalos Stone. Well, I had a few ideas, but first, I wanted to clean up this mess. If Rio really hid it in the Topworld, it would likely be somewhere near the gang's location, which is where we should head first.

I touched another body, transforming it back into human form as well. If the whole world was filled with Deadwalkers, I had a lot of work ahead. Perhaps Athena had an idea for helping the other souls who had already been affected. I hoped she'd have an idea, as she was our last resort. Of course, I feared she might tell me I had to give up Rio, but for now, I pushed that thought far back. I would see him again. I had to believe firmly in that, because whether I wanted to admit it or not, I already missed him.

"So..." a dark, sultry voice croaked from the bushes, and I jumped. "You can go ahead without me. I'll stay here for now."

I looked at Mal behind me.

He glanced at me, and then to the bushes.

"Who's that?" Mal inquired.

I gave him a nonchalant shrug and shifted my attention back to the bushes.

"Who's there?" I shouted toward the foliage. "Come out and reveal yourself."

"It's me, Lynne... Bory..."

"Bory?" I exclaimed. There was something odd about his voice. Very odd. "What's up with your voice?"

I rushed towards the bushes, where I had thrown him before the fight, but he screamed. "Hey, no... wait, stay where you are!"

"Bory," I whispered, slowing down. "What the hell are you doing?"

"I said, stay where you are!"

I crossed my arms. "Okay, either you come out, or I'm coming to you. Your choice."

"No. I, argh—Alright, alright," croaked Bory.

I bit my lip, my nerves getting the best of me. We were in the worst situation I can think of and Bory wants to play Hide and Seek?

"What is he doing in there? Did he get burned and now looks like a plucked chicken?" Ash chuckled beside me.

"You mean like your ass when it's cold?" Ebony chuckled, and I attempted not to cringe, wondering how she had any idea what his ass looked like when it was cold.

"Oh, shut up," Ash muttered back.

The bushes rustled louder, and suddenly, a man stood in front of us.

My eyes darted from his big feet, up to his slim legs, ignoring the center point that clearly indicated his gender, and got caught in his blue hair. No. God. Skull. No.

I let out a shriek that would have put a Wendigo to shame. I mean, I didn't even scream when I saw the Deadwalkers, but this was on a whole different level of terror. I frantically spun around, hoping this was all just a bad dream and I would wake up any second.

No, I refused to accept this. I covered my eyes, desperately hoping my suspicions wouldn't come true. It couldn't be, please, please, please, no.

The man cleared his throat behind me. "Uh, yeah, well... it's me, Bory the human..."

I heard a rustle and footsteps on gravel. I cautiously cracked open one eye, only to be greeted by the sight of him grinning awkwardly, running his hand through blue hair like he was auditioning for a human hair care commercial. And just when I thought it couldn't get any worse, he threw in a wink. A wink!

I wished desperately for a magically "Unsee" button to appear in front of me. This was too much. Way too much.

"Wow, you got a nice dick, man," Mal said and Ash nodded along.

"And your nickname Furball gets a new meaning,"

Ebony's smile widened, her laughter ringing out as if we had nothing to worry about.

"Okay," I said, throwing my hands up in the air and walking away. "I quit."

"You what?" Mal asked, his laugh all clear.

"This is enough!" I said as my feet buckled, and I sat down on the floor.

I pulled my knees up to my chest and buried my head in them.

This was all just too much. I could take lives and apparently give them back, too. The Topworld was crumbling. Rio was gone, and who knew if he'd even wake up again. And now Bory was a man! A human man!

"Lynne, I'm fine, I'm just a human—I think, because you touched me and—"

"Stop talking to me in that voice!" I snapped and shoved my head between my knees again. "You've taken everything from me, and now you've taken even my little... Ugh, I can't even use your nickname without being grossed out. Shit. I cuddle with you at night! He can't look like this and have a... a penis! He was cute! Full of fur and feathers!!"

"I think she's losing it," I heard Ash mutter, and I wanted to smack a stone against his stupid forehead.

"Lynne," Bory's new voice sounded, and I grunted. "Come on, it's really not that bad... I'm sure Cherry will like me this way!"

I felt a hand on my shoulder and flinched. "Don't touch me with that hand!"

And that's when I looked into Bory's eyes for the first time. They were blue too. His nose was a cute button nose, his face as friendly as ever, but... he was a human. A skulling human. This was a disaster.

"Lynne, touch me again, maybe I'll change back..." Bory mumbled, and I reluctantly poked him in the side with my finger, making sure to only look at his face.

But nothing happened, so I squeezed tighter, digging my nails into his stupid skin.

Nothing. I squeezed even more. He yelped.

"Ouch!"

"Argh! It's not working!" I hissed and stood up. "This is terrible! Why did I turn you into a human? And why can I do this?"

"You're the Goddess of Rebirth. You can turn back a lot. It requires some skills though," Any said, while he stood with crossed arms and a casual stance. I could see he was proud of it.

"And that means my hands do whatever they want? They turn humans into Deadwalkers and Burlacks into humans? Where's the sense in that?"

Ash burst out laughing, but his laughter got caught in his throat as I stared him down. Maybe he realized I could actually turn humans into Deadwalkers.

"She's creepy," I heard him whisper to Ebony.

"Your magic is much stronger here than in the Underworld,

where it's the weakest among all realms," Any explained. "In Olympia, it's at its strongest. It's trickier on Earth, though, because your magic doesn't know where it belongs. It requires training."

Which I didn't have.

I drew up my eyebrows. "And why didn't I turn Bory the last time I was on Earth? I touched him constantly." Well, this sounded weird now...

"You hadn't regained all your powers yet," Any said.

"Well, great. How do I get my sweet bear back then?" I said, almost tearing up at the thought of Bory looking like... this. "And do I need gloves again?"

"Yes to the gloves," Any said. "But, well, with Bory...we probably have to wait and hope the spell reverses on its own. I have no idea how your magic works. Everyone of us is different and so is our magic."

"And what's your magic?" Bory asked.

I stared at him incredulously. Unbelievable how deep his voice was now... I will never get over it.

"I am the deity of forgetfulness," Any said, and I scoffed.

"How ironic that I can't seem to remember anything..."

"That was not my doing," Any replied. "It's a natural part of reincarnation to forget about past lives."

"But you can give me back my memories, can't you? I know most of the curse's background now."

"As I said," Any continued, "we have to do it slowly. Because forgetting is a kind of fresh start, a way to push painful experiences aside, and if you remember too fast, we risk a lot. You could forget everything again and might end up insane. Toying with the mind is no joke."

"Didn't the Shadow King have a servant who made everyone forget who he was, and that's why he was so unknown compared to his sisters?" I said, and when I noticed that they all exchanged knowing glances, my jaw nearly hit the ground.

It was him all along. My brother was Rio's secret keeper.

I stood up, clenched my fingers into fists.

"You've been lying so much, maybe you should write a book. I could read it in a week and maybe finally know the truth."

"I would if I could, but don't forget that we're also cursed."

My brother and I locked eyes again until I couldn't take it anymore and exclaimed, "We're leaving. Let's find that stone and be done with it."

"And where are we going?" Bory asked.

His voice made me flinch. He repeated the question, this time in a higher pitch, which only made me glare at him more.

"To the Loops," I grumbled as I stomped ahead.

CHAPTER FOUR
LYNNE

As we made our way to the Loops' headquarters, Bory had initially wanted to help navigate, but I sentenced him to the very back. I needed time to process. Thank the Hellhounds, Mal offered him his cloak so he could wrap it around his naked waist.

We walked along the destroyed path and emerged into the city, Englewood. I remembered how great it used to be to stroll around here, seeing all the new buildings, but now chunks of abandoned house bricks littered the streets, their jagged edges threatening to trip any thoughtless step. The once-smooth asphalt was now a patchwork of deep cracks and giant mounds, creating an obstacle course for anyone trying to navigate through. I carefully stepped over a brick onto the uneven sidewalk, taking in the chaotic scene around me. The bent lamp posts cast eerie shadows in the fading light, some flickering weakly as if holding on to their last bit of energy. The only constant in this broken world was my beloved moon, its silver rays casting a haunting glow over the destruction before us.

We trudged forward when suddenly I heard a whimper.

I stopped, ignoring Bory's human stare, and then my heart almost leaped out of my chest. Oh, come on...

"Are you serious?" I said, and everyone turned to follow my gaze.

Behind us stood Soothie, huge and stuck in the twisted iron gate.

I facepalmed myself and hissed at him. "Soothie! What the skull are you doing here?"

He snorted, and the warm air sent my hair soaring. "You can't just come to the human world... you kinda stand out here... they have dogs, not dragons."

I carefully freed him from the iron bars, bending them aside.

The best thing about the Topworld was my strength. I was so much stronger here than in the Underworld.

"How did you even get here?"

Soothie let out another snort before tilting his massive head backwards, gesturing towards the once tall tower that I had climbed. It now lay in ruins, as if Soothie had charged through it without a care, leaving only a faint outline of his flight path behind.

I cuddled up to his spiky snout, my hand so small compared to his size that I could only stroke a third of his nostrils.

"You came right after us and crashed through the tower? For me? Gods. Did you hurt yourself?" I checked him over, and luckily, he seemed to have arrived in one piece.

"Well, great," Ash said and eyed Soothie critically from a distance. He probably had too much respect for my Sircha to get closer.

"What do we do with a dragon in the human world?" he said.

Soothie let out a small burst of fire, and I pushed him lightly. "Hey, cut it. We really shouldn't attract any attention..."

"Kind of hard with that gigantic beast," Ebony sighed.

"He just wanted to help," I said, petting Soothie.

"Exactly," Bory grumbled, approaching, and as he did, Soothie's eyes grew wider and wider. I noticed his yellow gaze scanning Bory from head to toe. Then, he shuddered and pulled back. I grinned with satisfaction. Soothie was just as taken aback by Bory as I had been.

"It's alright," I reassured. "He'll be normal soon...I hope."

"Hey, quit treating me like a plague!" Bory grumbled, placing his hands defiantly on his hips.

I envisioned my dear furball extending its fluffy arms in protest, longing for my old Bory to return. "Yeah, no, I can't cope. I'm sorry but I need some minutes—hours. Um. Okay, let's go get some clothes now."

"Um... you plan to bring the dragon along?" Ash said, stepping back a couple of paces as we moved forward.

Soothie strolled beside me, and a sense of comfort washed over me. Everything had changed, but he remained my anchor.

"Of course, Soothie's coming with us. I'm not sending him back, and with all the creatures running around here, he won't stand out that much."

Ash and Ebony shot each other a look, as if my brain was already mush.

"Not stand out?" Ebony scoffed. "He's almost as big as a house."

"Doesn't matter, we're here to save people, and if he wants to help, he can," I stubbornly stated.

"Yeah, they probably think they need to save their people from us..." Ash muttered, and we walked on until we reached a broken shopping area.

We stopped in front of a clothing store and before anyone could say anything, Ash used the hilt of his sword to break the window. Of course, the alarm went off, and even though I wasn't sure if there was still a police force here, considering everything was in ruins, I pushed Ash in and motioned everyone to follow. "Come on, let's just take everything we need and then get out of here!"

We stole some human clothes and a tablecloth for Smoothie.

Admittedly, it wasn't much better when he had a pink frilly blanket on his back, but I thought it made him look less threatening, which was what we needed.

We quickly changed out of our Underworld attire. As I removed the beautiful dress Rio had created for me, a wave of sadness washed over me once again. The rush of adrenaline in my body didn't give me much time to process everything that had happened. All I could do was hope that there was some way to bring him back to life. The thought of living in a world without him was unimaginable.

I put on a pair of baggy jeans and a crop top, not caring too much about how it looked. Human clothing had always been strange to me.

I heard the others grumbling as they also changed into the clothes we had stolen.

At least they looked funny too. Ebony wore a green dress that barely covered her ass, Ash had a gray shirt and shorts, Mal wore a zebra shirt and checkered shorts... Only Any seemed to look normal. He wore black pants and a black t-shirt. Well and Bory... Bory had a blue shirt and blue trousers on, which was okay, but there was a bit too much blue and not enough fur...

"They have strange clothing here," Ebony said, trying to pull the dress down, without much success.

"Yeah, they love dressing flashy," I said.

"That's not much use, though. Their clothes don't protect against the cold in winter, and in summer, you even sweat more in this weird fabric..." Ebony adjusted her cleavage.

"But you look good in them," Ash said, barely taking his eyes off Ebony.

"Oh shut up and stop staring."

As we strolled through the park, my eyes caught the vibrant pink neon sign of the 'Paradise Girls,' and my heart skipped a beat.

Would they all still be alive? Were the Loops and Dee's Girls the same as they used to be?

Most certainly not. People change and humans even more since their life is way faster than ours.

Well, there was no point in lingering any longer, so I gave myself a little push and led our group toward the Paradise Girls.

"It's strange that this building is still standing," Any remarked.

Indeed, all the other buildings were in ruins, but Rio's club and his entire block remained intact. I looked up and noticed strange little statues on the roof, hawks perched above. Odd. Had they always been there, and I just never noticed?

We decided that it was better to hide Soothie in the park. Only until we had prepared the Loops. We found a bridge under which we hid him. I promised that we would come get him soon.

Then, I knocked on Dee's pink entrance door, and we waited.

And waited.

Ebony leaned against the railing, crossing her arms as she asked, "Do you think your friends still live here? How long has it been since you've been back up here? Like twenty years?"

"I don't know how much time passed... But we've got to give it a shot," I replied, knocking again.

Suddenly, a small peephole opened, revealing a dark brown eye that blinked at us.

"Who's there?"

"Ly—Barbie," I croaked, ignoring the strange looks I received from the others.

"Barbie?" I heard a man exclaim in surprise. "No way!"

Then followed a muffled sound, a shout and we all took a step back.

Then, someone swung the door open, and there stood Punchy.

My gaze traveled from his feet to his head and a grin stretched across my face. Hell, he looked exactly the same, except for the slight hint of gray in his hair, leaving me to wonder how many years had passed.

"Oh skull, Punchy it's really you!" I shouted.

He laughed and then lifted me up as if I weighed no more than a bag of feathers. He pinned around with me and a hearty laughter filled the air. "Oh, Barbie! I was afraid you were dead!"

"Nope, weeds don't wither," I grinned, and he held me slightly away from him, a brown eye twitching as he observed me. "You... can... talk?"

I nodded. "I was under a spell last time."

"Wow, your voice is so different from what I expected," he said, giving me another squeeze. "Doesn't matter. Man—am I glad to see you. A lot of things have changed since you were up here and there are even more weird things happening right now. I think you being able to kill with just a touch wasn't at all the weirdest shit—"

"Hey, Punch!" echoed a young woman's voice from inside, causing him to release me as if a sudden icy shock had hit him.

"Who's that? Remember what I said about chatting with strangers?"

"Um, boss, this is—well—Barbie. A... friend of the...Baron."

"Baron, huh?" she rumbled.

But to my surprise, it wasn't an adult woman who pushed him aside now, it was a girl. She couldn't be more than eighteen, if even that. She had dark skin, her hair twisted up in the Bentu style, full red lips, and dark, captivating eyes that seemed to strip me bare. I cleared my throat and shifted in between Ebony and Ash, as if they could somehow protect me. From a girl.

"It's you," she hissed, her lips curling with an unmistakable edge of hostility, as if she'd just bitten into something sour.

I opened my mouth to answer, but her gaze turned to stone, an icy glint that could freeze a summer day. Then, with a sudden motion, she grabbed the door, yanking it with a force that made the whole frame shudder.

"Get lost," she said, and the door slammed shut with a solid thud.

I could hear Punchy's voice, attempting to talk some sense into her, advocating on my behalf. He was such a kind soul. She not so much.

"What's gotten into that bitch?" Ash asked, and I turned around, facing a sea of puzzled faces.

"Well," I began, scratching the back of my head. "That didn't go as planned. And believe me, I have no clue who that was. She's new."

"But she seemed to know you," Any said.

I shrugged. Whatever she thought, she had to be mistaken because there was no way I could have done anything to her. It's highly unlikely that she was even alive the last time I set foot on Earth.

"Why not give it another knock? They have to let us in," Ebony said, pushing me forward as if she were leading a charge.

"Yeah, if not, we'll smash our way through!" Ash chimed in with a grim expression on his face.

"Or we can use the back entrance," Any suggested in that soothing, almost velvety voice of his, always seeking the peaceful path in the midst of chaos. And just like that, it was as if my memory had never glitched, as if I'd always known that Any was the calm one, my sweet brother who tried to keep me out of trouble. I was the hot-headed half of the duo, always itching for those risky situations.

"Come on, Lynne," Bory said, edging forward to me, wrapping an arm around my shoulder.

I flinched. Again. I had to get used to human Bory. "We can do this. We just need to reach Cherry. She'll know what to do—"

By the Hellhounds, he truly had a crush on Cherry, didn't he?

I grumbled, strolled up to the door, and gave it another knock. This couldn't be the end of it. There's no way they'd turn down our offer to help.

"Let us in," I declared. "We're here for assistance., God damn it. Do you really want to keep those Deadwalkers around any longer? Don't be foolish. Open the do—"

The door opened and this time it was Cherry.

The feisty girl stood right behind her, arms defiantly crossed, while Punchy grinned as if he had two clothespins attached to the end of his cheeks, keeping his smile in place.

Cherry looked exactly the same, not a single strand of gray in her hair. Her gorgeous afro still rocked that half-pink, half-black. The only hint of her age, if you could even call it that, were those tiny lines next to her eyes, and the weary gaze she carried now. Maybe the slightly fuller curves up top, but it suited her just fine.

I was over the moon as she hugged me tight, her sweet scent wrapping around me, creating an instant sense of home. It was funny that the world could collapse, yet she still smelled like a blooming garden on a warm spring day. I hugged her back, closing my eyes and savoring the comfort of being close to her.

Oh, I've missed her.

It felt just like back then.

Only this time, there was no Rio, no watchful gaze piercing across the room...

CHAPTER FIVE
ARIA, OLYMPIA 1000 YEARS AGO

"That ain't gonna work," a deep voice chimed in.

My hands desperately clung to the makeshift rope I'd cobbled together from about twenty bed sheets I had stolen over the weeks. They always used three sheets per bed and here and there I stole one. Maybe they noticed, but no one asked me about it. So that's why I dangled from a balcony like a fish on a hook now, glancing upward at a stranger. And when my eyes met his, my heart nearly stopped.

"You—"

"Your majesty, you mean?" he retorted, undoing my rope from the railing.

My stomach twisted. What did he have in mind?

I desperately searched for something to hold on to. What if he let me fall?

"No, please..." I begged.

He held the rope firmly. "I appreciate the effort to escape, and believe me, I tried that plenty back in my day, but learn from my mistakes: The moment your feet touch the ground, you'll be burned by wildfire and thrown in the dungeon for days. The floor's enchanted. No apprentice is escaping from here."

He pulled the rope up a bit, letting me dangle with a smug grin.

"And what's your plan for me now?" I tried silently cursing the Academy. The building was made out of gold and silver, all shiny and slippery. Nothing to hold on to, yank my feet in... I was at his mercy. He could do anything, and he was unpredictable. I knew exactly who he was. Zagrios, Hades' son. The whole pantheon was buzzing because he signed up for this week's assembly. Nobody knew why he was here. What he was up to. But we all knew it had to be something evil .

"I'm still pondering," he said, hauling me up only to let me drop again as if I weighed nothing.

"What can help your pondering?" I gritted my teeth. By Olympia... he was indeed insane.

"A smile."

"Out of stock."

"Pity," he released the rope, leaving me to fall. I screamed and remembered I should be quiet. If the others found out what I did... I clung to the rope like it was my lifeline and he caught me again just a few feet from the ground.

I sucked in a deep breath. That asshole.

The display of his power was loud and clear.

"Fine then," I shouted up to him, curling my lips into a smile.

"You can do better, Little Moon," he grinned and pulled me back up.

I growled. "Little Moon?"

He pulled me up and lifted me over the railing.

I opened my mouth to add something, but he spun me around, pressing his body against my back. His grip on my face forced me to look down, and with his other hand, he let the rope fall, watching it unravel into a thousand threads as it hit the magic field. I swallowed. Okay, maybe it wasn't such a great idea after all.

He turned me back around, placing both hands on the railing beside my hips.

I instinctively retreated a bit, but the golden railing dug into my back, causing discomfort. His blue eyes locked onto me, and I couldn't help but notice how strikingly beautiful this man was. Within his iris, I saw small black shadows swirling, as if they were in some kind of dispute.

He grinned and flashed white teeth at me. "Like what you see?"

I swallowed. "Um... Why, Little Moon?"

"You have a round face, like the moon."

I widened my eyes, but before I could say anything that might get me in trouble, he laughed and said, "No, I saw you training. When you channel magic, your eyes glow white."

"Seriously?" I said, reaching under my eye as if I could still feel the odd sensation.

I knew they burned when I trained with Helios, but I didn't realize they glowed. Like all the other eighteen Olympian candidates, I had yet to discover what kind of magic I'd possess, but glowing eyes? What was I supposed to do with that?

"Yes, like a little moon princess," he said, toying with my hair.

But the moon made sense... I was the only one in the family with silver hair, and the glow of my eyes... "I thought I might develop more of a dark power," I confessed, not thinking much about who I was actually talking to. "My father is darkness, along with my mother Nyx, they devour the light of day. So..."

"Thanks for the explanation. I know your parents. But," he said, stepping back a bit. "You don't have to stick to the same magical lineage. Your magic reflects your character, and it'll reveal what it brings out in you. You seem to bring light to the darkness then," he smiled, and I had no idea what he was trying to tell me.

He casually leaned against the railing beside me, saying, "Now, girl, I could come up with a hundred guesses, but I'm curious why you chose to run. Care to enlighten me?"

I gave a half-shrug, not exactly sure how to put it. Should I tell the truth? Well, why not?

"I was bored," I confessed.

"Of course. But, what treasure were you hunting for in the depths?"

"Something other than the usual dance of polite gods, endless gossip, and glittery trinkets."

"Ah, you'd find more of the same down there."

"Alright, thanks for the knight-in-shining-armor act, but I should be on my way to resume my thrilling boredom," I brushed off the rail and started heading back inside, but he intercepted, grabbing my arm, and tugging me back.

"Not so fast. I request a little quid pro quo," he proposed.

"What?"

"You owe me a favor, as a token of gratitude for my heroic dungeon intervention. Nothing in life is free."

I tried to catch a glimmer of compassion or even a hint of mercy in his eyes, but it was a lost cause. "What kind of favor could I possibly do for someone like you? I don't have much to offer."

He flashed a wicked grin. "We'll think of something."

And then, it hit me. What he had in mind. "I'm not hopping into bed with you! I'm not some kind of... courtesan."

He squinted, acting utterly baffled. "Remind me when, exactly, I gave you the impression that I wanted to fuck you?"

I paused, blinked a few times. Well, he had touched me often, so...

A smirk tugged at the corner of his lips. "I'm intrigued because, according to the Fates, you're quite the hot topic. They took their sweet time deciding you're some 'special' case, and that's not your everyday occurrence. So forgive me if I'm a tad curious."

I squinted, trying to read his true intentions, but his eyes remained an enigma, revealing nothing. "And you're not gonna ask for some sort of... physical favor in return?"

"No need for that. You're practically a kid, still wet behind the ears. Trust me, I've got my hands full, no nursery raids necessary."

"Good to know," I replied, my skepticism not entirely gone.

He looked like he was about to say something, his gaze briefly drifting to my lips.

I cleared my throat. "Tell me, what would Zagrios, Hades' only son and the Shadow King, want from someone like me?"

"Maybe your fancy magic or perhaps I'm just here to sprinkle a little excitement into your life."

Now, he had my attention. "Excitement? What are you getting at?"

He stood to his full height, straightening himself, causing me to arch my neck upward to meet his eyes.

"I know they've shoved all those 'traditions' down your throat. Women are supposed to be pretty, dance to society's tune, and play sweet melodies, all wrapped up in a neat, obedient package."

I paused, pondering his words. Then, with a bit of a snarky grin, I said, "Well, that sounds like a real thrill."

He mirrored my grin, the tiniest hint of amusement in his eyes. "Oh, it gets better. Brace yourself for a taste of what real life can offer, my dear."

With that, he sauntered away from the wall, fiddled for something in his dark cloak and before I could muster up some courage to ask more about this deal, he threw a red pomegranate at me. I sucked in the air between my teeth. I knew what that was. My ticket to the Underworld.

"Come to me and I'll show you what life means," he whispered, sending a shiver down my spine. "

"Is that a threat?"

"A promise."

"And what is it that I have to give you because you saved me?"

"A favor. I'll keep my right to think properly about it. I'll tell you once you're fed up with your life here and come into mine instead."

"And if I may inquire, Your Majesty, what brings you here?"

"I'm stealing something," he winked, spun around, and suddenly the shadows engulfed him.

CHAPTER SIX
LYNNE

They let us in after sizing us up, probably thinking we didn't quite fit the chosen attire. Cherry held my hand the whole time, whispering about the changes that had taken place. As she told me about demons and Deadwalker onslaughts, I couldn't help but be blown away by their accomplishments. The gang had transformed into a task force, taking on whatever crawled up from the Underworld. They rescued numerous people, giving them a safe haven in all the buildings Rio owned. But the transformation of Dee's Paradise made my stomach turn.

Water trickled down the walls. The once-pink wallpaper was now worn and torn. With the chandelier gone, all that was left was the broken fixture and the hole in the wooden floor below, revealing its sudden fall. The staircase leading upstairs, where we girls had our rooms, was blocked and barricaded with crates. Wooden beams supported the walls, all doors were locked with iron bars, and extra furniture.

Then Cherry opened a thick iron door leading down to the basement. "This house used to be a military base. That's the only reason we're still alive. Many didn't make it during the first attack. The creatures came at night, catching us unaware."

As Cherry spoke in hushed tones, she held the armored door open for us to descend. The grumpy girl went first, followed by me and the rest of our group. You could tell from her posture she'd rather have us out of there.

"Can you believe these Topworlders? They're like a whole new level of bizarre," Ash muttered behind us, and when he squeaked, it seemed Ebony had given him a playful jab. "Honestly, their living setups are out of this world, and not in a good way."

"You act like it's your first time here," grumbled Ebony.

"The last time it looked completely different."

"Of course, it's called a different century, you moron."

We reached the bottom, and I was left in awe.

The stairs led into a deep, dimly lit chamber, the smell of metal enveloping us. It seemed like the walls were safeguarding the deepest secrets of the world as they were covered with steel plates. Some of these plates seemed slightly raised, hinting at access to hidden rooms. Pipes and cables disappeared into the shadows, revealing that there was more to see than met the eye.

One thing that left me breathless was the fact that she had scavenged a Deadwalker's head. It was already so decayed that the skin had become leather-like, no longer reeking. Its mouth gaped open, eyes sunken and dry, and all I could think was that this soul wouldn't find its way back anymore. It would likely roam the Topworld as a restless spirit forever. Just like so many others...

"Here's our communication center," Cherry said as we arrived, gesturing to a corridor leading to another room. I never knew Diva Dee's basement was this big.

I peeked in and saw computers and screens displaying

videos and maps of unknown locations. On the wall opposite from us there was a large map of Chicago, pinned to the wall, marked with notations and many sticky notes. All the red crosses told me that there had to be a lot going on in this district lately... I just hope the red exes didn't mean deaths or attacks because if so, there had to be hundreds of attacks on a daily basis.

Cherry opened another room, and several unfamiliar people greeted us, lying on a sea of cots. They didn't lift their heads as we entered, likely a constant flow of people seeking shelter.

Cherry and the girl conversed with them in passing, asking how they were doing, if they needed anything. However, everyone declined, expressing their gratitude. A few merely turned over upon hearing us and drifted back into slumber.

As Cherry led us to another door at the far back, I scanned the room, and my gaze fell upon a woman lying in the corner, her arm wrapped in a tight white bandage. Beside her, an elderly man lay with a splint on his leg, his face etched with lines of pain. A young boy rested nearby, his forehead adorned with a small bandage, evidence of a recent injury.

Cherry welcomed us inside, and within the room, we discovered two more beds, along with a desk and four chairs.

"This is where we sleep," Cherry stated, taking a seat behind the desk, motioning for us to sit as well.

Bory eagerly sat on the closest chair to her, flashing a grin at Cherry, who luckily paid no attention to him.

Ash, Ebony, and Mal refused to sit, leaning against the wall with arms crossed. So Any and I took seats next to Bory.

"I'll guard the door!" Punchy announced, closing it behind us.

"Anwyn," Cherry said, touching one of his snow white hands. "It's good to see you alive."

"Likewise," he said, a tiny smile tugging at the corners of his lips.

"Sadly, many have died," Cherry began, her gaze dropping.

"Diva Dee?" I blurted out.

"She's alive, but she's been through a lot. She has the room next to ours. Although she's in a wheelchair now, but she's doing okay."

"And Mellow and Cheetah?"

Cherry looked down. "Mellow is alive, but Cheetah…"

I could tell it was hard for her to talk about, so I changed the topic. "We're here to stop it, Cherry."

"How do you plan to stop it?" the girl sneered, arms crossed, continuing to scrutinize us.

"Cheeky little thing," Ash murmured, rolling his eyes.

And then, without a second to spare, Ash suddenly had a dagger right by his head. His eyes widened in surprise, and then he swiftly reached out and pulled the dagger from the wall. He pointed the sharp weapon menacingly at the girl, ready to strike if necessary. "Are you nuts? You nearly skewered me!"

The girl leaned over the table, piercing him down with her gaze. "I don't miss. Ever. I'm the number one Demonslayer around here, so watch how you talk about me."

Cherry sighed and drew a hand over her face. "Jamie, would you please treat our guests with respect?"

Jamie? The sound of her name made my stomach plummet. The grumpy girl was… Rio's daughter? It was like a sudden, sharp slap across my face. What did I do to make her so mad?

Jamie scoffed. "Guests? You do realize who you let in, right?"

I blinked. And blinked again. What. Was. Happening?

Cherry slammed a fist on the table. "Yes, damn it, I know. These are Lynne and Any," she said, and I flinched as she mentioned my name. It occurred to me that Rio had told her everything, who I truly was, where I came from... "and they're my friends, so treat them as such for fuck's sake!"

"Jamie? You're Jamie—Rio's and...and your daughter?" That was all I managed to say.

Cherry nodded, a sad smile gracing her beautiful face. She stroked Jamie's bun knots, but Jamie quickly brushed her hand away.

"Don't mention that man," she grumbled, and the room fell silent, heavy with tension.

My heart sank, burdened by the weight of her words. The sound of her grumbling echoed in my ears, each word piercing through me like shards of glass.

"W-why not?" I stuttered. The once vibrant colors of the room now appeared dull, mirroring the heaviness in my chest.

Her gaze snapped back to me. "You know why, he cheated on Mom with you."

I widened my eyes at her. "He did what?"

Cherry's hand flew to her mouth as she gasped in shock. Her cheeks flushed with embarrassment before turning to her teenage daughter. "Oh my God, Jamie! We've been over this so many times. You need to stop with these silly accusations."

She turned back to me, her face flushed with embarrassment. "Jamie found some photos of you in Rio's office and now she won't let it go. She's convinced you two had an affair and that he left her for you."

"But that—"

"Not just some photos, Mom," Jamie hissed, her face contorting in anger. "Naked pictures of her, tons of kissing photos, hundreds of them spanning several years! How is any of this okay? He was your husband."

I could feel the heat rising in my cheeks as I sank into the chair, wishing I could disappear.

Ash's high-pitched laughter echoed behind me, but I

couldn't bring myself to turn around. I could hear Ebony scolding him, but I kept my eyes fixed on the floor, feeling like I was living a nightmare.

Hell, I knew exactly which photos she was talking about. We took some less-than-innocent pictures during our short holiday, in the last few days I had before I was forced to leave and go back to the Underworld.

Cherry's voice lowered to a menacing whisper as she leaned in close to her daughter, the edges of her red lips curling into a snarl. She didn't want us to hear, but her words cut through the tension like a knife. "If you can't behave, I'll have Punchy come and drag your snarky self out of here. Do you understand?"

"But she—"

"I told you," Cherry cut her off. "Your father and I were together because of you, to give you a normal childhood. We didn't have a romantic relationship. She was the love of his life, and got whisked away to the Underworld."

"She was the one he left me for!" Jamie screamed, tears glistening in her eyes now.

I could see that it was still a sore spot for her.

Just like me, she was gnawing at his love for her, wanting to be the number one in his life. But she needed to learn that we all have very big hearts, capable of taking in and loving many more people. It wasn't me or her.

All of us could be dear to him.

A sudden pain pierced my heart, and it became clear that the old Shadow King could never have loved so many people. Everyone in this room. Cherry, Punchy, Jamie, Any, Ebony, Ash... me... he loved every single one of us now. I couldn't exactly remember how he was back then, but I think, that's something I don't miss. I don't know if I could fall for the man Zagrios was eons ago. Not only had he changed, but I did too.

"He didn't leave you, Jamie. Rio went to the Underworld to

save you, to rescue you from a Deadwalker's bite. He had to bring back a hundred souls for you, and he did it willingly," I said and noticed Jamie knew it was the truth, but she didn't want to accept it, probably because it was harder to accept the truth than to spin her own version of it. I knew that feeling all too well. I've been a master of spinning my own versions for years.

"And where is he now?" she asked, her eyebrows knitting together.

Cherry and Jamie exchanged curious looks, waiting for my response. I hesitated, glancing over at Any and Bory who were also looking at me expectantly. Could I trust them with this information? My heart raced as I debated whether or not to reveal that he was the Shadow King.

"He's in trouble," Any said for me. "And we need you all to save him, to save us."

"In trouble? Life-threatening? Cherry's face contorted, her eyes widening in disbelief, as if she had just witnessed a thunderous explosion. I shook my head. "Not at the moment, but—"

"We're all in danger," Mal interrupted, and we turned to face him. "Earth is crumbling, and so is the Underworld. The only world that will remain standing once the demons and shadow creatures destroy your world will be the realm of the gods, but even that is slowly decaying. Too many souls are ascending to the heavens, the circle can't be closed anymore, souls can't be sorted in the Underworld."

"And what can we do about it? We've been fighting these beasts for years," Jamie hissed.

"You can't defeat them," Mal continued, casually shrugging. "No one can, except Athena."

"Athena?" Cherry inquired.

"The supreme goddess," Any added. "She leads the gods,

and we need to reach her and implore her to intervene. Too much time has passed by."

"But why doesn't she do it on her own?" Jamie grumbled. "Surely, she can see that we're all here struggling for our lives. Why does she need you to remind her of her job?"

"She doesn't need us for anything," Any responded sharply, "but the gods are hesitant to interfere since it spiraled out of control during the Olympian era. They're likely already trying to find a solution, but thanks to a specific curse, they're somewhat constrained. However, we have a proposal we can present to her."

"You?" Jamie raised an eyebrow.

She looked at us, and I knew what she saw.

A group dressed oddly, like we were fresh out of a carnival. She didn't see warriors beneath these clothes and that needed to change. We had to show her what we were capable of.

I could handle that.

So, I clenched my fingers into a fist, slowly awakening my magic. It still felt strange, not needing bones or any anchors. I guessed Rio had managed to release that barrier, and I assumed my soul just remembered all the experiences and skills it once possessed. I closed my eyes, focusing on my magic, letting it stir.

"Mal?" I said. "Would you be a dear and fetch me the head of the Deathwalker from the antechamber?"

"Why?" he asked, and I turned around.

My eyes burned, and I knew they were glowing white as my gaze pierced his.

He swallowed, nodded, and rushed outside.

I took a deep breath and turned back to Jamie and Cherry.

Cherry sucked in a sharp breath as she saw me, but Jamie observed me, trying to understand what we truly wanted. Who we really were and what we were keeping from her. She was smart, very smart, and it filled me with pride knowing she was Rio's daughter.

The door slammed behind us, and Mal thudded the Deadwalkers head on the table in front of us. "Here you go," he grumbled, wiping his hands on his pants before returning to leaning against the wall as if nothing happened.

Jamie clicked her tongue. "What do you think you're doing? It's the first Deadwalker we've smashed, and it's a symbol—"

I stood up. My eyes were so bright now that they cast a faint glow on the deadhead. Oh, my magic truly was stronger here. I wondered what more I could do.

"Quiet now," I said, sensing an unexpected authority within me, a different aspect of myself.

Aria was more present today than ever, and the goddess within me was blooming, too. Hard to admit, but I loved it. I've spent far too many years not knowing who I was. It's high time I found out.

I touched the head, and a white beam of light shot out of my fingertips, draping over the entire head like a piece of cloth, then flowing like water into it. Murmurs spread through the group as the head transformed. Step by step, the yellowed bone turned brown, the decayed skin grew back again, pore by pore. The dead flesh tinted and darkened and became vibrant, alive. Then, the eyes grew, becoming fuller, filling with water, and the iris slowly turned into a glowing ocher. A piercing color stared back at us, reminding us of what was happening on Earth. The havoc we were exposed to. The Underworld might be a refuge for souls, but it couldn't handle the overflow anymore.

The hair upon her head grew thicker, dark and matted tendrils cascading past the table's edge. As Cherry recoiled in absolute horror, it struck me like a dagger through my soul. My blood ran cold. What unspeakable terror had we unleashed?

The woman before us wasn't just anyone.

She was Fox.

I stumbled backward in dread as the strength of my magic began to wane.

A moment of distraction, and my eyes felt normal again. My hand was cold, lacking the white shimmer. My magic gone again.

"No," Cherry uttered, her eyes meeting mine. "We didn't—"

I knew what Cherry was thinking. This wasn't fair. Despite the hatred, the betrayal, the lies, and the torment both of us had suffered thanks to Fox—she didn't deserve this. I gripped the chair's backrest—the wood creaking under the pressure. Bory stood up, placing his arm protectively over my shoulder, as we all stared at the now lifeless head. At Fox.

"You couldn't have known it was her," Any whispered next to me and I felt his steady grip on my shoulder. "Behind each Deadwalker is a soul, and once they're turned, they're stuck in limbo, they're not themselves anymore. It's not Fox you killed."

"This i-is horrible," Cherry whispered. "We sent so many souls into limbo…"

Jamie held her hand, and suddenly, she didn't seem so strong-willed anymore.

"But she has the power to heal them, to rescue them from limbo," Mal added from his spot in the back of the room.

I noticed Jamie's expression change as she watched, her features softening and her eyes trying to make sense of what was happening. For a moment, she looked like the young girl she should be.

"We have to stop this," I said.

"Intense," Ash blurted, and we all looked at him. He pointed at Fox. "What? That's wild."

Ignoring him, I turned back to Cherry and Jamie. "To

prevent this, we need your help. Rio hid something here, a key that will take us to Athena. We need your help to find it."

I sensed that Jamie listening more intently now. My plan worked and my grip on the backrest loosened a bit.

"Alright, and you're sure the attacks will end when we find that... key?" she asked.

"No one can ever be sure," Any said, turning Fox's head, so we now saw a fan of black, glossy hair. "But it's worth a shot, better than dying in misery."

I heard a soft agreement fill the room.

"What does the key look like?" Jamie asked.

"We don't know," I said. "It's supposed to be a large stone."

Jamie cringed. "Never saw father playing with stones."

Any fumbled in his pocket and retrieved a notebook.

He casually leafed through it, revealing pages already turned brittle. Then he unfolded the book and pointed at a stone that looked like a dragon egg, with a carving of a knotted net covering its surface. The sketch showed a hollow center, widening towards the base.

"That's the Omphalos Stone, an ancient relic. It doesn't really look like a stone, but more like a Greek jug. There is a city called Delphi in Greece and it's the mystical center of all our worlds. Back in the day, Zeus sent hawks on a cosmic scavenger hunt to find the center of our world, and when they crossed paths over Delphi, that's where he placed the Omphalos Stone. The stone had so much power that it connected all three worlds. Olympia, Earth and the Underworld. It got its power from Rhea, Zeus mother, since it was the very stone that she wrapped in swaddling clothes, pretending it was Zeus, in order to deceive her husband Cronus. He wanted to kill his own son and since that stone helped in saving her child, she transferred most of her magic into it, turning it into one of the most powerful relics of our worlds."

Any pointed a finger at a hand-drawn map of Greece. There was a huge circle showing Delphi.

"There, nestled on the slopes of Mount Parnassus, rested the Omphalos Stone. It served as a conduit for direct communication between the gods and mortals," Any explained. "And since Athena and the new gods shut all connections to Earth and the Underworld, this stone was turned into the only possibly way to communicate with the gods. For centuries."

"And why did Rio have it in his possession?" Jamie asked.

I flinched slightly when she referred to him by his name instead of calling him Dad.

Any smirked. "He stole it and destroyed the only thread connecting Earth and Olympia. Thanks to him, no god could leave Olympia and destroy his plans."

A dark flicker passed through Any's eyes, and a knot formed in the pit of my stomach.

As Any's eyes flickered with a dark intensity, a cold shiver ran down my spine. I could tell there was more to the story that he wasn't telling me. Why wasn't he angrier at Rio? Did he really steal that stone for my sake? No. It just didn't add up.

My fingers curled tightly into a fist.

Despite everyone else painting Rio as a monster, a small part of me felt like there was more I needed to know. I studied my brother's face, but he remained steadfast. Maybe I could catch him off guard or sneak up on him to find out the truth. The latter seemed like the safer option.

"This way no god could help us either..." Jamie whispered.

"Exactly. That's why we need to repair the connection and go to Athena." Any said. "So, please, would you be so kind and help us to find Rio's hiding place?"

"Yes," Jamie and Cherry said as if from one mouth.

CHAPTER SEVEN
LYNNE

After Cherry showed us our sleeping cots, Diva Dee nearly lost it when she saw me again.

I was surprised, given how much she had aged, her skin wrinkled, and the dark circles under her eyes were visible despite the heavy makeup.

Meeting more familiar faces, it became clear that the attacks had left their mark, yet Diva Dee bore the brunt of the impact.

She carried her fate with composure, but I could tell she missed the days when she danced on the stage in flashy dresses. Her current duty at the camp was to bring some joy and lightness to the somber group. In her wheelchair, she would move around, gathering everyone to play games, share stories, or sing whenever those they had rescued were consumed by grief. As usual, Diva Dee was the beloved center.

After a brief pause, we huddled around a map that Cherry had printed for us and began marking potential locations to search for the Omphalos Stone. While everyone else shared information about Rios' whereabouts, I turned to Any, hoping he would tell me whether there was more to the story or not.

But, of course, he clammed up, avoiding eye contact and fidgeting with his hands.

Feeling dejected and at a loss for what to do next, I shifted my attention to Jamie, hoping she would be more receptive. However, just like my brother, she kept her distance and didn't engage in conversation with me. She probably needed some time to process, and I postponed our talk.

To shake off the awkward tension, I brought Mal and Bory to dinner. At least those two were still easy to talk to. Ebony and Ash hung back in the common room, while Any brooded in the corner, lost in thought as usual.

Despite the tense atmosphere, Punchy remained his lively self, bringing some much-needed positive energy to our group. But to say the least, the food wasn't exactly gourmet—canned goods from the supermarket and noodles. The Loops also had plenty of packaged items like chips and candies stocked up in a room, in hopes that it would last until the end of the year. After that, Cherry told me they would need to venture out on another search. But as I looked around at my companions and thought about our situation, I fervently hoped that we would find that stone before then.

THE MEMORIES CAME and went as they pleased now, some leaving me utterly drained, others I just accepted. But every time I remembered a moment Rio, and I shared—I wanted more. I had to know who he truly was, because so far, I couldn't detect a hint of the evil man everyone always warned me about. The monster. Until now, he seemed educated and polite, and I wondered if I was getting all the details right or if Any was playing tricks on me once again. I tried to talk to him alone, but he avoided me as if he was finally sick of lying to me.

We spent the last two days with searching some spots we marked on the map.

Of course, we went to his old villa, the one where he used to live with Cherry and Jamie. The latter refused to accompany us there, so no chance of talking to her again. However, all that remained were a few ruins, and according to Any and Mal, we would have sensed the stone's magic if we were close. So, despite flipping nearly every stone three times, we found nothing.

On the way home, we encountered some more Deadwalkers, but they posed no real threat.

I reversed the transformations wherever I could, though I had to admit that wasn't always possible. Battles against shadow creatures were raging worldwide, and it seemed as if the entire demon realm had invaded Earth. Still, it mattered to me that I saved those I could.

We buried Fox in the park, or rather, Punchy did.

That thought, however, was better left pushed farther back.

And when Any took over guard duty at the entrance in the evening, I seized the opportunity to finally question him. Alone.

"So, what's the plan with Athena once we track down the stone?" I startled him a bit when I poked my head out of the entrance and sidled up beside him, arms crossed.

"That she rewinds time," he replied, shifting his weight to his other foot.

My eyes widened in disbelief. "That's impossible. No deity has the power to do that."

"Wrong. It's possible. That's why Rio stole it in the first place and we had to figure out a sneaky plan nobody would catch wind of."

I swallowed. Of course there was more to it. There always was. "Rio and you...You hatched the plan before our reincarnation?"

"The plan is to ask her to turn back time to a point where it can change the world. We'll undo a mistake."

I noticed he was dodging my question, giving me some roundabout answer to keep me off his back. And just when I was gearing up to dig deeper, Ebony snuck up behind me, nearly making me jump out of my skin. Figures, I'm not the only sneaky one around here.

"That's pretty dicey," Ebony said. "Would've been great if you guys had told us earlier that this quest was a lost cause."

My eyes shot up to her.

Similar to the rest of our crew, she was now decked out in military gear, because let's face it, we couldn't battle in those absurd outfits we'd scrounged up. Jamie and Cherry had generously supplied us with the practical gear.

"And it's against the law," chimed in Mal, emerging as well, and I pulled a face. Could I never have a private chat with my brother? "Athena won't be keen on rewinding time without serious consideration."

"She will. Trust me," Any said and I noticed them sharing a glance I couldn't place and I could have hit both of them.

"What's the deal? It's bedtime! You guys should be *sleeping*," I hissed.

"Well, we figured out pretty fast that when you slip away, it's better to follow," Ebony said with a smirk that begged for a smack as well.

I sighed deeply. This crew practically invited trouble.

"Too bad you didn't bring the whole gang," I retorted, rolling my eyes. Fine. Any slipped away once again, but I was determined to get him talking eventually.

"Well, Punchy and Ash are still locked in a battle of cards," Mal said. "And Bory's catching some Zs."

"Of course, he is," I sighed. My once blue bear was always the easygoing companion, never sneaking up on me like these guys.

But since he'd been in his human form, he'd been relentlessly pursuing Cherry.

Unfortunately, Bory didn't know how to flirt, confusing it with asking to serve her, and now he was like her personal lackey. Whenever Cherry needed someone to make the beds, he was there. If someone had to discard cans, he was there. We let him do his thing, and I sincerely hoped my silly minor spell would wear off soon because nobody could handle a smitten human-Bory.

"But how could Athena possess the ability to turn back time? I've never heard of her having the power to manipulate anything," I said.

"Legend says the Omphalos Stone has the power to change events in the past, but it's also extremely dangerous—that's why it was forbidden until we forgot its magical properties. But Rio found out so he stole the stone from Athena," Any explained.

"Why would he do that?" I questioned.

Any replied with a sly smile, "So that no one but us can use it until we're ready. Plus, without the Omphalos Stone the gods couldn't intervene on Earth since the connection was broken. It all boils down to planning and foresight."

I narrowed my eyes at him. "You sound like Hecate."

At that, Any's expression grew worried.

Our sister always spoke in riddles because of her visions, and I started to actually miss her. The more memories I had the more my heart ached for people I'd forgotten.

Any and I shared a knowing glance as Ebony chimed in with

a sigh. "I think using this as our salvation is risky. If we alter the past, there's a chance we might not even exist anymore—the world afterwards could be completely different."

"We'd be foolish not to try," Any said, glaring at Ebony. "Yes, there are dangers in altering history, but with proper precautions and limitations, it should work—just look around you." He gestured outside. "Nobody wants to live like this, and if we don't take action soon, there may be no worlds left. The doors have already been opened—we waited too long. We all gotta give up something if we're gonna save this messed-up world."

A thick silence hung between us, punctuated only by the sound of our breathing.

I avoided Any's gaze, my mind racing for something—anything—to say in response.

He was right and I felt a knot of guilt form in my stomach.

Mal pushed himself off the wall and stopped right before Any. I noticed his hand brushing against his, a brief touch that spoke volumes. My brother looked up at him, and I could see the longing in their eyes. The tension between them has been driving me crazy since I found out about those two, and I'm still desperate to know what had happened and why Any kept rejecting Mal despite his obvious love for him.

Mal cleared his throat and casually slipped his hands into his pockets."Well, it's probably better to risk changing everything than to have nothing left to change."

"Okay, okay...you may be right. It's just scary..." Ebony said.

"Alright. We're on the same page that the stone is our final option. Now, where do we go searching for it next?" Mal asked the group. "Any unexplored spots we haven't checked?"

Everyone's gaze turned to me, and I could only think of one place. "Um, maybe Reina's house?"

Any nodded. "Yes. I was thinking the same."

"Perfect, then let's ask the grumpy little one and the pinky haired woman tomorrow how the fuck we get there," Ebony said, turning to me. "And you stop sneaking away, girl or I'll cuff you against me."

As we approached Reina's house, we were met with a scene of destruction.

Even with Cherry updating me that Rio's family had made it out, it was tough to wrap my head around the downfall of their once glorious mansion. It now stood in ruins, its walls crumbled and shattered, the windows destroyed and scattered around. The grand entrance way was barely recognizable, with pieces of the ornate pillars and arches strewn across the ground. The walls, once a pristine white, were now blackened and cracked. All sense of grandeur was lost, and we found nothing but dust.

No matter how hard we tried, we scoured every nook of that crumbling house, and I even sprinkled a bit of my magic to brighten up the darkest corners. But our quest turned up zero, and we went back empty-handed, settling at the table with the gang as Cherry dished out the goods, warming up those canned delights. When Diva Dee cracked open her can, she told us about the trend of people moving to the rich areas in search of secret bunkers. They destroyed everything while fighting for their lives. As she delved into more stories about how the gang saved many people, my mind was roaming with ideas and where to search.

"I wish there was a guide telling us where to go. This is getting annoying." Ash complained, quickly finishing his meal of slimy soup, with his feet propped up on the edge of the table.

Ebony, sitting next to him, gave him a stern look. "Remember your manners, Ash." She gave his foot a sharp tap, causing it to drop to the ground with a loud thud.

Their voices grew louder and more tense, a heated argument on the brink of exploding.

As their banter faded into the background, it suddenly hit me. Ash had mentioned a "guide"—and we had a very certain book with us! Damn. Why hadn't we thought of checking it earlier?

I leapt up and rushed to the cot that Eb and I shared, digging through our bags until I found the thick, leather-bound book. Returning to the group, I gasped for breath as I announced, "Wait, guys, there's one more thing we can try!"

Ebony jumped as I showed her the old book given to us by the Blood Queen before she sent us to Earth. "This might have some answers," I said, trying to sound hopeful.

"God no, you must be kidding," Mal said. "Stop your sister, Any."

The others in the group murmured as I opened the book.

I noticed Cherry quickly ushering people out of the room to give us some privacy as I frantically searched for a spell that could help us.

"Aria," Any was suddenly by my side as I eagerly flipped through the weighty book, running my fingers over the elaborate symbols. "This book is wicked. I don't think we should—"

"—just let me have a look, God damn it."

The book was written entirely in the Old Language, a difficult tongue that we had been taught at the Olympian Academy. Despite my efforts, I could only understand fragments of it. Because of my stubborn nature, I wasn't able to stay in school for very long.

I glanced up at Mal.

He's fluent, but he stood far away from me, arms crossed

and refusing to even glance at the book. So, I wasn't even going to ask him because I knew he would say no.

I continued my search alone.

"I don't think there's anything useful in here," Any said just when I stumbled upon something about a Search Spell. Though I couldn't be certain, my hopes rose once again.

"Actually, there's a locating spell that could be of use to us," I offered, hoping I was right.

Any raised an eyebrow. "You do realize this book was hidden for a reason?"

"Oh, why don't you enlighten me?"

"According to legend, Lilith is the author of this book. She is known as the goddess of demons," Any explained, glancing at Eb and Mal for confirmation. "The spells contained within are a mix of good and evil, making it difficult to discern between them. Using this book puts us in danger of using the wrong spells."

"But the Blood Queen gave it to us," I interjected, realizing my argument wasn't exactly convincing.

Mal let out a frustrated sigh. "She probably intended for us to use it to close the gates, but we were too late."

"Or perhaps she gave it to us as a last resort," I suggested confidently. "She knew we couldn't close the gates without it."

"How can you call this a *last resort* when we haven't even started searching properly?" Ebony protested.

I shot her a glare. She should know better and not just take my word for it. "We're running out of time, that's why."

Everyone stared at me as if I had sprouted a second head.

"Come on, guys, let's give it a try," I urged. "I've used this book with the Blood Queen before, and I'm still alive. And if anyone doesn't want to join in, I can handle it alone." Since no one said anything, I read out out, "Inaeta a skala te ea ta Omphalos varea te."

The book vibrated in my hands, emitting a low tone as if a muffled male choir sang from its depths, repeatedly singing the same tune.

I couldn't comprehend what it was singing.

I looked up, my gaze meeting Mal's.

God, it was eerie.

Suddenly, the book closed itself, and I stared into its now completely animated eyes. The head in the middle was now prominent, as if an actual Deadwalker's head lived within. The vines on the sides swayed in the gentle wind, and the raspberries looked ripe for picking. Out of shock, my hands loosened, and I almost dropped it, but as if enchanted, the book clung firmly to me. I couldn't help but hold on to it. What the—

"You have summoned me," it declared with a voice echoing from the walls. Its mouth was fused, already in the midst of the decay process. The teeth were elongated, reaching down to the chin, and a tooth jutted out under the hollowed nose. Trustworthy was something else.

I swallowed, sensing Any, Ebony, and Mal positioning themselves around me to get a better look at the book. "I will reveal the location of the Stone, but it comes at a cost."

"What could a book possibly want?" Mal hissed, and Any elbowed him.

"Blood," the book hissed, and I noticed the others becoming uneasy.

"Whose blood?" Any asked, attempting to take the book from me, but it was stuck to my fingers as if glued. No one could pry it away now.

"Hers," the book said, its dark eyes focusing on me.

"No," Any protested, once again extending his hand beneath the book.

I pulled away, my gaze stern. "Stop bossing me around. If it wants my blood, it's going to get it."

"Aria," he said, "as we told you before, the book originates from the demons."

"Any," I snapped just like he did, "I'm aware, but tell me, Mr. Know-It-All, where are we supposed to search for the damned Stone, huh? It could be anywhere, and before we wander aimlessly and return home empty-handed, we should use what we have, and we have *this skulling* book."

"I think she's right," Ebony said. "Although I wouldn't really trust the Blood Queen, giving it a shot won't hurt."

"It could go *very* wrong and set us back hours again," Any said.

"Well, we won't succeed without taking risks," I said.

"Yeah, life is no walk in the park," Ebony added. I smiled at her and then suddenly, the book released one of my hands.

"Give me your wrist," it demanded.

I hesitated at first, but then I lifted my hand, placing the wrist face down on the book's mouth. Then it snapped shut, and the book's many teeth bit into my skin. I felt the blunt tips piercing me, and I screamed.

"Damn it," Any yelled, trying to take my hand away, but then he screamed and clasped his hand. "This damn thing burned my hand!"

Gritting my teeth, I clenched my fist around the book and pressed it harder against my skin. The sharp edges dug into my palm, drawing blood that trickled down my fingers. I closed my eyes, focusing on slow, steady breaths as the pain intensified. Finally, it released my grip, and I pulled away, revealing the deep red imprint of the book against my skin. The blood continued to flow, staining my hand and the pages of the book.

"For the Hellhounds, I'll get a bandage," Ebony said, about to rush downstairs, when Mal held her back.

"It's okay," he said, placing his hand over mine.

A warm sensation spread on my skin, and when he removed

his hand, my wounds were closed. I looked at his hair, and I saw a strand turning white. It always happened when he healed something—his hair got lighter. Suddenly, I could remember the first time I saw him. Strangely, it wasn't in Cave Town, but at a market in an alley... Back then, he had black hair and just a few silvery dreadlocks. Yes, exactly, his hair didn't always look like it did now. It was initially jet black, then slightly gray, and it kept getting lighter until eventually, all his hair would turn white. I had always wondered what would happen then. Would he still have magic when there's no hair left to turn white?

Neither of us knew the answer, so we were left to patiently wait and find out.

"Oh, Styx," Ebony muttered, taking a step back. "You guys are all sick. Creepy."

Mal swallowed and put his hand in his pocket, as if he needed to hide it.

He always hated his gift. In the Underworld, nobody wanted to be healed. There we're supposed to suffer, yet I found his gift the best of all. He could take away the pain.

"Thank you," I whispered.

We exchanged glances briefly. There was so much he didn't tell me. What he did with the Blood Queen, how he helped her, and what their relationship actually meant...Mal avoided my gaze at first, and then he looked at Any, making my anger even greater. The two of them had another secret. Something they didn't tell me.

The book licked its lips. The teeth were now stained red from my blood, and its lips were the same color as the raspberries growing along its edges.

"You are seeking the o," the book said. "A huge task."

Mal rolled his eyes. "Bloodsucker," he grumbled. "Just tell us where it is."

"The Stone was protected by a potent magic. It's not that

simple, Silverhair," the book replied, fixing its gaze on Mal now. "You must find the notes. He left a message for you."

"He? Rio?" I asked, feeling a pang in my heart when I spoke his name. Any seemed to notice, rubbing my back with his hand.

"He gave you the key," the book said, its eyes staring at me.

"What key?" Ebony asked, looking at me as if I had hidden from her the fact that I had known where the damn Stone was for a long time.

I threw one arm up in mock defense. "I have no key!"

"It's not an object," the book continued. "He told you where you could find them, but in a way that no one else could. Not even I."

"Interesting," Any said. "He must have done a lot during the short time frame in between reincarnation."

"But I remember nothing," I said, shaking the book out of impatience. This couldn't be all! I gave it my blood, and it talks more cryptically than the Oracle. "I have no idea about the key."

"Oh, but you do," the book said. "You know it. You know the letters; they almost align themselves day in and day out, over and over again."

I squinted my eyes. What exactly did this book want from me?

"Okay, she obviously has no clue," Ebony hissed, pointing her finger at the book. "Meaning, you can now spit out another hint, or I'll throw you into the fire."

"Fire can't harm me, sad nymph," it said, and Ebony blinked at its nickname. "The blood was delicious, so I'll offer one more piece of advice. You must journey to the Wadden Estate. Within its walls, you will discover crucial clues that will guide you to the stone. The words that will assist you in this quest have been ingrained in your memory from the moment you were reborn on Earth. You will recall the location of the hidden stone, as it was revealed to you, just before your reincarnation. Trust in your abilities, and you will remember everything you need to know."

The book suddenly shut its eyes, returning to its normal appearance as a slightly unsettling object.

CHAPTER EIGHT
LYNNE

"You're headed where?" Jamie's voice cut through the air as we packed our things in the common room.

"Goldcoast," Any replied, securing the gun Punchy gave him. Loaded with silver, it seemed capable of slowing down Deathwalkers, a kind of range control. "Richeleustreet."

"Who do you know living there?" Jamie's shock was palpable, her gaze darting to her mother, who nodded affirmatively at Any and me.

Jamie's jaw dropped. "You're that wealthy?"

"Were," Any corrected, his throat clearing. "Can we use your van again?"

Cherry nodded. "Of course. Punchy can drive you."

"I'll come along," Jamie chimed in. "There are quite a lot of demons in that area."

"Perfect." I smiled. Perhaps this was my opportunity to finally engage in a meaningful conversation with her.

The sting of her disapproval cut deep.

Admittedly, it must have been a strange pill for her to swallow. Growing up in a household where parents coexisted, their love a mere ember of friendship rather than a fiery romance.

Well, that was anything but the norm. But where else could Cherry have turned? Money was tight for her, every cent stashed away for her schooling. Her mom got caught in the crossfire of gang mayhem, leaving Dee's Girls as her only support system. And while Jamie wrestled with the raw reality that she didn't quite fit the whole picture-perfect family mold, the kind her friends seemed to slide into effortlessly, there was no doubt that it was the best call Rio and Cherry could make. She had everything a kid needed, until, well, the gates to the Underworld cracked open. Courtesy of her dad.... and me.

Sure, she had every right to be mad, but not for the reasons she thought. I'd get it right again. I just had to. She's Rio's kid, after all.

I quickly gathered our belongings and stuffed them with Punchy in the trunk, mostly bladed weapons, since Death-walkers needed to be beheaded in the end.

Punchy's van lacked the polished gleam of the cars Rio had and appeared rather worn. It sported many dents, dried blood-stains, and scratches etched into the metal. Suddenly, an image of Punchy zooming the car through a group of Deathwalkers flashed in my mind—and a shiver ran down my spine.

Ebony and Ash immediately took seats at the back.

Trying to make it clear that the middle row was reserved, Mal headed to the front with Punchy. I wanted some private time with Jamie. Since I couldn't take a step alone, the middle row was all I had.

"God, I hope this time I don't feel sick. I hate these things," Ash said from behind as Jamie buckled him and Ebony up since they struggled.

"You'll end up enjoying it," she said. "It beats strolling by a mile, and trust me, if we walked, we'd be toast. These zombies are a major pain in the ass."

"Zombies?" Ebony asked.

"Deadwalkers," Bory chimed after he said his goodbyes to Cherry. "It's a term from the movies. You know that moving picture they have in the common room?"

"Ah." Ebony gave Jamie a puzzled look, as if she'd just stumbled upon something strange and wasn't quite sure what to make of it.

Bory seemed like he wanted to snag the seat next to me, yet a slight nod from me directed him to the front, alongside Punchy and Mal. I craved a bit of room and tranquility—essential to draw Jamie into a conversation.

When Any snagged the seat next to Ash, Jamie heaved a sigh and moved to the front row. Her face fell when she found all the seats occupied, and that's when a mischievous grin played on my lips. She looked at me, cringing. When I patted the seat next to me, she realized the lack of options. Jamie made her way toward me, and took the only available seat left. Ha. Victory.

With a slight grunting sound, she secured her seatbelt, and Punchy took the wheel. In that moment, Punchy's gaze met mine in the rearview mirror, and I couldn't resist breaking into a wide smile. It felt like back in the day, when he used to drive me around, take me to the shooting range because Rio wanted me to be able to defend myself and that's when my smile dropped again. Just the idea of him and where he might be hit me right in the heart—a pang that stung worse than all the blows I took from the Deadwalkers.

The only solution to stop my incessant thoughts and longing for him was to constantly reassure myself that he was simply sleeping, and everything would be fine once I located that stupid stone. At least, that's what I hoped for. I couldn't afford to waste time grieving over him. My main focus was to save him before I had to experience genuine sorrow.

Emotions could wait until later. Until I held him again.

Punchy switched on some music and cheerfully sang along with a female voice.

Oh, how I loved Punchy.

"Punch," Bory piped up, earning a glare from him, as Punchy was in the midst of belting out a tune, and we all know he took his singing seriously.

"Huh?" he grunted.

"What could I do to put a smile on Cherry's face? A surprise, maybe?"

I couldn't help but roll my eyes. Bory was on this mission to create the perfect gift for Cherry, but considering everything was falling apart, chances of finding anything remotely gift-worthy were slim.

"Um, how about chocolates and flowers?" Punchy suggested with a half-shrug, resuming his singing. "Yeah, I thought about those. Even considered making the chocolates myself but I couldn't find any ingredients besides canned food—everything else is so moldy, you know?" Bory said.

"Hmm... Yeah," Punchy pondered, his finger tapping his chin as if contemplating the mysteries of the universe. "What about a necklace?"

I let out a snort of laughter. "Where exactly are you going to find a necklace in this wasteland, Punchy?"

"We could shop—oh, well the store is destroyed too. Yeah, I think we won't find a pretty necklace, Bory." Punchy sighed.

Oh my, Punchy was a sweetheart, but to be honest, he wasn't exactly the go-to guy for brilliant ideas, but Bory tried it nevertheless and kept on brainstorming with him.

I caught him sighing and glancing back at Any before refocusing his gaze on the street. His shoulders slumped as he took in the scene. I had to insist on a conversation with both my brother and Mal. This situation is getting out of hand.

As Ash and Ebony launched into a discussion about slaying

Deadwalkers more efficiently, I seized my chance. "So, Jamie, I'm truly sorry for everything that's happened." Well, that wasn't the best kind of start.

"That you took Dad away from me, you mean?" She shot back, her tone unforgiving. She turned to face me. An icy glare bore into mine.

"I didn't take him away from you," I explained, hoping she'll understand. "He stayed on Earth because of you. Just look at your scar." I motioned towards the mark on her neck. "Remember how the Deathwalkers attacked you? You're alive today because he struck a deal with the...Bone Queen." It's difficult to say her name, but I managed to choke it out. "He wanted to come for me, but not before you were grown up."

"This doesn't make it any better."

"He loves you, Jamie. With all his heart, he talked a lot about you in the Underworld and he misses you."

"Still, he had more photos of you than Mom or me," she said, staring outside.

"I'm sorry. I understand it's a complicated situation. But your mother told you they didn't have a romantic relationship..." I trailed off. Gods. What else could I say? I really wanted her to like me. Rio loves her so much. "Okay. Look. What I wanted to tell you in the first place, your father loves you. He would do anything to be with you again," I began, gently touching her arm, relieved that she didn't pull away. "He's shared stories about you, like how you're crazy for Paw Patrol, how you used to dance like no one was watching, and belt out songs like a little popstar."

A hint of a smile flickered across Jamie's face, but it dropped as quickly as it showed. "He only knows the version of me up to when I was five. I hate dancing and singing now."

My smile dropped as well.

"He loves you, Jamie," I said again. The weight of each

passing moment he cannot be with you weighs heavily on him. Believe me. It's true. You can be as angry with me as you want, but please, not with him. I hope he gets the chance to tell you how much he loves you again soon. " I hoped I could tell him how much I loved him soon as well.

A quiet nod from Jamie followed, though I wasn't sure if my words were penetrating the walls she had built around herself. I just wished. It would have broken his heart knowing how she thought of him now.

She turned her gaze away, and as her eyes settled on the swirl of dust kicked up by Punchy's van, I caught sight of a single glimmering tear tracing a path down her flushed cheek.

Positioned in the car out front, Punchy was ready for a quick getaway if any issues cropped up.

Oddly enough, the house itself stayed the same, mirroring the one etched in my memory. As I approached it through the wrought-iron gates, its striking presence lifted my gaze.

Even though it appeared a bit worn now, like all the other buildings on Earth nowadays, the exterior of the estate still kept its stunning beauty--I suddenly had my father in my mind, telling us that this was the most beautiful colonial villa in the city. And I believe it was. The three stories seemed to stretch toward the sky, while the windows, tall and arched, offered glimpses into the shiny and spacious rooms within. Unfortunately, the white bricks appeared aged and tired, and the previously green ivy that entwined the walls had become blackened by the accumulated dust.

With every footfall upon the cobblestone path, each stone worn smooth by countless footsteps, I felt a subtle connection to my former self walking here. I knew I've lived in this house, sneaked away to Rio through the garden, playing soccer on the lawn with Any... In simple terms, I felt the tug at my heart and the weight on my old soul. So, I stopped and just looked at the entrance. It was still flanked by imposing columns that seemed to whisper tales of my forgotten life. But I didn't need all my human memories back to know that living like this wasn't normal. We truly were rich as skull.

"You good?", Any suddenly said, his hand on my back, rubbing gently as we both stared at our former house.

"It's odd to be back. How is it for you? You have so many more memories of this world than I do."

He sighed as we continued along the path.

Bory's voice carried clearly from behind, claiming that Punchy was a genius, that flowers and chocolates might not be his forte, but a necklace could work, given the state of the house. Oddly, Jamie even chimed in, helping him out by describing the jewelry her mother liked.

"Well," Any said cautiously, "I only lived here until I graduated high school. And after you died, our family fell apart. Mom escaped her grief through constant vacations and pills, while Dad was hardly present. I didn't understand why at the time. My memories of the Underworld and Olympia were erased as well, of course. But then, before everything with you and Rio happened, I found out that father was a Titan. I saw him vanishing and discovered that magic exists. And when he couldn't offer much help after your death—I took matters into my own hands. I traveled, studied ancient civilizations, challenged my father until I figured out what had happened. Unfortunately, it was after I struck a deal with the Blood Queen."

"You were lucky it wasn't the Bone Queen," I remarked.

Any nodded. "Yeah, but it was Dad who pointed me to her. He would've never handed me a spell that led me to the Bone

Queen. He wanted me to strike a deal with his lover, a little nugget of information I stumbled upon much later, naturally."

"Weird that they have a thing." The thought of Cyril being my father still made me cringe. His true name was Erebos, but he apparently changed it to stay under cover... but every time I saw him at the Blood Court, it made my stomach churn. Given that he hit me numerous times as a kid, I now understand why I hated him so much. I guess my soul remembers all the scars he left there. At least when he was around, the queen's temper was less fiery. She used to be so snarky and difficult when he was gone. And in the end, he received a punishment for being cursed as well. To be honest, I was relieved. He couldn't stay with us in our human lives because of his own curse. He wasn't allowed to remain in any realm for too long, constantly crossing between them. But thinking of it, it was strange that Athenas's curse also affected him. I thought it only controlled those close to me... There was another factor that simply didn't add up, causing my stomach to churn even more.

"We never had a great relationship with him. I don't think he's capable of having healthy bonds," Any added. "Maybe the Blood Queen fits better than our Mom ever did, human or Titan."

"Did he love Mom? Nyx, I mean?" A heavy sensation settled in my gut.

I knew I loved her, even though I sometimes feared her power. Darkness frightened me back in Olympia, it always had. I needed light everywhere, always needing a flame, which Any gifted me with candles, teasing that I should marry Helios' son, the Sun God. A smile tugged at my lips at the thought. He used to mock me about that. Good that the darkness loves me now.

"Yes," Any said after a long pause. "But Mom's magic caught up to her. She grew more distant, her power uncontrollable. Athena finally intervened, taking her to the Underworld, where her magic expanded to where no light reaches the world anymore, and she—" Any's voice got stuck.

"Died?"

"Yeah, sort of." He took my hand and squeezed it tightly.

I squeezed back.

I couldn't help but feel his sadness as he looked directly at me. "They turned her into a giant beast. We actually saw her. Do you remember Tisiphone's beast?"

My stomach dropped. "That's Mom?"

Any nodded. "This was how I first met Rio, in asking him to bring back our mother, but it was a lost cause. Only Athena could reverse this spell and she wouldn't."

"Why?"

An exasperated sigh escaped Any's lips as he spoke, his voice heavy with frustration. "It's a punishment because of Hecate," he explained, his eyes downcast. "Because of her vision. It changed everything, and she punished our mother for her unsteady magic." He paused, his tone taking on a bitter edge. "But it was easy to get rid of her. Just give a warning to the other gods and punish her for her lack of magical wisdom."

My eyebrows furrowed in confusion, and I couldn't help but ask, "Athena punished Mom? That doesn't seem like something the goddess of wisdom and justice would do."

Any let out a humorless chuckle. "Our names are just interpretations of our powers, Aria. There's always more to a person."

I sensed that he didn't want to talk about it anymore, but I couldn't resist prying. Who knows when I'll get another chance to ask him like this? "Do you think Athena would free Mom if we lift the curse?"

"I hope so," Any replied quietly. "Living like this is not an option."

He pulled away from my grasp when I tried to comfort him.

"What about Hecate? I remember the three of us being close, but my memories about our family are so distant," I said aloud, realizing that Any never truly talked about our sister.

"She died," was all Any said before pulling away completely.

I was about to ask some more since that answer was anything but satisfying, but then Mal appeared, and at the sight of him, Any sighed and marched ahead alone. Great. My time frame for real talk was over then.

Mal let out a heavy, resigned sigh and I saw him clench his jaw. Recognizing the opportunity to change the subject, I turned to him with newfound curiosity. "Alright, spill it. What's the deal with you and him?" I said, my eyes following my brother as he paced in front of the imposing double doors, giving them an occasional shake.

"What do you mean?" Mal grumbled and I could have slapped him.

As Ash and Ebony hurried over to assist Any and search for a way inside, I grabbed Mal by the shirt, pulling him a little away from Bory and Jamie.

"You're into my brother," I whisper-shout.

Mal's eyes rolled dramatically as he brushed off my statement, but when he caught my determined glare, his shoulders slumped in defeat. "Must we always go at full speed? Normal people take things slow, get a feel for things first, ask if they want to talk about it. And thanks for asking, but I don't."

He spoke with a sense of defeat, as if we had gone through this same disagreement countless times before. Maybe in his head.

"Normal people have time. We're on a clock here. So, come on, how do you two know each other, and why is there such an awkward tension?"

Arms crossed, I made it clear I wouldn't back down until he told me what was going on. This was a fight I could win.

He sealed his lips. That bastard.

And that's when Ash's voice cut through. "We're not getting in here. We should split up and search for another way," he yelled.

"Fine, Mal and I will head to the back door together," I shouted back, grabbing Mal's shirt again and pulling him toward the garden. Behind us, the others gathered, discussing where they'd head to.

"Okay," I said as we reached the back door by the terrace, as if it was only yesterday that I celebrated my sixteenth birthday there. "Now what's up?"

"Look, there are things that are better left unsaid. You don't want to hear about your brother's sex life," he began as we ascended the stone stairs.

I halted, grabbing the brass railing. "You had sex?" Shit, I thought they were in the talking and longing stage.

"See? It's already too much for you," Mal grumbled as he stormed towards the white terrace door that apparently got replaced with clear glass. He shook it forcefully, realizing it was locked. "Can I break the glass? This house doesn't mean anything to you anymore, does it?" he said.

"No, it doesn't. Go on, give it your all," I said.

Mal drew his sword and thrust it into the door, causing it to shatter into countless fragments. He gestured for me to enter, and I reached inside and opened the door from within, allowing us to enter smoothly.

"So, where did you two first meet?" I asked again.

"At the Blood Queen's palace during the Dance of the Dead," Mal replied stiffly.

"We had a fling back then. But he stopped showing up when I started working for the queen. Until we met again when you and Rio came to Cave Town."

"Yeah, but there must be more to it," I murmured as we stepped into the villa.

"He was always afraid of something serious," I said, recalling memories of him with Tina and then a girl named Sierra Mojica.

Out of everyone, she was the only one he truly had a relationship with, and I really liked her. He was completely in love with her, but when things started to get serious, he would suddenly cut off all contact. That's when she turned to me for help, but unfortunately, I couldn't do anything. At that time, I didn't know that he leaned towards men.

"It's sad. Whenever things get serious, he always shuts down," I said.

It was strange how I was starting to feel more like Aria now. Initially, I had resisted even hearing that name, but now it felt like my own. Almost as if it were me, and that feeling continued to spread within me as I regained more memories. The more I remembered, the more I could accept being Aria.

With a grin, I stopped in front of him and said, "But you're in love with him. I've never seen you act this way with anyone else."

He muttered under his breath and forcefully shoved me aside, storming through the orangery where we could hear the rest of the group talking. I reached out to grab Mal's arm, trying to stop him from leaving in such a rage. "Are you really just going to walk away?" I asked, my voice rising with frustration, but he paused, gasping for breath.

I placed a hand on his shoulder. "Mal, maybe I can help. He's my brother, I know him." A bit. And to be honest, I struggled with him too, but I hated to see Mal struggling like this.

He turned towards me with tears in his eyes. "I told Any that I love him and he said he loves Zagrios instead. Happy now?"

My heart sank. I had a feeling this was coming, but I didn't expect it to hurt so much. "Mal, listen. My brother may have issues, but I know deep down he cares about you."

Mal scoffed. "How would you know? You're constantly fighting."

I took a deep breath, trying to keep my emotions in check. "I've seen the way he looks at you, the way he lights up when you're around. He's just scared of his own feelings, pushing you away instead."

"His walls are impenetrable. I don't know how to break through them."

"Well, he's my relative, and it's clearly a family issue. We're all stubborn in our own ways. But if you truly love him, give it a chance. And know that I'm here for you, no matter what."

His shoulders tensed and then dropped, his face contorting with a mixture of grief and relief. He wrapped his arms around me, his fingers digging into my back. When he finally pulled away, his hair was disheveled from running his hand through it repeatedly. "Sorry we had to lie to you, but it truly was for your own good. I packed up and moved to Cave Town just for you. What more do you need as proof of my love? It's like a giant "I love you" sign that I wear around my neck at all times."

I chuckled. "Cave Town sure was something, wasn't it?"

"Now, would the two of you back there mind coming over here? We have a quest to tackle," Ash called out to us from the hallway.

I gave Mal a last final pat and then we moved over to the others.

Ebony's arms were tightly crossed as she asked, "Where do you think he hid it?"

I shook my head, feeling the weight of all the expectant gazes on me. "I really have no clue," I confessed, trying to think of possible hiding places and items that could be hidden.

"Well, that book said he told you everything," Ebony said.

Ash waved his hand dismissively. "Yes, she has amnesia," he said with an exaggerated eye roll. "Just like you every morning when you forget how lucky you are to wake up next to me." He flashed a toothy grin while Ebony stood one step further away from him.

"Dream on," she retorted. "I never wake up next to you."

"You did thrice." Ash said and I think Ebony was trying to kill him with her look.

"Lynne," Bory spoke up. "What if we check some rooms? Maybe something will trigger your memory and help us find what we're looking for."

"That's a good idea," Any agreed.

"But what exactly should we be looking for?" I asked him, hoping he would have some insight. After all, he knew Rio better than any of us. My memories of human Rio were few; most of them only showed us being flirty or skipping school together.

"He used to sleep over at our place often," Any began, leaning against a staircase leading to the second floor. "Usually he just had his duffel bag with him—some clothes and nothing more."

"But what if it's not related to human Rio at all?" Ebony chimed in, causing all of us to turn and look at her. "I don't see how he could have known anything about his previous life during his reincarnation... "

"Zagrios hid it before the reincarnation. He planned it all out,"Any added.

"That's similar to what the book mentioned," I said. It seemed nearly impossible to figure out where Rio could have hidden anything in this massive house.

"But maybe everything is connected... we should start by searching the rooms where the three of us spent the most time—my room, the living room, and... your room," Any suggested.

I grimaced at the thought. In my room, it was just Rio and I...

"And the storage room," I quickly added.

"Which one?" Any asked.

"The one behind the bathroom. I remember seeing you and Dad disappear in there once."

"Oh yeah," Any recalled. "He took me with him to the Underworld to meet with the Blood Queen."

"He must have had Zagrios' approval, then," Ash interjected.

"That's odd," Ebony added.

"Hey, what are you guys doing here?" Jamie yelled from across the room, finally joining us with Bory in tow. "I thought we were searching? We already roamed through the kitchen and living room while you guys chatted?"

"Not cool," Bory grumbled.

I threw up my hands in mock defense. Well. Guilty.

"Okay, you guys are right. Come on, we split up. Lynne, you search and touch as much as possible," Any said. "The rest of us will look for books, notes, anything that might lead us to what we're looking for. This could take all day."

CHAPTER NINE
LYNNE

We roamed through the entire house, and Bory insisted I touch everything to make sure nothing was missed. We were divided into teams to be more efficient. Jamie was with Any, Ebony was with Ash, and Bory and I were accompanying Mal.

"It's crazy how much money you had," Mal remarked as we strolled through the second floor.

"Lynne, give the curtain a little *love tap*," Bory said and pointed to the white dusty curtains to our sides.

I rolled my eyes. "He wouldn't have hidden the stone in a damn curtain."

"You never know," he retorted with a shrug.

"You're impossible," I said and touched the curtain and nothing happened. So we went on.

No matter how much I pondered, I couldn't figure out where Rio had hidden that skulling stone, especially knowing he told me. I could pull at my hair for not remembering. But something told me I should try the storage room, even though Any was convinced I wouldn't find anything there. Bory was right, we never knew, although the things Bory suggested usually were the most hideous.

"Yeah, we were never short on material things. It's crazy how much we possessed," I said to Mal, touching the portraits on the wall.

Suddenly, Bory returned with five items he had piled up in his arms.

"Touch these. They look peculiar."

"Do they..." I said and stared at the objects in Bory's hand.

It was a strange feeling to be back in this place after so long. The last time I was here, I had no idea what these objects were for or what they were called. But now, it all suddenly made sense to me. I knew those items were not the ones we needed, but for Bory's sake, I pushed myself to reach for the stapler, vase, and Any's Power Ranger doll. As expected, nothing happened. I let out a sigh and shared a grin with Bory, whose disappointment was evident in his blue eyes. He reached into his pocket, and it was like watching a magician trying to pull something out of thin air letting none of the items fall to the ground. I couldn't contain my laughter at the amusing sight.

"Bory, I don't think he would have put the stone in a keychain..." I stared at the small plastic dangling in Bory's hand.

"What's a keychain?" Mal asked, taking the green cloverleaf that Any and I had brought from the summer camp in Ireland.

"It's something people attach to their keys to make them easier to find,"

I coughed softly, ignoring Bory's disappointed expression as my touch didn't do the trick, and casually continued down the hallway. It was quite dark, with just a few windows here and there, playing hide-and-seek with the light. The hallway seemed endless. I looked at the many white doors on our right and left, wondering why we had so many rooms and what was inside them. I vaguely remembered that Dad had a sports room, Mom had an art room, a game room, a cinema room... as I said, humans loved having a room for everything. But I knew Rio wouldn't have hidden the stone just anywhere. It had to be somewhere I could find it. Somewhere Aria would go. Something I would remember.

"Maybe we should have taken Any with us," Bory said, bringing me another handful of items.

I touched a teddy bear, a plastic apple, and a nail file. Bory and Mal stared down at me and honestly, I had no idea what everyone expected to happen, but nothing did. Absolutely nothing.

So, I turned and went ahead. We had to go to the bathroom and search for the hidden room there. I just felt it deep in my chest.

"Do you even know where we're supposed to go?" Bory called out from behind, as he continued to amass a growing collection of random objects.

"Try channeling your inner Rio," Mal suggested and I couldn't stop a grunt.

"Yeah, visualize him," Bory chimed in. "Maybe he'll pop up like a genie."

I came to a sudden halt. "Could you guys cut me some slack? This isn't helping." Popping up like a genie? He couldn't be serious. I missed him so skulling much and I would have loved if he popped up but he won't and I would love to shout and cry and demand my husband back—but I skulling can't.

With an apologizing smile, Bory extended more objects to me. God. These two were impossible.

I didn't touch the objects this time and continued forward. Mal and Bory shared a look as I walked by, and for some reason, I felt drawn to the left. Without hesitation, I followed my instincts and reached for a doorknob. The gilded handle was rough under my fingertips, covered in dust. I pushed it down and stepped into the room, as if compelled by an unseen force.

It was my old room.

As my hand gripped the doorknob and I stepped into the room, my heart thudded in my chest and I froze.

I felt the plush white carpet under my feet, worn from years of childhood playtime. A twinge of sadness hit me as I remembered how Any and I played with plastic construction toys on this very spot. The walls were still painted in a comforting shade of white, adorned with fairy lights that used to twinkle. Amongst the lights hung a collection of Polaroid photos, each one capturing a cherished memory...

My gaze swept to my white bed with its playful canopy, to my cluttered desk, covered in stacks of books and trinkets from my past, still commanding attention in the center of the room. But it was the towering bookshelf that made me gasp. Every shelf was packed to the brim with books of every genre, a testament to my insatiable appetite for stories and adventures. As I looked around, I could almost hear the walls sigh under the weight of countless tales and feel the weight of longing in my heart. This room was my sanctuary.

And then, my gaze was drawn to a simple box resting on my bed, labeled with the words "Top Secret."

"Is this some kind of secret police box? I think I've seen something like this in a TV series," Bory said, standing next to me as I rushed to it and lifted the lid. Inside was a purple plastic ring, and my heart seemed to stop for a moment.

Even if I wanted to, I couldn't do anything about the memories that formed in my mind now.

I heard Bory say something, but my thoughts were overwhelmed by the sudden images in my head.

Rio and I entwined in my bed, our bodies pressed together as we explored each other's every curve.

CHAPTER TEN
ARIA, EARTH 20 YEARS AGO

"You know what?" he whispered, his breath hot against my neck as his body pressed against mine. My legs wrapped tightly around him, pulling him closer to me. "What's that?"

"We could do something wild," he murmured, his blue eyes glinting mischievously in the sunlight. "Something reckless and thrilling."

"Crazier than our breaking into the school for a pool party?"

"Yes," he said, his expression suddenly serious. He cupped one of my breasts, making my heart skip a beat. "Do you know that feeling when you hear cheesy love songs on the radio?"

"Rio," I laughed, "what are you talking about?"

"And every cheesy song suddenly is about you?"

My laughter was abruptly cut off as I felt the intensity in his gaze.

Without a single word, he closed the gap between us and devoured my lips with a fierce kiss that sent shivers down my spine.

"I fucking love you," he growled, ravaging my mouth with a raw passion I had never experienced before.

My hands feverishly tore at his shirt, desperate to have him closer. "I love you so much that I want to do all the dirty things people warn us about," he whispered against my skin as he pulled down my stockings and gripped under my school skirt. "I want," his tongue sought another kiss, "to ink your name on my skin," another kiss, "gotta brand myself with you 'cause you're all I freaking want. Forever, no escape."

"Rio," I moaned as he nipped at my neck, his fingers digging into my ass cheeks.

"I want to take a huge loan with you, binding us in all contracts there are, I want to do Graffitis with you, I want—" I kissed him back, almost ripping his shirt as I tore it down from him, sighing as his skin touched mine. "I want to marry you. When all this is over, marry me, Aria."

That's when everything came to a halt, our hands tangled in each other's hair, chests rising and falling as we tried to catch our breath.

He searched my eyes for an answer, silently pleading for me to say yes. "Marry me."

I had to take a moment to process his words because they felt like something out of a dream. As I gazed into Rio's beautiful face, I saw the gentlest soul in his eyes and I knew I could love no one else. "I do, yes, yes, yes and a thousand times yes."

He flashed a wide grin and reached into his pocket; the pants hanging loosely on his hips. I hadn't had a chance to get rid of them yet. He pulled out a plastic ring, purple and almost glowing in the dim light. It had a simple, yet elegant design with a small gemstone in the center. "I'll buy you the most beautiful ring there is," he declared as he held it out to me. "It's just temporary."

I eagerly extended my fingers towards him and when he slid it on, there was a slight tension between us that made my breath catch in my throat.

"I don't need shiny things. I need you."

"I'm still worried about..." he trailed off, his fingers drawing circles on the plastic ring.

I silenced him with a kiss, not wanting to think about the dangerous drug deal he referred to. We both made the decision that I'd deliver the drugs and I was determined about it. He had to get out of this shit and he would.

"Don't worry," I whispered against his lips. "I trust you."

As his nose brushed against mine, I could feel the slight trembling in his hand as he protested, "But you'll be out there alone. I still think we shouldn't do it. It's not—"

"I won't. You'll be there to protect me."

He winced.

"We'll be fine, and then we can get married in a simple chapel, just the two of us." I couldn't think of anything more romantic. My parents were always flaunting their wealth, but what good is money if you're not happy? It means nothing. They had every opportunity in the world, but still hurt each other. Rio had nothing, yet he was the most caring and lovable person I've ever known. No one or nothing else was necessary for us. We just needed each other. We had to complete this one last job before we could start a new life together.

Without hesitation, he responded to my words by capturing my lips in a fierce kiss, his tongue exploring every inch of my mouth.

I moaned into the kiss, feeling the familiar heat pooling between my legs.

"You have no idea how much I want you right now."

My body shivered with need as his fingers traced a path down my body, teasingly brushing over all the places that made me quiver.

"Please, fuck me."

I could feel Rio's breath quicken against my neck as he whispered, "Your door isn't locked."

"I don't care."

This was no mere request. It was a plea, a demand for him to claim me completely.

I felt him shiver against me as he pressed his lips onto mine, his tongue probing deep into my mouth.

"I need you, Rio," I moaned.

He gripped my hips tightly as he pulled me closer, grinding our bodies together in a primal dance of desire. "I know, darling."

He ran a rough hand through his messy hair before leaning in again to capture my earlobe between his teeth gently. "Tell me what you want."

I couldn't resist any longer. "Fuck me hard against the wall," I whispered back, biting my lip submissively.

His gaze flickered with a fiery desire as he reached out, his muscular hands taking hold of my waist and effortlessly lifting me from the soft mattress.

Instinctively, I wrapped my legs around him as we walked towards the wall. He pushed me against the cool surface, and I felt a thrill run through my body. In one swift motion, he pulled down my panties and his boxers. "Isn't this your parents' bedroom wall?" He asked with a smirk on his face.

Rio positioned himself at my entrance while I muttered under my breath, "My father is such an asshole. It's his fault for putting his room in that spot, not mine." He paused for a split second to brush aside a strand of my hair. "I like your way of thinking," he said with a grin.

And when I arched my hips so that the tip of his cock slid inside, he let out a low growl, finally pushing himself inside of me in one swift motion, filling me up completely. It felt so good - so right - that it almost hurt. His hands roamed southward, cupping my ass cheeks possessively and pulling them apart as he moved forcefully against me.

The sound of skin slapping against skin filled the air.

I gasped between moans and groans while clutching at his shoulders.

"You're so wet and ready for me," he whispered against my ear.

He thrusted into me with one powerful stroke, meeting my moan with his own feral growl. My nails scratched lightly at his back, leaving goosebumps in their wake, and I loved the way he fought against coming.

When my gaze met his, his hips pumped harder against mine, setting a brutal pace that I matched perfectly. Every time he drove into me, I felt a jolt of pleasure shooting through me, electrifying my core.

And when he moved his thumb to my clit, circling it, I knew I wouldn't last any longer. I dug my nails into his neck and when he slammed into me over and over again, I lost myself in the blissful agony of our union and cried out in pleasure. My walls clenched around him and it seemed to be all he needed, because with a primal roar, he buried himself to the hilt inside of me and held still, letting me ride out the last of my climax before joining in my ecstasy with a feral growl. As he came inside of me, he bit down on my neck, his hand trembling against my hips. Our bodies shuddered together, writhing in the afterglow of pleasure—panting, sweat-drenched, and satisfied.

"We're destined for one another," he whispered against my pulse point.

I nodded in agreement, my breath coming in short gasps. "Forever," I replied, almost on the verge of crying because this force of a man was mine.

Suddenly, I was back in the present, and my eyes welled up with tears as I stroked the plastic ring in my hands.

Forever, sadly, lasted less than twenty-four hours.

They must have taken the ring from my corpse as well as the rest of the things in the box. My yellow summer dress... my cell... and some other small things. Maybe the cops gave this back to my family, and they just put it here.

Rio and I never stood a chance. Never.

Shortly after our engagement, Rio shot me because the Blood Queen wanted me in the Underworld. A tear trickled down my cheek as I slid the plastic ring onto my finger.

"What's that?" Bory asked, holding me tightly.

"My engagement ring..." A desperate laughter bubbled up in my throat.

I turned, signaling Mal and Bory to follow me since we wouldn't find anything else in here. "Let's go to the storage room."

As we made our way down the hallway, we could already hear voices, and in the bathroom, we found the others.

"Did you find anything?" I asked.

Jamie shook her head. "No, just a bunch of useless stuff."

I smiled. "You'll find plenty of that here as well."

"Oh, and a necklace for Mom," Jamie said, showing it to Bory.

It was a dusty gold chain with a red ruby. It had once belonged to my mother, but wherever she was now, she wouldn't need it.

"It'll look lovely on Cherry," I said, and Bory's eyes lit up when he saw the necklace.

He grabbed it and quickly tucked it away. "It's perfect, thank you Jamie."

"Now what?" grumbled Ash.

"We couldn't find anything, and since you mentioned there might be something here, we decided to go for it," Ebony added.

"I believe I know where," I responded, twirling the plastic ring on my finger.

The words were etched in my mind...

I needed to find out where he had left a message for me, and a feeling of unease crept into my stomach. The Blood Queen claimed she had to eliminate him because he posed a threat to the world on my behalf. But could it be that I caused his descent into madness? It didn't add up with what I knew about him. What if there was a crucial piece missing from the puzzle? My knowledge was limited to fragments, far from a complete picture. What if he truly was the antagonist in this story, and my love blinded me to the truth? Confronting this possibility would be difficult, especially if he was the mastermind behind it all. I pressed my ring against my collarbone and took a deep breath, hoping for clarity.

Leaving behind memories of Rio and our kisses in this very bathroom, I made my way to the storage room at the end of the hall. It was still filled with boxes and extra bedding. This was where I had first caught Any and Dad with that strange golden light, and I knew then that something was wrong.

"We used to hide here whenever we traveled to the Underworld," Any reminded me as we entered the room.

"How did you go to the Underworld so easily?" I asked, raising an eyebrow.

All eyes turned towards Any now. "After you were reincarnated, Dad conjured us to Earth, but I wasn't really there—I wasn't born here like you. Thanks to my abilities, though, we made everyone believe we were born as twins on Earth. That way, we sneaked into all their memories. Your birthmother became my mother this way too, but since my magic is way stronger up here, I ended up forgetting the truth as well, and I got reincarnated in some sort."

"So, he wasn't my birth father on Earth?"

According to Any, there was no way of controlling who'd be your new parents once you get reincarnated. therefore... Therefore, he had to intervene to maintain his involvement.

"All of this," he gestured around him, "was manipulated. We pretended to live a normal life until we got you to the Underworld again. Dad wanted it to end quickly, to get you down there as soon as possible but we had to wait until you aged, at least until you reached the same age as you had before your reincarnation and then Rio found us, and made everything even more complicated."

Any sighed, forcing himself to grin. "My soul got confused for a while about what was real and what was fake. Dad had maintained the illusion so well that I eventually believed we were humans living here, growing up, going to school. But once you died, I made it my mission to understand what was going on, to find out where Dad went every other month. But my soul was so confused that it wasn't until I got back to the Underworld that I realized what had been done to me. What father and the Blood Queen had planned. They wanted me to kill Rio, so that he'd come back to the Underworld, but I couldn't do it."

He didn't need to say it out loud that he fell for him too. The sadness in his eyes was clear, proof that he felt like a failure. So, I touched his shoulders, squeezing softly.

He clenched his fingers into fists.

Mal cleared his throat awkwardly, and honestly, I didn't know what to say either. We both loved the same man and lost him.

"Well, Rio's ideas aren't always the best," Ebony said, and when Ash nodded in agreement, I realized they still held a grudge against him.

I tried to avoid getting into another argument and just started rummaging through the shelves. I had a hunch that Rio had hidden something for me in this room. We both found out about Dad and his weird abilities right here. This was where it all began, so if he stashed something for me, it just had to be in here.

"But why would he hide it here?" Ebony asked, and the others joined in, tossing everything onto the floor.

"Because we used to meet here," I confessed.

"What do you mean, 'used to'?" Any asked, irritation in his voice.

"Well," I sighed as I tossed another crate to the ground, "whenever he stayed with you, we'd meet up here, and..."

"We can imagine," Mal interjected.

"It's a miracle no one heard you. In the palace, the two of you fucking was pure torture," Ebony added, and Ash burst into laughter.

"Yeah, we always played some card games and the loser had to stand guard at your door."

Jamie cleared her throat, and I noticed her blushing cheeks.

"Alright. I think we get the picture..." I nervously chuckled, realizing my fingertips were tingling. "I'm sure there's something here. I can feel it."

"I'm not finding anything," Ebony grumbled as we continued to throw items onto the floor. "Except..." She reached her hand all the way to the back of the shelf and took out a book. "I think it's a diary, maybe. No idea." Ebony flipped through its pages, and I noticed Any's widened eyes.

"This is one of my journals... What's it doing here?"

He took it and scrutinized it. "This is strange. I passed it on to Rio after I went to the Underworld."

"We've been here before," Jamie suddenly spoke up, and all eyes turned to her. She looked around with squinted eyes. "I remember little, but I know we were here, just before Daddy..." Jamie swallowed, and I noticed her shifting her weight from one foot to the other. "Before he left."

"Why would he hide my notebook here?" Any asked, looking at me.

I shrugged. "As if I would know. You guys seem to know everything."

"I can only imagine that he had some sort of revelation," Mal suggested, nodding at me. "You should take the book. See if it provides any clues. He clearly left it here for you."

I took the book, and the black leather binding seemed to tingle as if it wanted to sear my skin.

We waited for a few heartbeats.

"No memories," I said, disappointment lacing my voice.

"Well, that entire trip was a waste then," Ash grumbled, and Ebony nudged him in the ribs.

"Why don't you check the pages?" Bory suggested. "Maybe he left you a message in there."

"Yeah," Jamie added. "Dad worked with that book a lot..."

I glanced at the pages but couldn't discern anything at first glance. "Maybe we should look for something else..."

"It'll be getting dark soon," Jamie said. "It'd be better if we're home when that happens."

"Alright," I sighed. "Let's take one more look around and then head back."

CHAPTER ELEVEN
LYNNE

We drove back home and had dinner with the others. Punchy lightened our mood with a funny story about how the Loops once stole a food truck from another gang while Diva Dee sang some songs. Afterwards, we retreated to our rooms. While I shared mine with Ebony, the guys were all together in a larger one.

We laid on our cots, flipping through the books.

I talked her into checking the Book of Silva to find something useful, while I flipped through Any's book for some notes. Eb had a better grasp on the Old Language than I did, so I was glad she agreed to touch the creepy book. But our efforts were in vain. It was frustrating to come up empty-handed. All we discovered so far was this diary—and since my fingers burned like hell as I touched its pages, it had to hold some significance.

I was so sick and tired of all these riddles we needed to solve.

Why did I have to be the one to fight through it all?

It made no sense.

I was paying for everything. My mistake was falling in love.

Was that really reason enough to be pursued and punished for decades?

I snorted and examined every drawing by Any.

He had always been a talented artist, sometimes spending hours sketching, especially when he needed some space. I could always go to him, even at night when he was asleep, but when he painted, he needed his time, usually to process something.

I stumbled upon a sketch of myself, a near-perfect depiction with smudged water droplets, almost like a photograph. Running my thumb over the page, I discovered it was the most worn one in the book and I realized it was Rio's notebook too, given to him by Any.

My heart took a wild leap as I traced the smudged lines.

Those water droplets, just stains on paper, suddenly hit me with a wave of deep sadness. The thought of him staring at my picture, remembering Any and me, got me all choked up. The moment Any and I had to go back into the Underworld, Rio lost his best friend too, and the pain he must've felt hit me hard.

Suddenly, my eyes welled up, and I gripped those pages so tight my fingers trembled.

Skull. I missed him like crazy.

All I wanted was to be wrapped up in his strong arms.

Sighing deeply, I averted my gaze to Ebony, trying to somehow distract me from missing Rio because it might be death of me otherwise.

"Eb?"

"Yep?" she said, sounding irritated as she flipped through the book with a scowl on her face.

I put the book aside and decided to just ask her straightfor-wardly. "Why do you all hate me so much?"

Her eyebrows shot up, and she glanced around as if there was someone in the room confirming how absurd my question was.

I held her gaze.

Her brown, ocher-colored eyes avoided mine, and then she dramatically exhaled, hurling the book aside. The book promptly threw a tantrum, closing itself with all seven seals, making an over-the-top metallic clank, and even growling like a dog.

"Enough!" I exclaimed, wagging a finger at the book, which now lay next to Ebony. Perfect. It will never allow Ebony to touch it again.

She stared at it with an expression as if she was preparing for an intense exorcism session. The book couldn't resist one final theatrical growl before conceding defeat, closing its eyes and feigning a deep slumber.

I turned my attention back to Ebony. "So, why are you Horsemen so sour on me?"

"Look, girl," Ebony said, resting her head on one hand." We've been privy to the whole drama from the beginning. Zagrios saved us all in a way and offered us a place as his four Horsemen. It wasn't exactly a job posting. We wanted to help him and have been fighting by his side ever since, becoming friends in the process. Briz joined us later. Originally, it was his father," Ebony swallowed, "in his place, but when he died, Briz took over. He really wanted to serve Zagrios, so we all swore an oath to serve the Shadow King, loyally and utterly grateful. Even though we were aware of his weaknesses, we loved him the way he was. And then you came along."

"And disrupted your love?" I said with a mocking tone.

"No, you took him away from us," Ebony said, her voice tinged with ironic laughter, as if she found her own words amusing. "It might sound silly, but for a while, it was just us. We fought demons, brought monsters that shouldn't roam free back into captivity—and then came the time when Zagrios changed. From one moment to the next, he became different,

Some jokes weren't funny to him anymore, he left parties abruptly, didn't want to stay for board games, and eventually, we found out he'd stolen away a young goddess from Olympia months ago and apparently showed her the ropes down here."

Ebony shook her head, and I clutched the picture of me tightly, as if it could transmit Rio's touch or his tears.

"He had only you on his mind. Ash and Isix warned him, I advised him to do whatever made him happy, but I had no idea where it would lead us all. I'm sorry; you're not really to blame, but Rio disappeared from our lives, and eventually, he was so in love with you he ignored everything and everyone else. Every one of us, even our opinions. We warned him about the curse and that he should hide his love for you better. At first, he refused to admit that he, the great Shadow King, had fallen in love with you, but he did. I think the bond between you two suddenly became so strong, and then when your father discovered the two of you, it got even worse. He went mad, seeing enemies in everyone. He even had a fierce argument with Ash once, causing him to vanish for a month. Zagrios apologized to him, but they still had disagreements, especially over you. And when he would have sacrificed us all for you if necessary, we weren't a united front anymore. Then he left, reincarnated. And we were alone with his fucking court. We stayed loyal and saved what could be saved, waiting for him, but it wasn't until Any came to us, with your father, and promised the King would return, that we had hope again. We had been lost for a long time."

"But you worked for the Bone Queen in the meantime, right?" I said, not entirely sure what to make of this information.

"Not really, we just took on some minor jobs to stay fed," Ebony replied. "Afterwards, we pushed aside that version of the narrative and come up with a new one in order to avoid setting off the curse. We couldn't reveal the truth - that Rio was actually the king of the shadows and we were his soldiers. This was something Zagrios desperately wanted to keep from you, as he has always been fiercely protective of you."

She winked, but I could still sense the lingering pain, knowing that I meant more to him as his friends.

"I'm sorry," I said sincerely.

"As I said, it's not really your fault, and I guess we're all here because he saved our lives. Hell, I was a mere shell of myself when he found me."

I wanted to ask her what had happened, but the look on her face told me I shouldn't push. It was hard, though. I was a genuinely curious person.

"He kinda saved me, too," I began, an unexplainable depth filling me. "I lived through him. Thanks to him—he opened up worlds for me I couldn't reach on my own. He brought light to my darkness, and—"

"—you brought light to his," Ebony finished my sentence. "It took me a while to realize it, but he was incredibly lonely behind that tough exterior. I think he was crying out to be loved the way his mother loved him before she died... And he answered that cry for love with violence. Zagrios could see everyone's wishes and exactly how he could help them, just not himself. When he found me in an alley..."

Ebony paused, as if contemplating how to describe the image in her mind.

"Eb, you don't have to open up if—"

"No," she interrupted me. "I want you to understand. Why I am how I am now. I trust no one—Zagrios and the Horsemen are the exceptions—because they brought me back, and anyone who threatens them, will have to deal with me." Ebony's gaze hardened again, as if she wanted to tell me I was part of the reason her family was in danger. "Understand that I wasn't always like this. I was cheerful, naïve, I was a Nereid once..."

"A Nereid?" I interrupted, raising my eyebrows. "Those are the sea nymphs, right?" And they were known for being deadly.

"Yes," she said, her eyes darkening as she gazed into the distance. "We lived in the water, and our purpose was to draw evil souls into the waters to help the cycle, to separate the good from the bad so everyone could cleanse their sins. One day, before I was even ready to join the elder, trained Nereids, I snuck away, believing I could capture an evil soul myself and explore the shore. I was like you. I thought my powers were bigger than they were and my knowledge more profound. In truth, I was just a silly girl. I ran away, and a soul trafficker ensnared me. He imprisoned me, used me as an attraction to show everyone what the Nereids looked like because hardly anyone knew. Barely anyone ever saw us, and when they did, it was in the waves, appearing like humans riding on horses, only it was the white foam of the dark sea upon which we rode. A horde luring souls with our songs and then dragging them into the sea. The man kept me in a cage, and once Nereids stay on land for seven days and seven nights, they grow human skin. That's what happened to me. I was no longer a Nereid. Without my scales, the soft texture between my fingers, and the faint bluish tint of my skin vanished. He tried to throw me into another body of water, the Seven Rivers, the Black Sea, to change me back but every time, I just sank like a piece of lead. That's the punishment for Nereids who changed. I can never go back to the sea again. And when the Ravenman realized I was useless to him, he started looking for another way to use me."

Ebony lowered her gaze and began picking at the dirt under her nails. I stood up to sit down next to her on the bed, and placed a hand on her shoulder.

As I shifted my position, the diary belonging to Any slipped from my grasp and landed on the floor with a soft thud in the background.

"I'm sorry, Ebony."

Her eyes glistened in the dim candlelight as she shook her head. "From one day to the next, I was torn away from my family, thrust into a world that was foreign to me. On land. I didn't even know how to walk. I had to learn to walk first, only to be captured by that man and abused because that was the only thing I was good for. I was a body with holes that he filled, and he filled every hole. Every. Damn. Hole."

A tear rolled down her cheek, and I felt my own eyes burn.

"I know what you're thinking—how could this happen to someone like me? A warrior. But I wasn't always a warrior. On land, I was helpless, and that was the worst part for me, the knowledge that I couldn't do anything. I couldn't even walk, lift my feet, or use my fingers. Back in the sea I could do anything. I had my fin, moved with the waves, with the tide... Suddenly, I was trapped in a useless body, good for nothing but to be—" She stopped for a heartbeat, breathing against the rising lump in her throat, "—raped."

Her voice grew softer. "Until I learned to walk. Until I learned to wield a knife. Until I stabbed him and ran away." She spoke so quietly now that it was almost inaudible. "I was so inexperienced in combat that I didn't mortally wound him and I regret it every day."

"He deserves Tartarus," I said.

"Yes, but you mustn't forget who's in Tartarus. Compared to them, he's a lamb. What am I compared to thousands?"

"He wanted to make him suffer forever... but Zagrios mustn't upset the balance. We all have our destinies given by the Fates. He can intervene, but only to a certain extent. I convinced him I wanted to be the one to kill him, giving him the last punishment. No man should be my shining knight. But I was helpless, allowing someone else to do whatever they wanted with me, to change me, to bring me to another world, to take everything and everyone I loved from me, and yet, I still want to end him. Not Rio. No one else should punish him. Rio helped me, yes, but only so that I can help myself in the end and I will."

"You want the favor I still owe you to lead you to him?" I asked.

Ebony shook her head. "No, I know where he is. Do you remember the night in Catterville?"

I nodded, my cheeks turning red like a beet. I would probably never forget that night.

"There, Zagrios told me that his shadows had found him, and Ash and I searched for him. He always had raven feathers in his hair. I sometimes called him the Ravenman. He never revealed his real name to me. You know we can do too much with true names. But Ash and I found him. Of course, Ash wanted to bash his skull in immediately, given that he kept slaves like Ash..."

"Ash was a slave?"

Ebony nodded. "A Shadowslave."

My eyes widened. "How did Rio save him from this?"

"It's not my story to tell. If Ash is ready, he will tell you himself, but that's why he's not taking any shit from anyone anymore."

I swallowed hard. Ash despised me more than anyone else. He'd never tell me his story.

"Anyway, we know where he's hiding, and I know exactly what I'm going to do with him once we've resolved all this crap. And then, only then, when I have him by the balls," Ebony said with a wry smile, "I'll make my wish come true. I want the Raven Man, and I want to take care of him on my own, with no help, to prove to myself that I'm strong. That no one will ever use me again. I'm a warrior. I'm strong," she said, her face filled with a pride that made me admire her. She had survived.

"And... what would you wish for?" I asked.

"That you—somehow—bring me back to the sea," she said so softly that I could barely hear her. "That I can ride with the Nereids again."

Her eyes glistened, and I caught a tear. "I will do everything I can to get you back to the sea. But a wish like that will cost you something from off your life."

That was how wishes worked. Life gave us what we wished, but we had to give something back to life. Time. The only payment our soul knew.

Ebony nodded. "Yes, I know, and it's okay. I've made a life for myself here, learned to love life in the Underworld. But every time I see the sea, every time I drink water, every time I flush the toilet up here, it reminds me of how I swam in the sea with my mother, my sisters..."

I smiled.

That was why she never really let Ash and Illiam into her heart. She wasn't ready to commit on land. She didn't want to stay here and lose her heart.

"I'll help you," I said again, knowing full well what it meant to not feel in the right place.

"Thank you," she said, and suddenly warmth filled her gaze.

She opened her mouth to say something else when she suddenly looked down behind me at the floor. "Aria," she said, and her eyes widened. "By the Hellhounds, look at the book. This page looks strange."

I turned around and saw that the notebook had opened to a peculiar page when it fell. It was a blank page, and a few letters seemed to shine through the paper.

I couldn't quite see it, but the way the lamp illuminated it made it stand out vibrantly.

"That's really odd," I commented and picked up the book.

I ran my fingers over the page, and the letters became darker. I stroked it again, and more letters emerged, as if they were growing out of the book.

Ebony sucked in air through her lips. "I'll get the others."

As she hurried out of the room, I lingered on the page, caressing it with my fingertips. The breeze that followed her exit tousled my hair as I continued to trace every edge of the page. Suddenly, a poem materialized in an ancient language. I couldn't decipher it, but Rio had written it. No doubt. I could recognize his handwriting anywhere.

"What happened?"

I heard a voice asking, and when I raised my head, Mal, Any, and Bory were clustered in the doorway, peering into the room with eager expressions.

"That wasn't there before. I know this book inside and out," Any said, rushing in and taking the book. "And Rio didn't know the ancient language as a human..."

"He must have added it before the reincarnation," Mal suggested, touching Any on the shoulder, which made him flinch and move away from him.

I gave Mal a knowing look and sighed; his pain was an open book for everyone, but that was Mal. He was not one to keep secrets. He wanted to show his heart to everyone. Unfortunately, Any was too closed up for that. Maybe he acted differently with Mal alone, but as soon as we, or rather I, was there, he closed himself off.

"Yes," Any said, his voice catching in his throat. "Rio gave me this book as a gift during our high school days. He knew I loved special journals. Maybe he wrote this poem inside just before his reincarnation, hoping that his soul would find it and pass it on to me. But that poem must be a hidden message meant specifically for you, Aria. Only you can decipher its meaning."

He handed me the book.

"Well, great," I grumbled, taking it from him. "But I have no idea what this—" I tapped angrily on the yellowed pages, "—is supposed to tell me."

"Maybe we should translate it first," Bory suggested and stroked my hand, trying to calm me down.

Mal let out a sigh and snatched the book from me. "Alright, I believe I'm the most familiar with it among us..."

He was right, but I couldn't help but wonder where he'd gained such a profound knowledge of the ancient language.

If my guess is accurate, it could only be achieved at the Olympian Academy.

Ebony and Ash's skeptical eyes were directed towards him, as if searching for answers. Ebony then turned her gaze to me, as if expecting me to provide the missing pieces. Unfortunately, all I could do was shrug. I had known him for years, but he had never revealed this side of himself to me until recently. Yet, I was determined to uncover the truth and leave no doubts in my mind.

Mal's brow furrowed as he read the words aloud, his eyes darting back and forth across the page. The rest of us leaned in closer, anticipation building with each passing second.

A nagging feeling tugged at my gut, a sense that something was off.

Mal's frown deepened as he picked up speed, his voice growing more urgent.

"Mal?" I asked, sitting up straight. "What's happening?"

Any stood next to him, peering over his shoulder at the book. "What's going on—oh."

"I don't know," Mal stuttered. "The words..."

"Mal, let me see!" I exclaimed, practically jumping towards him out of curiosity.

He turned the book for me to see and I gasped.

The words seemed to be shifting and changing before our very eyes, transforming into English.

We exchanged a look of disbelief.

Damn. This was some kind of strange magic.

"Can I get it?" I reached out my hand and Mal passed me the book, his skin covered in goosebumps. As I took hold of the book, I saw Any briefly touch Mal's shoulders before quickly pulling away.

I dove into the poem, captivated by its mysterious power.

Whispering winds weave a tale,
Hushed secrets in shadows they trail,
A mystery in ancient bones reside,
Tales of the past ruler, they confide.
Through time's unyielding embrace,
Howling echoes of history's call,
Eerie riddles within walls enthrall.
Skeletons dance in moonlight's gleam,
Kept secrets, they forever teem,
Unraveling the past's scheme,
Listen to the whispers' theme,
Listen to me to save you in my dream.

"Okay, that doesn't ring any bells," I said.

"Show me, please," Bory insisted.

I handed him the book and Any chimed in, leaning in to stare into the book as well.

"Oh! That's pretty," Bory said. "I didn't know Rio had it in him to write like this. Such a little poet!"

"He could be anything he wanted," Ebony added, glancing at the poem as well. "That bastard is way too talented."

"It's like he's trying to tell us the bones are from Zeus, a threat we already know about," Mal said thoughtfully. "But that last sentence..."

Ash interrupted, "It hints at him saving you, probably only Aria, as we mean shit to him."

I blushed. "Ash, he cares about you, too. He might say these bones have their own story, like a riddle."

"Looks like you two are the puzzle-solving duo," Ash said, grinning sheepishly.

"Maybe we can break it down, word by word," I suggested, still unsure of what the poem truly meant. What he meant by *saving me* in his dream.

CHAPTER TWELVE
LYNNE

No matter how many times we wracked our brains over the poem, it made no sense.

Not even close.

Exhaustion had set in, leading us to read meanings into every word.

It could suggest that there are more bones to be found, holding secrets within them. Perhaps the bones I collected already hold significance... or maybe the moonlight holds a hidden message. The possibilities were endless, and we eventually grew frustrated.

Meanwhile, the Deadwalker attacks were growing stronger, so we filled the gaps between our attempts to solve Rio's puzzle by going on missions with Jamie and Punchy. During these outings, I tried to release as many souls as possible.

Jamie had been opening up to me since our conversation. She started sharing stories about Rio as a father, making me miss him even more. He had been an amazing dad.

Jamie also helped us with the book, but like the rest of us, she couldn't make sense of it.

At one point, I laid in my bedroom, staring at the ceiling and crying. In the Underworld, Bory would always cuddle with me, but here it felt as though I were alone. Cuddling with Human Bory was strange, even though he held me close whenever he could.

At nightfall, I would take Soothie for flights.

The group was unfazed by the sight of a black dragon as they had faced far worse creatures. They readily welcomed Soothie into our fold. He served as our early warning system, perching on the rooftop and sensing Deadwalkers and other dangerous creatures well before Punchy's alarms could alert us.

I fell asleep thinking about what the book was trying to tell me.

I knew the words. I knew the words.

What the skull were the words?

WE GATHERED in the meeting room the next day. Cherry and Jamie were studying a map, trying to pinpoint places Rio had visited often before he left for the Underworld. We searched everywhere and were thorough. The evening before, Jamie, Bory, and I had visited the Shooting Range and Dr. Meinhard's office but with no success. All of Rio's siblings now lived scattered across the world, thankfully, each in their own bunkers with their respective families. It would take months to safely get to each of them...but to be honest, I didn't think he left any clues with his siblings.

So I stayed focused on the journal, reading the poem for the hundredth time.

Some memories resurfaced: my time on Earth in middle school, becoming the school's most popular student, fighting for Any, and going on a skiing vacation with Rio. He insisted on paying for everything, and I later discovered he had sold masses of drugs just to spend a week with me. Back then, I had no idea how poor he was, being as spoiled and naïve as I was. I only knew our bubble, and even though he told me he had little money, I didn't understand what that meant. However, no phrases or clues came to mind that could help me now, not in the Underworld or in Olympia.

"Oh, what the skull!" I shouted, tossing the book against the wall.

I was done with that shit. If Rio wanted me to find out, maybe he should have just written it out. In a normal sentence. Like normal people do.

Everyone turned to look at me.

Jamie was showing Mal how her phone worked and which apps she used to love but no longer functioned because the Wi-Fi was broken. Something about Snobchat or the like.

"What does that even mean?" Jamie asked, placing her phone on the table and stacking her feet on top of each other.

"What?" I said, frowning at the cursed journal. I was tempted to ask Soothie to incinerate it. Maybe I would.

"What the skull. It sounds odd, but you say it all the time," Jamie commented.

"Jamie!" Cherry cried out. "Don't be so rude."

"Oh, no need, Cherry," I said, waving a dismissive hand. "That's just a common phrase we use in the Underworld, like 'what the fuck' or something."

"Um, actually it's not," Ash said, meticulously cleaning his sword. "No one says this."

"What?" I said, straightening up, cringing. "Of course, we all say it. It's perfectly normal in the Underworld. Bory says it, Mal."

"Well," Mal chuckled, "I picked it up from you, but really, nobody else uses it."

"Nope," Bory chimed in from his spot next to Cherry, who was wearing his chain. "I learned it from you, too. It's not a normal phrase in the Underworld, but I never thought about it."

I furrowed my eyebrows. Only I said it? As I thought about it, I realized they were right. Nobody else used those words except for me.

I shrugged and looked at Jamie. "Well, okay, I've always been a freak. Whatever."

"But...hold on...you only started saying it after you made the Drop, never in Olympia or on Earth..." Any whispered, and we all fell silent, turning our gaze to the book and as if possessed, Any and I rushed to it. I snatched it up, flipping to the poem, and we both hovered over it as if it were our lifeline, and perhaps it was.

"Fuck," Any said.

"What?" Bory shouted, squeezing in between us.

"What is it?" Mal asked.

"The initial letters of the poem spell 'What the Skull...'" I whispered, my heart pounding up to my temples.

"It's an acronym... he fucking hid an acronym in that poem," Any whispered.

"So, these are the words I know? What the skull? Is he serious?" I exclaimed, throwing my hands up in frustration.

My anger towards this mission was growing by the minute.

My finger was pointed at the ground, and my neck was tense with rage. "He's down there, sleeping, and we have to solve this crap? With nothing more than a 'what the skull'?" I couldn't believe it. Here we were, searching for clues, trying to piece things together, and what was supposed to help us turned out to be my personal curse.

"Now, calm down," Bory said, sitting back down. "Maybe we can even form a word with it... Rio seems to enjoy hiding everything and—"

"—making it more complicated!" I shouted.

If he were here right now, I'd spank his fucking beautiful ass. What a dumb idea. I crossed my arms.

"He had little choice," Any chimed in, always quick to defend him. "He couldn't give any hints because of the curse, so he had to hide them well. Probably, during the reincarnation, he couldn't take much time and had to hurry. But if he forms acronyms, he might even hide the true meaning in an anagram."

"He had to hurry and wrote a crappy poem in the meantime? You can't be serious."

"You know he's fucking smart. He'd probably come up with it in a couple of seconds,"

I couldn't deny it, as much as I hated to admit it: Any was right. Rio was a genius.

"I think it's beautiful," Cherry said, and I shot her a glare.

"Why didn't he just write 'What the Skull' in the damn diary?" I wondered. "It would have been easier."

"He was being watched, for sure," Any explained. "And if he gave you such a simple clue, we all, including the Bone Queen, could have figured it out. You mentioned it before anyone else, and it was so well hidden that we couldn't make sense of it. I doubt the Bone Queen saw anything more than a meaningless declaration of love for you in that poem. It's smart of him."

"Or he was trying to make others believe he was giving a hint about the bones and Zeus," Mal suggested.

Any nodded. "Yeah, he did it for security reasons. That's clear."

"He's always one step ahead," Ebony said.

Punchy brought us filter coffee and a block of pens and we all tried to string the letters together somehow, but all we found were "Shall," "Hawk," "Talk," or "Hush."

"What if the entire sentence is a hint?" Jamie asked, clearly motivated to solve this puzzle.

"Skull..." I thought for a moment. "I don't know which skull he could refer to. There were plenty in the Underworld... There wasn't a particular one that stood out... unless—" I scanned the room in search of the Book of Silva and located it on a different table nearby. No one dared to lay a finger on it because it would throw a tantrum at the slightest provocation. "The only important skull I can remember is the Book of Silva. "

"Hmm... yeah. It's a pretty ugly but a prominent skull indeed," Ebony said.

"What if we go bug the book again?" Mal suggested with a mischievous grin. "I mean, it's a skull, right? Maybe it's the one responsible for solving the 'what'."

"To solve the what?" I asked, raising an eyebrow in confusion.

"You know, the part of 'What the skull...'" Mal replied, trailing off.

"Um... yeah," I said, scratching my head. "That's the worst combo ever."

"I think it's not that bad," Any chimed in, and I could swear Mal's eyes lit up as he said it. "Rio has a weird sense of plotting, so maybe that's the clue he was giving us."

"I found a clarity spell recently. Maybe that's the right one," Ebony said. "But I'm not touching that thing anymore. You'll have to do it."

She nodded at me.

Sighing deeply, I took the book and looked at it.

It was the only book with a skull... maybe they were right. I opened the seven seals, and the book's eyes opened.

Ebony shivered slightly next to me before moving further away from the book. "That thing is so creepy."

"So, Silvia, spill the beans," Ash called, pointing his sword at the Book of Silva. "Give it your all."

It hissed, and I turned away from Ash just to be safe. Still, I couldn't help but smile. Silvia.

"Would you help us with a clarity spell to figure out what Rio meant by that sentence?" I pointed to a piece of paper where 'WHAT THE SKULL' was written in large letters.

The book pursed its lips, eager to drink my blood.

"If you pay me, then maybe yes," the book said in its rough voice.

With determination, I extended my hand and allowed the book to bite into my skin, its sharp teeth piercing my flesh again. The initial shock sent a searing pain coursing through me, and I winced, squeezing my eyes tightly shut. But I held steady, letting the book feed on my blood until it finally released its grip. The satisfaction in its gaze was unmistakable. I swallowed as it licked its lips with an otherworldly hunger, its milky eyes remaining fixed on me.

"Read," it hissed.

The book sprang open in my hand, and a gust of wind rushed through its pages, causing them to flutter and dance in the air. As if guided by an unseen force, the sheets swiftly settled, halting precisely where the correct spell now awaited my gaze.

I read, "Ti simineo afto aste a evera."

A warmth coursed through me, and suddenly, I felt a gust of wind emanating from the book. It lifted my hair, causing it to dance like serpents in the breeze before it parted from me and flowed towards the scattered papers on the table. The wind merged with them, shifting the pens, and the silence in the room became palpable. In an instant, nobody dared to speak, breathe too loudly, or make a move.

We all stared at the wind, which picked up the letters and rearranged them. Within seconds, the words on the paper read: Cut all the Hawks, and further to the right, with some distance, stood CA.

"Cut all the Hawks in Chicago," I whispered, looking at the others, who stood there in astonishment. Rio had likely transmitted this message to me before we took on our physical forms. Our mission: find the hawks.

"But which hawks?" Bory asked.

Before I could respond, the book clapped shut on its own, let out a brief yawn, and then settled back into slumber. Its seals closed by themselves, and I carefully placed it on a table beside me.

"I think I've seen some on the rooftops," I said to Cherry and Jamie.

"Yes, but we've got a few of those scattered around the roofs of Chicago," Jamie said, and I realized what Rio had indirectly taught me all along: Parkour. We had spent a lot of time together on the rooftops of Chicago. Perhaps that was already an indirect hint. A warm feeling enveloped me. What if my visit to Earth had far more significance than I had ever imagined? What if everything we did had a purpose? What if it were our two souls guiding us all along?

I leaned on a chair, my knees suddenly as weak as butter.

He had hidden the stone for me, so that if I needed an escape, I had a way out, and only I could find it. Something told me that the hiding places of these hawks were also connected to the places and experiences we had shared on Earth.

"How could he place all the hawks?" I asked.

"It's a spell," Any said.

"Well, then." I turned to Jamie. "Have you learned Parkour?" I asked with a smile on my lips.

She returned my smile. "Of course."

"Then get ready to search the rooftops of Chicago for these hawks."

CHAPTER THIRTEEN
LYNNE

We went as a trio.

Any was eager to join us, but, admittedly, his climbing skills left much to be desired.

It was Mal, Jamie, and me, along with Soothie. My sweet dragon flew us to higher grounds, deftly avoiding the dangerous Deadwalkers as we maneuvered through tight corridors in search of the hawks.

It wasn't long until we stumbled upon the first hawk, it was perched directly above the Paradise Girls building. I had noticed it from below before, but never paid much attention to it. It was a Stone Hawk, intricately connected to the structure, as if it had been built with the very house itself.

It didn't look significant and probably wouldn't have caught my eye. Weathered and worn, we had to knock it off the building with a swift sword strike. After inspecting it thoroughly in the base and finding nothing to stand out, Ash suggested that the sought-after stone was likely concealed within the hawk.

With a burst of raw energy, he shattered the stone.

We protested, worried that he might cause damage, but it

was too late. Ash was always impulsive like that - acting before thinking. The hawk now lay in pieces, and as we looked on in surprise, the stone crumbled easily into dust, revealing a small clay jug at its core. Strangely enough, the jug appeared untouched by Ash's powerful outburst. Yet I could sense the immense magical power emanating from it without even touching it. That jug was my connection to the world of gods - my true home, and it made me wonder how much time had passed since I last walked the halls of Olympia.

My memories of this place were the ones I missed the most —how the world looked, what it felt like to walk in the grass, where magic thrived on the strongest among all three realms. We kept the clay piece in Cherry's office and continued our search.

With every piece we found, my heart sank deeper into despair. As much as I wanted to rescue Rio, the thought of facing Athena filled me with dread. Would she even listen to our plea? Would she see us as weak and unworthy? The fear of rejection gnawed at me, but I couldn't let it consume me. I had to believe that this was our only chance, even though the possibility of failure loomed over us like a dark cloud. What would happen if we were turned away without Rio?

I pushed those thoughts far back into my mind and tried to relax in the evenings with the others. Jamie and Cherry introduced us to some games they'd salvaged, and we played cards with Punchy, Diva Dee, and a few others. Mal got along famously with Diva Dee, and she lamented the loss of her club, wishing she could show Mal what it was like to be in beautiful drag. We all mourned the absence of Diva Dee's Paradise, but I promised her we would rebuild it.

Slowly. Soon.

Hopefully.

The evenings were filled with camaraderie, and I was

grateful to see Jamie opening up to me, sharing bits and pieces of Rio's memories on Earth when we were separated and how she strived to emulate him. She had taken over the gang alongside her mother and Punchy when she turned sixteen, when the demons took over their world. Cherry had made it her mission to put an end to drug trafficking and focus on the city's safety instead. They had become a homeforce, fiercely protecting Englewood from demons and searching for the wounded, providing them with shelter and rebuilding their lives.

They had become a community full of love Rio would have been proud of.

WE FOUGHT off a few Shadowslaves and Deadwalkers, along with other menacing creatures that belonged in the Underworld, as we continued our search for the hawks. To expedite our mission, we split up and flew to different rooftops on Soothie's back. We combed through each rooftop methodically until we finally found another piece of the clay jug at our headquarters.

It pained me to realize that every location I had visited with Rio also had one of these hawk statues sitting on its rooftop. I couldn't help but wonder if Rio was aware of that when we would meet later or if he chose these places randomly. Perhaps our souls were drawn to them, connected by a shared past that bound us together. Maybe Rio, as the Shadow King, had handpicked these places for us, binding us even closer together. Our existence on this planet was never truly free. We were constantly being guided, yet also destined to fail.

We even found a hawk at Leonardo's now-destroyed clothing store.

It brought a tear to my eye to see that nothing remained of the once magnificent shop. None of his clothes... not even a tie lay anywhere. The buildings were blackened, charred, as if they had been consumed by a raging fire. We left it behind and found more pieces at Cherry's childhood home, two more above the opera house, the shooting area, the former pie store, at the auction house, the cemetery, Rio's house, near Reina's house, the prison, the hotel where we stayed before Project Raging Bull began...

As the night wore on and our spirits were dampened by yet another round of mundane board games, Mal and Diva Dee suddenly emerged wearing gorgeous vintage dresses they had found in a hidden chest. They beckoned us to sit and watch as they sang and danced, their voices sweet and harmonious, sending warmth spreading through our chests. Even Any smiled. A little but still.

We clapped and laughed, grateful for this small moment of escape from our worries.

Yet, we still lacked three hawks.

That's why we headed for the place I loathed the most in the early morning.

Governor Jenson's villa.

As the destroyed rooftops of Chicago stretched before us, a maze of concrete and steel reaching high into the sky. Sunlight danced off the shattered glass facades of skyscrapers, and a gentle breeze swept through the city.

I stood beside Jamie and Mal, our gaze fixed on the vast expanse of rooftops. In my hand, I held a rough sketch we had prepared, various marked locations on it were already crossed out.

"So, that's the Goldcoast," I said, gritting my teeth as we stood in the same spot where I sat with Rio, looking at Jenson's villa. I glanced at the window where I stole the Van Gogh and my fingers clenched around the paper in my hand. I hated this memory. The memory of his betrayal.

"Where to?" Jamie inquired, her gaze fixed on me.

"Over there is a hawk. Do you see it? Right above that window." I pointed in its direction, and she followed my fingertip.

"And back there's another one," she said, then cleared her throat. "And there's the third."

"The last ones," Mal said.

I grinned, relieved that we finally had all the hawks.

We traversed the rooftops to Jenson's roof, leaping over the gaps and leaving Soothie on guard.

"Do you think he'll wake up again?" Jamie asked as Mal passed us thanks to his long strides, and her question struck me like a blow to the chest. It was a question I asked myself at least a dozen times a day, but I had to give her the answer I needed to hear. My silent prayer. Wether they were true or not.

"Yes," I said, my voice resolute. "He must. I need him."

That wasn't a lie, not even close.

My heart, perhaps even my soul, I was never entirely sure, just didn't feel complete without him. It was like that when I worked for the Bone Queen. Storm Day was my only happy day when I watched him. Just being near him. It was the same after, without him at the Blood Queen's. I felt incomplete. As much as I didn't want to admit it, I needed him.

"Me too," Jamie said, and I rubbed her back.

"I look forward to him seeing you again. He'll be proud of you."

"Do you think so? I was angry at him for years. I thought he had just left us, Mom and me. I didn't believe her crazy stories until the demons smashed our windows. That's when I realized her witch stories, demons, and other worlds were probably true, and yet I still firmly believed that Dad abandoned us to... well, to find you."

I forced myself to smile.

We hardly differed in those thoughts. I had thought the same. "He knows, Jamie. No matter what thoughts you had, he'll forgive you. He loves you with all his heart."

A smile spread across her face, and I felt a surge of warmth in my heart. As she gripped my hand, I noticed the ring on her finger, the one Rio had given her. He would be happy to see she was wearing it again. I could still hear him questioning if she was mature enough to have it...

"He was very sad in the Underworld," I said. "Because you weren't with him, you know."

"I'm sorry," Jamie said. "I'm sure you wanted to have him with you without his mind being somewhere else."

I shook my head. "We all have big hearts, and there's room for everyone. He should let more people into his heart." He had done it too little over the years...

Suddenly, darkness enveloped us.

We halted and heard screams, followed by a loud clatter and crash.

I turned around and saw Soothie flying above us, with two Deadwalkers clinging to his wings.

"Soothie!" I shouted, pulling Jamie down into a crouch as he flew narrowly above us, his claws just mere inches from our faces.

We huddled on the rooftop, weapons drawn and senses sharpened, as a monstrous creature from the Underworld emerged from the shadows behind us. It had terrifying claws and glowing eyes that gleamed in the darkness. Its body was covered in black, scaly armor, and its mouth oozed with corrosive, green slime.

"What the hell is that?" whispered Jamie beside me, holding her breath.

"A Shadow Devourer," I said, glancing at Mal, who had intercepted Soothie several feet behind us, just above Jenson's apartment and was currently battling two Deadwalkers on the rooftop with Soothie. I could see in his glance that it took everything from him to not scorch them, but he knew I would want to save their souls.

Soothie was the kindest.

For a moment, it reassured me that Mal was assisting Soothie, but the Shadow Devourer in front of us quickly dispelled any sense of calm within me when it flashed its horrible teeth. I didn't tell Jamie, but these sinister beings could condense the darkness around them and use it to their advantage. With their dark and eerie appearance, they could fill the hearts of people with fear and tiptoe through the shadows before striking. They were feared hunters in the Underworld, and the green eyes with slits like a snake told me they were sent by the Bone Queen. A subtle hint that she was still in the game, ready to strike wherever we were. That she would devour the Shadow King and his queen.

The creature roared, a bone-chilling scream that echoed through the passageways and made the walls tremble.

Then it lunged at us.

I tried to push Jamie aside, but she shoved me back, her weapons already drawn, pointing at the roaring beast.

"I won't turn my back to fear," she said through clenched lips.

And even though I knew Rio wasn't her biological father, I could swear that his courage, his determination, flickered in her eyes as the beast descended upon us.

In that fleeting moment before the creature lunged, our connection, our bond, became palpable. It wasn't just about defending ourselves. It was about protecting each other, and hell, I would do all I could to make sure she wouldn't get hurt.

The Shadow Devourer struck with lightning speed, its inky-black claws slashing through the obsidian darkness it conjured up. Jamie's reflexes were lightning-quick as she deflected its initial onslaught, her sword ringing out as it met the creature's menacing appendage. Despite the bone-jarring impact, she stood resolutely, her eyes filled with unwavering determination.

Simultaneously, I harnessed the magic coursing within me, summoning forth a tempest of swirling, glowing white winds that enveloped the beast's head. The ferocious gusts whipped around it, disorienting the creature as it let out an enraged, otherworldly shriek. It thrashed about, its gleaming, serpentine eyes temporarily veiled by the tempest.

Seizing the opportunity, Jamie lunged forward with a dancer's grace, her blade gleaming in the dim light. Her attack was precise, aimed at the vulnerable underbelly revealed during the beast's frantic retreat, and the blade pierced its flesh with a grotesque squelch, drawing forth another anguished howl.

As I maintained the swirling tempest, the creature writhed and contorted, the pressure of the gales preventing it from mounting a coherent counterattack. The winds howled in response to its agony, and the shadows clinging to its form recoiled, as if the very darkness itself shrank back.

In that moment, it felt as if the world stood still.

I knew the beast would meet its death now, and it was aware of it, too.

But at the precise instant when Jamie struck again, driving the knife into the creature's heart, causing it to writhe and spew—its serpentine eyes fixated on me. The green irises danced, as if attempting to ensnare me, their white and green threads pulsating like a living heart, and within those dark pupils, I recognized her.

The Bone Queen.

She watched us.

I bit down on my lip, channeling my magic upwards, a bolt of energy crackling in my fingertips as I pictured her face right in front of me.

"If you're enjoying watching us, then watch as I take you down. We're mere seconds away from putting an end to your schemes, Melinoe."

I struck, and as Jamie twisted her sword, the wet, squelching sound resonating in the night, the creature exploded before our eyes. Engulfing us in a torrent of black sludge. Slime and blood coated our faces, thick streams running down my cold cheeks.

I wiped it away from my face, checking Jamie for any wounds.

To my relief, aside from the gruesome sight before our eyes, the blood on our faces, and bodies... she was unharmed. We shared a breathless moment, our hearts pounding in sync as we marveled at the grotesque aftermath of our battle, at our hands, at the pungent liquid on our faces, our hair clinging wetly to our bodies, the smudges of blood on our faces looking like Pollock paintings......And in that eerie stillness, the air tingled with a sense of foreboding.

I could sense something else lurking nearby, something equally menacing, and my heart might have just stopped for a fleeting second.

Jamie's eyes met mine right before our gaze swept to the ground where a low growl rumbled in the distance, a guttural sound that sent shivers down my spine. There were more Shadow Devourers, creeping out from the depths of the cemetery of Englewood. They looked like vermin, like black roaches crawling up from the graves... up from the Underworld.

My heart raced as I realized that the battle was far from over. I looked towards Mal, his face etched with fear, clutching the hawks tightly in his hands as he ran towards us. Soothie circled above us, ready to bring us to the others.

Warn everyone we can.

CHAPTER FOURTEEN
LYNNE

I dismounted from the dragon, Jamie hot on my heels.

"Mal, come on!" I shouted, clutching the hawks nervously in my hands. When he didn't move, I spun around and saw him sitting on Soothie, shaking his head.

"No, you go, put all the pieces of the stone together, and I'll head to the cemetery to deal with those creatures."

I slumped. I knew someone had to take care of it, but...

"Mal, you can't do this alone."

"He's not alone," I heard Ebony call out, emerging from the club in full gear, a fully equipped crew trailing behind her.

Punchy aimed arrows, Ash gripped his sword, and then Jamie handed me the third hawk.

"Here, I'll go with them."

I struggled to hold back my tears, but they escaped my control as she smiled and reached out to touch my arm. Cherry's reassuring words gave me the courage I needed. "It's all right, Lynne. We've got this. You go ahead." Ebony and Ash nodded in agreement. "Hurry!"

Tears welled in my eyes as I rushed down the narrow staircase and burst into Cherry's office. Bory and Any were already inside, waiting for me. The almost-finished Omphalos Stone sat on a table behind them, its massive dragon egg shape looking deceptively ordinary.

My hands shook as I carefully placed the hawk figurines on the table. Without another word, Any unsheathed his sword and struck each one with the hilt, shattering them into pieces. We carefully gathered the remaining shards and fit them back into place on the stone, completing the complicated puzzle.

As we stepped back, a radiant golden glow emanated from the now-complete Omphalos Stone. Its warmth filled the room, making it feel as if we were standing before a roaring fire.

Suddenly, a loud buzz filled the air and the colors on the stone began to dance and swirl like a kaleidoscope. They merged together, forming a solid piece of smooth, dark basalt that dwarfed the table beneath it. It was as if the stone had never been broken, restored to its original form before our very eyes. We couldn't help but take a step back in awe at this mysterious power before us.

I looked at it, not sure what we'd do once we have it but suddenly my muscles didn't work. I felt paralyzed. Hell, my breathing became erratic and my whole body trembled. My friends were out there fighting.

Jamie was out there fighting.

Rio wasn't here.

Panic set in as my nerves constricted and my breathing grew shallow, I couldn't breathe. I–

Bory took my hand. "Lynne, it's alright. We're almost there. Just touch it. It will all be fine."

"A—and it'll take us to Olympia? Are you sure?" I asked, my voice unusually thin.

"Yes. We'll go together," Any said and took my other hand. "Let's go. We'll touch it at the same time, okay?"

We reached for the stone, and all of a sudden, it felt like the ground ripped open, and I was plummeting deep, deep, deep into the unknown.

"Oh, no, no, no, no, no!" I heard Bory's voice calling from a distance.

I shot up from the grass, my body tingling with a burst of adrenaline. There was a meadow stretching out before me, a patchwork of vibrant colors and textures. My vision was filled with the vivid hues of various flowers, ranging from the delicate petals of wildflowers to the bold blossoms of sunflowers reaching towards the sky. The air was thick with the scent of nature's perfume, a sweet and intoxicating mix that seemed to dance around me. I could feel the gentle breeze caressing my skin, carrying with it the soft rustle of grass and the cheerful chirping of birds. It was as if I had stumbled into a secret garden, a tranquil oasis hidden away from the chaos of the world.

"Oh, no, no!"

I looked around and saw no one. I could hear him, but where was he? "Bory? Any?" I called out, but got no response.

I almost tripped as I stepped into the tall flowers. And when I saw the lake stretching before me, my mouth hung open in awe. The water was a mesmerizing shade of azure blue, reflecting the fluffy white clouds above.

The scenery before me was like something out of a painting. As I tilted my head back, I couldn't help but gape at the sky above, filled with vibrant oranges and pinks that resembled watercolor brushstrokes. Olympia was undoubtedly the most stunning place I had ever laid eyes on. I noticed several areas where the water cascaded down in a waterfall-like fashion, forming serene lakes. The water was crystal clear and shimmered as rainbow-colored fish swam gracefully within its depths.

"Ouch!"

I froze in place, my feet planted firmly on the ground. It was then that I noticed Bory lying right in front of me; I had almost stepped on him while lost in thought. My hand flew to cover my mouth, and I quickly took a few steps back to give him space.

"Oh, shoot, Bory, I'm so sorry."

It was only now that I noticed something was drastically different. It was my Bory.

My sweet blue Furball! I let out a squeal, picked him up, and hugged him tightly. "It's *you*. You're back!"

"Yeah. That's my problem."

I held him slightly away from my face. "Why would that be a problem?"

"This way, Cherry will never marry me."

My eyebrows shot up. "Marry Cherry?"

I laughed and hugged him again, his grumpy face playing no role. My Bory was back.

"Lynne," he gasped. "You're suffocating me."

"Oh," I held him away again. "Sorry. Where's Any?"

"Here," he said, and I jumped, spinning around to see him standing right behind me. "Perfect. At least we all made it here safely. This place... it's... wow." I couldn't find words. Olympia was amazing. "But where do we need to go?"

"Up there," said Any, pointing behind him to a serpentine path leading up into the mountains. That was the famous Olympia, the mountain of the gods where the Pantheon lived. The temple of all gods. It reached so high that I couldn't even see it. It disappeared entirely into the bright blue-glowing lake above us. Any took my hand and led us forward, diagonally across the flower field.

"Come on, we need to hurry. Down there, it's literally chaos."

We ran across the flower field to the path and ascended it. Along the way, I noticed strange flowers with colors I didn't know how to describe. They were so peculiar. I also noticed that the path, which meandered downwards, had water up to my ankles. However, the water flowed upward, and with each step, it lit up in all the shades of green and blue that I could imagine. My breath caught.

"The water in Olympia is fluorescent. It emits light after being charged with energy from our magic," Any explained.

"Why is the water flowing upward?" I asked, my gaze fixed on my feet, parting the water as I walked.

"It propels us, like a kind of escalator, to get us up faster."

I had no choice but to marvel at the natural wonder around me as we mastered the ascent. At some point, though, I felt watched. My back felt cold, and my neck was sweaty. I turned around, and my pulse quickened.

"Any, I don't feel well."

"Those are the scouts," he said, nodding upward.

I tilted my head back and saw a dozen men in golden armor standing above the water's surface, arrows aimed at us. "They're making sure no one enters the Pantheon, who isn't welcome."

"How do they know we're welcome?" After all, Athena wanted to kill me.

"The gods don't seem to mind us coming. So it doesn't bother them either."

I swallowed and locked eyes with one of the scouts. They looked like what humans would describe as angelic, with enormous white wings. Their faces were stern as they monitored every step we took.

"Since we passed them alive, it means the gods want to see

us," Any said, and only now did I realize that some tension had left him. Had he been afraid?

"Were we in danger?" I squeaked.

"Well, they could have easily shot us."

My eyes widened, but Any just kept walking straight ahead, leaving me dumbfounded. With a furrowed brow, I followed him, never taking my eyes off the scouts.

As our footsteps echoed against the green grass, it gradually transformed into a mosaic of ancient stones that seemed to stretch endlessly towards the sky. The Pantheon loomed ahead, its towering pillars and intricate carvings rising like a fortress before us. As we drew closer, the individual rocks seemed to fuse, creating a massive and awe-inspiring palace in front of our very eyes. It was as if the stones and buildings were one entity, seamlessly blending into each other. And then, as if by magic, an arch made entirely of water appeared before us, beckoning us to pass through. As we did, we found ourselves transported to the other side, now standing high above the mesmerizing structure below us.

"This is what makes the human sky so blue," Any said. "People believe that there's something up there. Another world. But if their souls aren't ready, they don't pass through this threshold, they don't reach Olympia. They only see black. Infinity. Just like their possibilities for their lives. Infinite."

"Even though everything is finite..." I whispered and lowered my gaze as the water flowed up to our feet and became part of the arch. We had passed the first hurdle.

I took Any's hand and let him lead us forward.

We left the scouts behind us.

Ahead of us was a palace so vast that I felt like an ant. When we stood before it, all I saw were these white columns. They were like giant grids lined up behind each other. I turned around. The water converged on stone slabs, and as I turned back, I saw the water flowing downward, making it look like I was standing on a precipice, a cliff, of enormous infinity pool proportions.

"It's overwhelming," Any said. "I hold my breath every time."

I was forced to pause and take a moment to devour the breathtaking scene in front of me. It was as if I stood atop the highest peak in the world, surrounded by endless stretches of crystal clear blue water. The surrounding air was ablaze with vibrant ribbons of light, just like the aurora borealis—in all its glory. My senses were overwhelmed by the sheer beauty.

"Come on, it's not safe to linger," Any said and turned me around.

I had to do everything in my power to keep going, not allowing myself to be carried away by the natural phenomenon. Before us, a gate loomed as large as a hundred men in a row. There was no lock, no handle, and I knew well that there couldn't possibly be anyone capable of opening such a massive gate by hand.

"How do we get in there?" I asked, realizing that I seemed to come up with nothing but foolish questions.

Before Any could even open his mouth to reply, a gust of wind and a dark murmur arrived, and the gate swung open.

Athena stood with her arms crossed, the muscles in her arms flexing as she gazed at us with piercing blue eyes. Her bronze hair cascaded down her back in soft curls, framing her face like a halo.

Her silver armor reflected the vibrant light of the scene, causing me to shiver.

CHAPTER FIFTEEN
LYNNE

Seated on her imposing throne, she gazed at us with her icy eyes and asked, "What is the purpose of your visit?"

Her expression clarified that she loathed me. Every thought and memory of my actions, as well as Rio's, was surfacing in her mind at this very moment.

Any cleared his throat. "I believe, with all due respect, Athena, that you know why we're here."

I flinched.

Why was Any speaking to her this way?

Then I remembered he had already spoken with her extensively, discussed and debated for centuries...we both knew her. We both lived among the gods.

"The world is falling apart, the people are in pain, and soon, aside from us deities, there will be nothing left," Any said.

A muscle in Athena's jaw twitched. "It's not like I haven't foreseen these centuries ago, is it?"

Any huffed out a laugh. "You can't be so stubborn and refuse to act."

"It's not about wanting, boy," Athena hissed the last word.

I clenched my fingers into fists. "You wouldn't betray every-one, would you? You defied Zeus—you fight for fairness. How can it be fair to desert all of humanity?" I said through gritted teeth.

Athena laughed, a cold, mocking laugh. "You, of all people, want to tell me I'm wrong?"

Suddenly, her expression darkened, and a chill ran through me.

She stood up, and I felt a wave of power, like water ripples, emanating from her body, washing over me.

"You and Zagrios defied my orders," she stepped closer to me. "You conspired against humanity, putting your stupid love above all else." Another step and another. "He stole years from us, stole the Omphalos Stone, the only connection between Earth and Olympia. So tell me how should I have acted without that bridge to the mortal world? So, I ask you now: don't you think the speech you're giving should be reserved for someone else? "

She stopped in front of me, only half a head taller, but I felt as small as a child next to her.

She looked down at me, her eyes gray and cold as death itself. When she extended a long, elegant hand, she gripped my chin, forcing me to look her in the eyes as she said, "The man who claims to love you has plunged us all into the abyss. For what? For you. You should have had the time I granted you. Instead, you wanted everything. Everything but saving those humans, even though you could have. And now I have to listen to you, scolding me for the very wrongs you two committed. No, I don't think so. "

Looking away, I said, "I tried to stop it...When, I saw it, I almost—" I remembered how she gave me the poison, and an icy shiver ran down my spine. I drank it. I accepted to die.

"Almost is the right word. Since then, you've tied our hands. History has taken a course we can no longer stop. Zagrios got what he wanted, like always, and we'll have to figure out how to deal with the new world we'll soon have."

Tears welled up in my eyes as I imagined Jamie, Cherry, Punchy dying... "No," I cried, "we can't allow this. There must be something."

Athena laughed, finally letting go of my chin. "What, little one? What solution is there? The prophecy has been fulfilled. All gates to the Underworld are open. Now, people will die and our worlds will collapse. Maybe we should focus on doing better after the apocalypse."

She said it as if it were the consequence. As if billions of humans wouldn't matter...

Any's gaze landed on me, and a sly grin spread across his face. His eyes sparkled with determination and cunning. My curiosity piqued as I tilted my head, wondering just what scheme he had cooked up now.

"There's another one," Any said firmly as he stepped toward Athena. She averted her gaze, focusing on him now. "According to legend, the Omphalos Stone has another function."

Her eyebrows shot up. Perfect curved lines. "Which would be?"

"It can rewind time," Any replied.

Athena laughed.

"You know it's true. The legends say so."

"The legends," she hissed, "also say that the stone will be destroyed forever if we are to use it. Don't you think the gods would have used that ability at some point if the consequences weren't so unbearable? We can't destroy the only connection to earth—"

"—Perhaps we should sever all ties with humans," Any said. "That way, they would be protected and no longer under the influence of the gods. They could live however they choose."

"But humans desire our help," Athena snapped.

"Do they? Do we help them? All we did was use them for our fun and I thought that's what you despised most about your father. Our help is unfair. We listen to some and ignore others. Without our interference, life takes its course as it should."

Athena wrinkled her nose.

"Why do we need a connection, Athena? All these years, we've managed without one. We don't need the humans to hail us. But what we need is to save them from us. The misery they're in now is our fault. Without our influence, we wouldn't be where we're at now. We need to act, because none of us know what will remain if the Bone Queen triumphs."

Athena nodded. "If she awakens the Bone God and his revenge falls upon us..."

"The Bone God?" I asked.

Athena bore her eyes into me again. "When Zeus is reborn, he won't return as Zeus. We all tried to capture him with magic, and because magic always has a negative consequence, it's said that when he's resurrected, the Bone God, the greatest Titan of all time, will return. He'll storm Olympia and end the rule of the gods once and for all."

"So, everything would be destroyed..." I whispered. "The Bone Queen wants to erase all three worlds? Even the gods?"

"She hates me because I didn't help her, so yes."

Athena nodded thoughtfully. "Yes, she wants to end everything and erase the evil. All of us."

"Why didn't you take any action? Why did you let it go this far?" I whisper.

"Like I said, ask your husband. Ever since I've known him, he's been working against me, against us. He's inherently evil."

"That's not true," I weakly replied.

"Oh, really?" Athena touched my forehead, and suddenly I saw Rio. How he punished souls like the Shadow King with a whip of fire, how he shot the Blood Queen across a throne room, how he created creatures that instilled fear.... how he strangled and suffocated thousands of souls with his shadows, and the longer it took for them to die, the more his eyes sparkled with joy.

"No!" I screamed, trying to break free from her grip, but she didn't let go. Her hand dug into my forehead, and I couldn't deny what I saw any longer. Rio wasn't like this. Rio was good. "Understand it already," she said. "Rio is evil. Hasn't he proven that to you over the last decades? Maybe he believes he loves you, but in reality, all he loves is the idea of having you, possessing you. I thought you're wiser than acting like a damn object."

Suddenly, I remembered Nana's words, and my heart pounded in my temples. No, I couldn't accept it. Rio wasn't evil.

He couldn't be.

He was my Rio.

He helped the needy on Earth... he—

"Rio has killed numerous people on Earth," she said as if she could hear my thoughts. "He lied to you, made deals to avenge himself against the gang bosses. Maybe they were evil people, yes, but they also had people who loved them. What about all the lives he ended?" Athena's hand pressed harder against my forehead, and images flared up again.

Zagrios, being celebrated after killing a lover of the Bone Queen.

Crowds of demons and monsters cheering for him.

Zagrios on a mountain of dead souls.

Zagrios pushing a woman into Tartarus with a smile on his face...

I collapsed to the floor, my body trembling. "Stop. Please, stop."

I couldn't bear to see Rio like this anymore.

Every fiber of my being loved him.

I couldn't. I just couldn't.

"Ah, I see," Athena suddenly said. "Anwyn, you might be right. There's a solution, but it's our last," Athena said, stepping away from me as if I were no longer worthy of standing beside her. I heard her stop in front of Any. "If we can travel back in time, then and only then do I see the solution as killing Zagrios, the son of Hades, before he plunges our worlds into disaster. Before he meets Aria. Before he fulfills Hecate's prophecy. We must nip it in the bud."

"Kill?" my voice croaked, barely audible as I spoke the words. "I can't kill Rio. Please, I..."

"You've come to me," Athena said, her voice echoing through the room. "You wanted my help. That's the only solution I can see."

"But the Council," I began, mustering all the strength I had left, my hope fading, my fingers trembling. "Maybe the Council knows another solution. We could ask all the gods and decide after—"

"Aria," suddenly Any spoke up and came to me. "We don't have time. We need to act."

My heart sank. He couldn't be serious. "Any, you don't mean to say that we should... that I..."

My throat constricted as I struggled to say the words. It was too much to bear. How could this be real? The thought of ending the life of my soulmate was unimaginable. They couldn't seriously expect me to do this.

His expression softened as he watched me struggle, and he took a step toward me, but I backed away, shaking my head.

"I can't do this," I whispered. "I can't. How can you even

consider it? How can you ask me to do this? I thought you loved him, too."

"I do… but remember, I tried to kill him on Earth and before he was reincarnated," he said calmly. "It's the only solution we have. He's gone too far."

"You sound like Nana," I said, and he winced as I mentioned her name.

"Nana was right," he simply said.

"B-But we can't kill gods…Rio he's immortal."

"We can," Athena said, and both of them looked at me. "With Zeus' lightning bolt."

"All his bolts ended up in Tartarus with him," I said.

Athena shook her head. "No. I have one. I will give it to you, and you'll have to stab it into Rio's heart."

She couldn't be serious. "No."

"Has he influenced you so much, Aria? Goddess of Rebirth. You used to be the embodiment of justice. Where is that sense now?" She gestured to the world below. "Do you want to sacrifice everything? Every second we spend, people are dying. Do you value your love over the lives of others? This also puts you in the villain's role."

I swallowed.

My heart raced.

This couldn't be happening.

This couldn't be my life.

Athena's head tilted slightly, giving the impression that she suddenly felt sorry for me. "He's evil, Aria. The evil that will destroy us, and only you can get rid of it."

"Your lives were intertwined by the Fates," Any said, taking my hand.

I looked into his eyes, and something flickered within them. I couldn't identify as if he wanted to tell me more through it, but… it was like another language. I couldn't translate it. "Only you can reach him. You know what he dreams of. He trusts you, and you—"

"—will be his death," Athena finished his sentence.

I wanted to withdraw again, but Any held me tightly, his gaze penetrating deep into me. "You are the key."

A tear rolled down my cheek. "I don't want to be your key..."

"That's not up for debate," Athena said, and she went to a soldier, whispering something to him.

As he left the room, she snapped her fingers.

And right there the Omphalos Stone appeared before us.

The item had been repaired, now displaying a huge jug resembling a dragon's egg that emitted an eerie glow akin to a halo. As she extended it toward me, I glimpsed something white within, yet it was all warped, so I couldn't really tell what it was.

"When you use it to turn back time, the stone will be damaged afterward. We can never go back in time again, so we must ensure you get it right. I'll choose a time when you two didn't know each other yet, but you could likely captivate him. Perhaps your first year at the Olympian Academy..."

There was a knock at the door, and Athena went to answer it, taking an elongated box before returning to us. She didn't need to open it for me to know what was inside.

Zeus' last lightning bolt.

I swallowed hard, my heart pounding wildly as she approached.

With a snap of her fingers and three taps on the box, she opened it to reveal a delicate necklace inside. Upon closer inspection, I could make out the shape of a lightning bolt, but I never would have guessed that it represented Zeus' powerful weapon.

Her fingers carefully lifted the delicate gold chain from its velvet box and placed it around my neck, the cool metal giving me goosebumps all over my body.

"Keep it there at all times, and when the moment comes, as soon as he's close to you, stab him in the heart with the necklace, and we'll be rid of our problem. The future will change."

I blinked, finding it hard to breathe because of the pain this thought brought me.

"I know it's difficult for you now, but don't worry. Once you experience the real Shadow King, it will become easier. Zagrios has deceived you, tricked you into being on his side. In reality, he's a heartless bastard who only values his ego and himself. He's incapable of genuine love. You'll see. Now, come." She took my hand and led me to the o. It vibrated like a beehive.

"Something is off," I said and Athena scoffed.

"What nonsense, little one."

My hand trembled in Athena's calm, warm grasp.

"No it didn't vibrate like this the last time, Any," I turned my head around to look in his face. "Any something is wrong."

"It may be the time spell, Aria. All good, keep on breathing."

"Bory, do you feel it?" I said and checked on him in my pocket, but he only shook his head, afraid of speaking in front of Athena.

"Honey, don't be silly," Athena said, and we came to a halt in front of the stone. "You'll wake up, initially not fully aware. Your body will continue as if nothing happened, gradually bringing you to your senses in the situation. You won't feel different at first, just living your life as Aria, and I can't tell you how long your body needs to adjust to your memories, living it all over again. But then, at some point, you will remember and can act clearly. But be cautious. Be aware that every change impacts the future. That's why time travel is highly forbidden. It's very dangerous. Unfortunately, we're in a situation that demands the inevitable. We have no other choice."

Athena lowered her head and guided my hand toward the stone, but I was trembling so hard that she paused briefly.

"What about Bory... can I take Bory with me?" I said.

"Bory?" Athena asked.

I nodded to him in my pocket and when he stuck out his head, showing her his little furred head, she cringed. "That would be difficult, as only your consciousness can travel back to your old body. Bory didn't exist then."

"They could try it," Any said. "It's a theory that hasn't been attempted. The course of history has shown that it is possible to wander in one's dreams, so why should a new soul not have the same capability?

"But we don't know what will happen to you when you touch the stone," Athena said, looking intently at Bory. "You could die. You could get stuck in the past..."

"No," I said, reaching to take Bory out of my pocket. "That's not an option. Please wait here for me, and—"

"—Lynne," Bory said, his expression suddenly so serious that it nearly broke my heart. "I want to go with you. You need me. I'll never leave you alone."

"I won't let you die for me."

"I'll never leave your side. If you leave me here, I'll touch the stone right after you."

"Bory..."

"No, I want to be brave, too. I'm coming with you. I firmly believe that I'll wake up there with you."

"I can't—"

"Touch the stone," he said, pointing to it.

"No, I can't. I can't do this. I..." My throat constricts and my lungs seize up.

And before I could convince Bory to stay behind, Athena grabbed my hand and forced it onto the jagged stone, sending a searing pain through every inch of my body. It felt like a million needles piercing my skin at once, leaving trails of fire in their wake. I couldn't hold back the scream that escaped from my tortured lips as tears blurred my vision.

Bory.

Please save Bory.

CHAPTER SIXTEEN
ARIA, OLYMPIA 1000 YEARS AGO

The sunbeams tickled my face, and almost simultaneously, the temple bells rang, followed by a knock. Oh by the Fates.

"Goddess of Rebirth?" echoed the soft voice of my Herald. "You need to get up."

I've been confined to my golden chamber, feeling like a caged bird waiting for someone to set me free. Finally, I heard the familiar click of the door unlocking and Iris entered, dressed in a gown that seemed to shift and change colors with every movement. Her hair cascaded in shimmering red curls, reflecting the soft hues of the spectrum. From her back emerged wings of multicolored light, embodying the otherworldly splendor of the celestial phenomenon she controlled.

She was known as the Goddess of the Rainbow and served as the Herald of the gods among many. I admired her gift, being able to conjure rainbows out of nothing and soar across our realms. Sometimes I saw her in divine ceremonies, presenting cups of nectar to the gods.

I couldn't help but admire her gift, though I wished for it myself. Her presence was a relief in the otherwise dull and lifeless Olympian academy. At the upcoming Festival of Entry, I planned to speak my mind to Any and Hecate, who had been absent from my life thanks to the strict rules of this academy. I never realized just how rigid and authoritarian this school was before arriving here. The idea of finally discovering my magic under the guidance of the gods seemed exciting, but it turned out to be slow and stifling. My life came to a halt since arriving here—and I hated it with all my guts.

"Isn't she ready yet?" Nana's gruff voice startled me. Oh no. Here comes trouble.

She was the sole remaining link to my home as I attended the divine academy. My chaperone. Like every divine offspring, I was assigned a nurse responsible for raising me according to divine expectations. Needless to say, it didn't work out well for me. I hated all the rules and constraints.

The Olympian gods followed a hierarchy led by Athena as the head. Respect and acknowledgment for Athena's authority were fundamental principles of our nation. Hence, every day started with honoring Athena, which is why Nana held the stone owl up to my face before I even stepped foot on the ground.

I kissed it three times and saw Nana pout.

"What?" I hissed. "I honored her, didn't I?"

"Look at yourself," Nana hissed back. "You should be ready; your classes start soon, and we still don't know what class you have today."

Iris grimaced.

Her words echoed through my head as I slowly emerged from the bed. My eyes struggled to open, and the morning light seemed almost blinding after hours of darkness. Nana stood over me, her disapproving gaze fixated on my disheveled appearance. She had always said that I was difficult to wake, a trait that often earned me scoldings. Without giving me a chance to respond, she ushered me to my table and forced me into a chair. As I sat down, my silk toga threatened to slip off my shoulder, revealing my wrinkled nightclothes beneath. Ignoring my protests, Nana placed a small, palm-sized gold cube in my hand. When I glimpsed myself in the mirror, I understood what she meant - I looked terrible. My hair was tangled and matted, and dark circles marred the skin under my eyes.

Despite my desire to make a good impression and prove my worth, I couldn't shake off the exhaustion. The Fates had seen potential in me and Athena was convinced I could perform great magic, whatever that meant. But after a year of trying with no success, doubt crept in. My peers were growing impatient and even Athena seemed frustrated with my lack of results. Each day she demanded a demonstration, and I just couldn't bear to see the disappointment on her face anymore.

My hair was in disarray, and long, white, wavy strands stood in every direction. I wanted to straighten them, but Nana screamed, "Child! Cube! Now!"

I let out a heavy sigh and shook the dice in my hand. As always, the cube spun with an almost magical force, growing stronger with each rotation. Its gold glow was like that of the sun, casting warmth onto my skin as it came to a stop. And just like every day, I was disappointed by the result—a harp. The worst class.

"Oh, no."

"Don't be so ungrateful."

"I don't want to play music with the Muses."

"They are the nine goddesses of arts and sciences!"

"More like the goddesses of lulling to sleep..."

Nana slapped my hand. "Enough now; you should be more grateful. You are here to gain and develop your divine power. Be happy you won one of the strongest powers since—"

"—the Mighty Trinity. Since Zeus, Hades, Poseidon... yes, yes, I know, Nana."

She squeezed her eyes shut, and I could almost feel her wanting to hit me, hoping I'd be as grateful as Hecate. Damn. I couldn't imagine how Any dealt with this school. But I wouldn't know for several more months. The men were housed elsewhere than the women, and we weren't allowed to see each other until we completed our training. Then the years of Merriment began, where we were matched for marriage based on our abilities.

With each passing day, these girls became more and more bothersome to me. They were like mindless dolls, easily swayed and controlled by outside forces. It appeared they had no independent thoughts or morals, and I grew disinterested in their company. All that occupied my mind was the longing for home.

Ever since Mom and Hecate were no longer by my side, I had learned to manage on my own. But being alone still hurts. It might have been easier if I had friends here, but Iris was the only person who would talk with me, and even then it was only during her duties as a servant.

There was also Nana, but she seemed to push me towards a different version of myself constantly. Someone I never wanted to be.

"Come on," Nana said, tugging on my arm and pulling me up. "We need to get you cleaned up. Today, of all days."

"What's so special about today?" I asked nervously as she led me towards the bathing area, a corner made of golden partitions and tiled floors. She ushered me behind the partition and clucked her tongue in disapproval.

"Athena is coming to your class today; she wants to see how far you've come."

How far I've come. Yeah. That interested her. I clenched my fingers into fists.

Apparently, everyone had high expectations of me. The Goddess of Rebirth. I should be able to prolong life, give humans eternal life, scare away death... I didn't need to mention that Thanatos hated me because my mere presence questioned his power.

Athena had faith that people would eventually turn to me, involuntarily praying for my help in saving their beloveds. Thanatos, the God of Death, privately feared that once my abilities strengthened, I could hear these pleas... something he dreaded above all else.

Unlike Hades' children, who ruled the Underworld and received the souls of the dead, Thanatos represented death as a force of nature and fate. Thanatos was forever young and looked no older than me, just eighteen years old, even though he was over a thousand. His skin was black like umber, and he had jet-black hair, always carrying an inverted torch or a broken sword. Every time I met him, he swore that my time would come too. Whatever that meant.

Nana began listing in the background what a young goddess had to do and avoid, and what I did wrong, starting from my dirty nails to my reluctance to put on makeup...

Iris smiled sympathetically and took off my linen shirt. She snapped her fingers once, and as always, small golden birds flew in through my large arched window with small bronze pitchers in their hands. They circled around my head and poured the water onto my head. It was warm and enveloped me like silk. Iris gave me a sponge, and I washed myself. The birds flew out again and came back in with small towels in their beaks, handing them to me to dry off. Iris helped me into my dress, a white A-line dress with transparent sleeves and a waist cord tied around the stomach. She snapped again, and the birds flew around my head, blowing my hair dry with their wings.

"Aria, after you've mastered the art of music—" Out of

nowhere, Nana let out a piercing scream that sent a jolt through my entire body. Iris, who was sitting next to me, shot up in surprise. "—By all gods and the Underworld, Aria, what the hell is a pomegranate doing here?"

Nana held out the blood-red fruit, her face serious and disappointed as she gripped it so tightly that her nails dug into its flesh. Iris sucked in air next to me, and I had to hold on to the wooden frame of the partition. Damn.

I should have concealed it more carefully, but how did she discover it? My eyes darted under my bed and I noticed a leaf that I had missed. Nana came closer to me, causing an instinctive step back from me. "Nana, I'm not sure—"

"Don't deceive me," she hissed. "Was he here?"

"He?" I gripped the wooden frame tightly. Iris placed a comforting hand on my shoulder.

"Zagrios," Nana hissed.

"Why would he—"

"Don't! Everyone knows those seeds of misfortune are his. Dealing with him leads you to the Underworld, and he traps you there. I hope you weren't so stupid as to eat one, or he'll have you in his clutches forever."

I swallowed. "No, I have taken nothing."

Nana stared at me for a few seconds, as if she had to test me, as if every sound from me was a lie. "How could you be so stupid and talk to him?"

"I needed a little variety."

"Variety," she said and looked at Iris. "Not a word to anyone."

Iris nodded and took her hand off my shoulder.

"Go. I'll take her to class myself."

Iris nodded, picked up the wet towels from the floor, and ran out.

After the door latch clicked shut, Nana raised her hand and

slapped me on the face. The blow turned my head to the side, and I stumbled back until I crashed into the wall. Lifting my head, I breathed so heavily that my chest rose and fell.

"Where did you meet him?"

I couldn't exactly tell her I wanted to escape... so I averted my gaze, hoping she wouldn't hit me again.

"I say it again: Where did you meet him? He hasn't been seen here for weeks!"

I took a deep breath and exhaled, determined to keep my thoughts to myself from now on.

Nana's gnarled fingers dug into my shoulders. Her grip was so tight that I winced.

"Child, don't be so stubborn! You can't associate with Zagrios. He's evil. Do you know what he has done? He sends assassins to his sisters to have them killed. He wants the Underworld for himself. The King is evil incarnate."

I took a deep breath.

Everyone knew the stories about him—he could create a whip from shadows and enjoyed punishing evil souls himself. And Tartarus was his playground.

Hell, I knew of his vengeful nature and disdain towards his sisters. I knew he slept with anyone who gave him a second glance, but most importantly, I fucking knew he could offer me an exciting life, something different from the monotony here. And that's why I just couldn't stop thinking about him, about the pomegranate...

However, I was a coward, which is why I didn't dare to visit him—until today. When Nana took my chance away. I should have taken it as soon as I could.

Nana grabbed my wrist. "Your role is too significant in this world for you to associate with the wrong Gods. Come. We have to go to the arts."

Nana dragged me out, and I stumbled into the hallway of

the divine palace at her hand. It was like everything in this godly realm, golden and gleaming. But for me, it was a golden cage with rules that would determine my entire life. The moment I entered the divine academy, my free will was taken from me.

I stared at a picture of Athena and wished she could see the suffering she inflicted on us. She promised improvement after overthrowing her father, but she formed a rigid regime where freedom was only possible in dreams. We were her tin soldiers. Nothing more. Yet, the Fates saw in their threads of destiny that she would bring about significant changes. We all acknowledged the power of the Fates and had to accept the predetermined destinies. Even we gods could not act against destiny. If we did not accept them, it was equated with hubris and considered the gravest offense in our world. Excessive pride or disrespect toward the gods was strictly punished, and Zagrios took over the torture personally. Legends say that he sneaked into the bodies of the victims with his shadows and destroyed them from within.

Again and again. It was like Prometheus' punishment. Prometheus was a Titan who helped humans and acted against the will of the gods. He stole fire from the gods and gave it to humans, providing them with warmth, protection, and the opportunity for development. This act earned him the wrath of Zeus. As a punishment, Prometheus was bound to a rock in the Caucasus, where an eagle daily ate his liver, which regenerated overnight. And Zagrios punished from within, just like that.

"You will avoid him. Don't speak to him anymore, understood? Or I'll tell your father."

I sucked in the air. Not father. "I will stay away from him."

"Good. Eventually, you'll have to become smarter."

We raced through the corridors of the academy, admiring its majestic structure. The building reached for the sky with its heavenly columns adorned in golden trimmings. Its design exuded timeless grace and a perfect blend of divine splendor and elegant aesthetics. The facades were crafted from a radiant material that shimmered under the light.

Large doors welcomed us into an entrance area guarded by stately statues representing various gods. As I stepped onto the floor, I marveled at the flawless mosaic of celestial imagery gleaming in beautiful hues, depicting the creation of our worlds.

Nana led me to a grand door which opened up to the class-room of muses.

I loathed my existence.

CHAPTER SEVENTEEN
ARIA, OLYMPIA 1000 YEARS AGO

*A*lways *dress modestly, ensure that attire covers the body appropriately.*

Unmarried interactions with the opposite sex must be chaperoned.

Obedience and submission to parental and later marital authority.

Proficiency in cooking, cleaning, and sewing is essential.

Adhere to strict social etiquette and manners.

Preparations for courtship and marriage are paramount.

Embrace traditional gender roles as a homemaker and caregiver.

I fucking hated all these stupid rules.

Flopping onto the bed, I was unable to contain my frustration as Iris locked the door behind me.

Today, I revived a puppy.

They killed it right in front of me, and then I had to touch it to bring it back to life. It drained all my magic, and I felt like utter misery. Athena was ecstatic, and I knew once I honed my powers, I'd become an extension of her, because my power wasn't always positive—misuse created Deadwalkers. I learned it the hard way, because the next puppy turned into an undead dog. I will never forget it.

When I saw the dead dog, with red eyes staring at me, I thought I'd drop dead from shock.

It was grotesque, and I couldn't bear being treated like a pet as well—waiting to become Athena's puppy. I saw it in her eyes today. They were ice cold.

As usual, I lay awake for hours before finally drifting off to sleep, only to be rudely awakened by morning to live the same day over and over again. I resented Nana for not listening to me.

Angry at Iris for being too scared to talk to me anymore, leaving me without a friend. Angry at Any and Hecate for painting a false picture of this academy and not revealing the truth to me. Angry at Athena. Angry at this damn academy.

And on top of it all, I suffered from constant headaches. Something wasn't right. I couldn't shake off the daydreams and flashes in my mind, like a recurring image of something blue with feathers. It felt like I was forgetting something important. As if I should remember, but couldn't.

And then I saw something red under my bed.

I leaned over the edge and pulled out a... pomegranate seed.

Despite my hopes for more, there was only one pomegranate seed.

My heart raced in my chest as I fixated on the small fruit, remembering Zagrios' offer.

I glanced at the window, seemingly open but surrounded by traps that could burn me alive at any moment. Then to the door. Solid gold. No way out unless someone let me out.

I held the tiny red seed in my trembling hand, my breath catching in my chest. I hesitated before trying to shove it into my mouth, but my hand shook so violently that the seed slipped and fell to the ground.

I grabbed it swiftly. This was my way into the Underworld.

But could I do it? Should I? Probably not, but his words echoed back in my mind: *I know they've shoved all those 'traditions' down your throat. Women are supposed to be pretty, dance to society's tune, and play sweet melodies, all wrapped up in a neat, obedient package.*

I was the neat, obedient package.

My fingers clenched around the pomegranate seed.

Come to me and I'll show you what life means.

I looked at my bedside table, filled with books on embroidery, singing, and dancing... and felt nauseous.

Come to me and I'll show you what life means.

Suddenly, there was a flash before my eyes and I saw that blue-furred bear once more. I shook my head in disbelief. Was I losing my mind? Yes, I couldn't take it any longer in this place.

I put the pomegranate seed in my mouth and bit down. A hint of sweet fragrance wafted from the interior as I expose the sparkling seed. The small, ruby-red jewels yielded as my teeth gently embraced them. The sweetness, intense and lively, danced on my tongue, mingling with a hint of subtle acidity, and darkness engulfed me as it pulled me deep into the Underworld.

I couldn't fully comprehend what was going on, but it seemed like a void appeared before me and I was plummeting into it.

I FOUND myself enveloped in shadows and mist, standing in the middle of a gateway.

It didn't take long for me to realize it was the door to hell, opening up as soon as one entered a portal to the Under-world. Before my foot even descended, an entirely different scene unfurled before my eyes. It was like little pieces merging together until I walked straight into the Shadow Court.

I whirled around and saw the entrance to the castle, but the drawbridge was lifted and there were guards dressed entirely in black, standing watch as if nothing had happened. It was as if I hadn't just slipped past their defenses undetected.

My heart thundered in my chest, and I forced myself to go into the city. The air grew heavy with an otherworldly chill as the winding path led me to black stone walls, weathered by passaging eons. Towers and spires soared towards the dimly lit sky, casting long shadows over cobblestone streets that echoed with each of my steps.

I hesitated, unsure if I should turn around and go back. But then I remembered that there was no going back. I wouldn't even know how to. Suddenly, a loud creaking sound caught my attention, and I looked up to see a murder of crows flying over-head. My sudden movement caused me to bump into a man passing by.

"Watch where you're going, fucking cunt!" he spat, striding past me.

As he rushed past, his words stung like a slap to the face, and I stumbled backwards. My heart raced as my eyes darted around, taking in the shocked stares of strangers. The once comforting blue sky now appeared sickly, casting a haunting glow on several skulls and bones scattered throughout. A shiver ran down my spine as I pushed forward through the maze of ramshackle buildings, their menacing shadows closing in around me. This was what I had asked for, right? Why did it feel like a nightmare coming to life then?

To my right and left, houses towered above me, constructed from a sleek, obsidian stone that appeared to consume any source of illumination. The atmosphere was so dense and oppressive, as if the very shadows of these passages were smothering me.

I suddenly felt all too light and touched my white hair, looked down at my white dress...it was a mistake and suddenly the people staring at me became a visible threat. How they watched me. Watched my body move. Watched my breasts bouncing under my heavy breathing. I walked faster, past Gargoyles perched on balconies, their stone forms frozen in eerie poses, watching over the city with a silent vigilance. Then, a man touched my hand, and I ran past the candlelit windows to a market. I think I once heard about it. It's the Night Market. A dark place where smugglers bought forbidden goods. Market stalls lined the narrow streets, adorned with rich fabrics, exotic trinkets, and goods not of this world. Merchants, draped in cloaks that seemed to defy the darkness, beckoned me towards their wares. The scent of unfamiliar spices and the distant hum of chatter created an atmosphere both bustling and arcane. Cloaked figures, their faces obscured by hooded mantles, glided through the shadows. I turned again and crashed into another man.

He spoke, but his words were cut off by a dark cloak. I caught glimpses of one strand of silver hair underneath." What's someone like you doing down here?" he asked.

"I—I just wanted..."

He pulled me towards him and spoke urgently, "Come with me. It's not safe for you here without a cloak." My heart raced with fear as I tried to resist his grasp on my arm, but it only tightened.

"Either you keep quiet now, or I leave you to the others. I don't want to draw attention to myself. I won't harm you."

"Don't they all say that?"

A smile flashed beneath his cloak. "Probably, but you've

seen my hair. I come from Olympia too, but no questions until we're at my place."

As we walked through the bustling central square, I couldn't help but feel small next to the colossal statue towering over us. Its stone features were chiseled with precision and its outstretched hand seemed to beckon me closer.

My guide led me through winding alleys and I couldn't help but wonder why a forgotten god would live in this underground realm. After all, it wasn't common for deities to linger in such places.

He stopped in front of an old wooden door and gestured for me to enter. I hesitated, knowing that it was unwise to enter a stranger's home in this unfamiliar world. But the thought of traveling alone was even more daunting. With a deep breath, I stepped inside.

"Quick. You stand out like a parrot."

"Like what?"

He grunted, closing the door behind us, and tossed his hood back, uncovering his black dreadlocks. I couldn't help but notice the scattered silver strands among them. His dreadlocks flowed down to his hips. Despite appearing winded, a constant reddish tint adorned his terracotta skin. Suddenly, something that felt a lot like a distant memory surged into my mind, causing me to press against the wall in shock. Instead of seeing him standing here, it was in a cave. A scream burst from my lips as I clutched my head in confusion.

"What's wrong?" he shouted, rushing toward me.

"Not sure. I've had this for days. I see things, and just now, I saw you."

"Me? You just met me."

"I-I saw you in a cave and by the gods, you seem familiar, b-but I've never seen you before!"

"You haven't. I'm sure."

I took a few deep breaths to shake off the strange feeling. "I'm sorry. Maybe I mistook you for someone else," I stammered. "What is your name?"

"Malachtit," he said, a friendly grin spreading across his face.

"I'm Aria. Nice to meet you."

"Likewise. Here, Aria." He handed me a cloak from a shelf. Finally able to look around, I saw it was a single-room space with a bed, chamber pot, a small kitchen by an open hearth, and a shelf with his clothes.

He didn't have many possessions. I doubt he could spare any of them. "You're giving me this, but you probably need it—"

"Take it. I can't have a goddess walking around like this in the Underworld."

I hesitantly slipped into the heavy cloak, grateful for its warmth. "Thank you."

He raised an eyebrow. "What's your business here?"

I couldn't help but feel a sense of unease at his words. "Just passing through."

My gaze traveled over his muscular form and landed on the small pouch at his waist, no doubt holding valuable trinkets from our world. "You carry herbs and potions. Are you a healer?"

He shifted uncomfortably. "How do you know?"

I smirked. "My sister has healing powers and swears by enhancing them with herbs like mugwort. You also have a pentagram, sage, and myrrh here. Either you love potent smells or you heal."

"Smart."

I gave a knowing wink. "But I've always heard that the inhabitants of this realm atone for their sins, not seek redemption?"

"Depends on what you're willing to pay for."

"Ah, so you're a smuggler."

The forbidden spells and powerful artifacts we deities hoarded back in Olympia were highly sought after in this realm, and it seemed this man had made a lucrative business out of smuggling them across.

His expression turned guarded. "That's dangerous information to have. I hope you'll keep it to yourself, or else I may regret saving you."

"I didn't need saving," I retorted confidently.

A wry smile tugged at his lips. "It would only have taken five minutes for you to find yourself in serious trouble. Everyone knows that white-haired people have high magic."

As I ran my fingers through my hair, Malachtit's words echoed in my mind.

My mom had always told me that our unique hair color would bring power and attention from others in our world. She explained that sometimes, our magical abilities drain us of melatonin, leaving us with this rare hair color.

I turned to Malachtit, who had been watching me intently. "I should go," I said.

He raised an eyebrow. "Where?"

"To the castle," I replied. "Zagrios wants to talk to me."

Malachtit's eyes widened in surprise. "He rarely seeks visitors."

"Well, he asked for me specifically."

Malachtit rose to his feet, pulling his hood up to cover his head. "Come, I'll lead you there. I have to meet a guard for a trade, anyway. One more good deed won't hurt, right?"

CHAPTER EIGHTEEN
ARIA, OLYMPIA 1000 YEARS AGO

"Why aren't you in Olympia anymore?" I asked as we climbed through more dark alleys.

The Shadow King's castle loomed into view, seemingly emerging from the darkness of the mountainside before us. Its silhouette stood out sharply against the deep night sky, with a slender tower that reached so high it almost seemed to touch the skulls.

There's a thick protective shadow etching against the castle's obsidian stone, lending it an eerie presence.

As I gazed at the structure, the windows appeared dark and indistinguishable and the several towers sharp like knives.

"You're not supposed to ask strangers such things," Malachtit said, and pouted.

"I ask these things. So?"

Malachtit grinned. "Well, things were never as simple for me up there as for other gods. My only power is healing, and Athena and I... let's say we didn't get along very well."

That piqued my interest. "Why?"

"That, my dear, goes beyond my willingness to reveal my secrets to you."

I lowered my head, thinking if only he knew I had been imprisoned for months, having seen no men other than Zagrios and my teachers, and that all my conversations revolved around gods, their stories, and legends. His were the most interesting ones in a long time.

I watched as he darted his eyes in my direction, his expression morphing into one of guilt.

"Why don't you start and tell me your story first?" he said as we ascended a winding path, reaching black brick floors before the castle gates.

Instead of speaking to the guards, Malachtit simply flipped his wrist, and the heavy oak door opened slowly, creaking on its rusty hinges.

"I made a deal with the Shadow King," I whispered, and Malachtit twitched slightly, almost imperceptibly.

He straightened up immediately, continuing as if nothing had happened.

"Are you crazy?" he whispered back, offering me his arm as we walked through the archway.

I linked mine with his. "Probably." Comes with being imprisoned.

"What led you to it?"

"You won't reveal anything about yourself, but I'm supposed to spill everything?"

His lips curled into a smile under his hood.

The entrance hall exuded a touch of mustiness and bygone eras. Along the walls were a dozen of portraits of Hades and Persephone. I blinked at the gorgeous drawings. Hades had long hair and blue eyes, almost like Zagrios, and Persephone was so beautiful...blonde, long curls and a face that resembled an angel. I inhaled deeply and stopped dead in my tracks when I saw a portrait of Zagrios. His beauty was well known, but seeing it on the painting almost took my breath away. He took after his mother. Holy hell.

"You have a crush on him," Malachtit suddenly said next to me and I jerked. "Is that why you made a deal with him?"

"What?" I snapped my head to him. "No, never."

I almost choked on the 'never.' Well, since our last meeting, I might have thought about him occasionally. Especially at night. But I didn't even know him, and finding someone good-looking didn't equate to developing feelings.

"You've got drool there." Malachit laughed, pretending to wipe something off my lip.

"Hey," I swatted his hand away, and we both burst into laughter.

"You're easily embarrassed. I always thought he was hot too, but he'd be too tall for me. I prefer the shorter men. Besides, he's arrogant as fuck."

"Why arrogant? What did he do?" I asked.

"You really know nothing, do you? What did they do to you up there?"

"Locked me up like a bird," I said, and wanted to bite my tongue. Shit, I couldn't keep anything to myself.

"So that's why you ran then. You want to explore the worlds?" he put on a knowing smile as if he once was in the same position as me.

I shrugged. "Maybe."

Malachtit was just too likable, but I was telling him too much. What if he actually meant harm? I couldn't know, and just because I found him likable didn't mean he was well-intentioned. Maybe he'd kidnap me and ... well, I didn't even want to go this far.

He laughed again, and for some reason, I was sure he wouldn't harm me. "He's probably in the throne room. It's where he holds court."

My heart pounded up to my temples. I had never seen a court session. We lived far away from the Pantheon, and we rarely even discussed other gods. Mother and father always said they had chosen country life for a reason. They hated the city and divine decadence. Especially with mother and her nightly excesses, not that simple for us. And now that she was dead...

"Is everything okay?" Malachtit snapped me out of my thoughts, and I wiped a tear from under my eye, nodding.

"Everything's fine." Nothing was.

I let my eyes roam through the castle's insides, stumbling upon a surprise maze of dark wood-lined hallways and rooms stretching to either side of me. Heavy velvet curtains in deep burgundy hung at the tall windows, allowing only sparse light, casting the hallway in a muted, mysterious ambiance. To our sides stood the Shadow King's guards, all clad in black armor adorned with his emblem—a combination of black smoke and swirling lines that formed an intricate pattern, ultimately winding around a pomegranate. Zagrios' symbol.

We waited in front of the reception hall, and Malachtit announced me.

"An official audience?" I grinned.

"I wouldn't know how else you could talk to him, but do me a favor, watch out for yourself. I can't accompany you in there. I have an appointment of my own, but not with Zagrios."

I knew he wouldn't tell me more, so I just nodded. "Maybe we'll see each other again."

"Maybe." He turned away, and I was almost disappointed that he didn't bid me a friendlier farewell. Then, he paused and seized my hand, slipping something into it.

I gasped. "What are—"

It was hard, small and when I opened my closed hand, I saw a small finger bone. My stomach dropped.

Malachtit placed his hand on mine. "Shh. Bones are magical, and if you rub it three times, it'll show you where I am. Just in case." He winked. "Put it in your pocket."

"Aria, Goddess of Rebirth," someone behind me said, and I turned.

I left the door ajar and turned my head, but Malachtit had vanished. A queasy sensation churned in my gut as I wondered how he knew about my abilities...

"Please enter," a stern-looking guard said in front of me, and I stepped into the reception room.

The corridor was lined with a heavy carpet, muffling the sound of my steps. Torches floated above my head, casting a vague light in the room.

My eyes were drawn to Zagrios, who sat before me on a throne crafted from shadows that seemed to pulsate and writhe like elusive eels. I couldn't help but take another look, just to confirm what I was seeing; and yes, there it was, a throne made entirely of shadows. The deep, inky blackness contrasted with the dim light of the room, making Zagrios appear even more impressive. His fingers tapped rhythmically against the armrests as he regarded me with piercing, sapphire eyes. This was no ordinary throne—it held a power beyond my comprehension.

His gaze was so cold, as if nothing could faze him.

As he nodded over my shoulder, the heavy wooden door creaked shut behind me and I jerked a little.

To his right, a roaring fireplace commanded attention with its elaborate carvings and towering height in the grand hall. The dancing flames cast haunting shadows on the vaulted ceilings, where stern portraits of long-dead nobles appeared to glare at me.

I saw Zagrios raise his hand, and a wind blew around me as my hood fell back, exposing my face.

"Little Moon," he said, and his voice made my heart beat

even faster. "Your escape abilities are getting better. What have I done to have you here?"

"I owe you something, right?" I said, pretending to be brave.

I approached him with cautious footsteps, aware of his fixed gaze on me. It felt as though he was undressing me with his eyes, and when he lifted his hand, I noticed the strings of my cloak were coming undone.

As I walked, the strings of my cloak came undone one by one until it lay abandoned on the ground next to me.

"Nice dress. But a bit too modest for my taste."

"Oh? How would you prefer it then?"

"More revealing."

The wind picked up and my dress fluttered against my body; the straps slipping down my shoulders. I tightened my grip on them and gave him a stern look. "We agreed that nothing scandalous would happen here."

I felt the wind again, but I held the fabric so tightly that nothing shifted.

A smile played on his lips. "That's not scandalous. You said you want to know how we live down here? We know no boundaries."

"Yes."

"Tell me your heart's desire, and maybe, just maybe, I'll make your dreams come true."

"We have a deal..."

"Ah, but most folks forget to jog my memory." A mischievous grin played on his lips.

"I'm thinking I made a wrong turn," I admitted, turning away, my nerves crawling up the back of my neck. I tried to bolt, only to collide with a wall of inky shadows that halted my escape.

"Thinking you can stroll in and walk right back out? Darling, you're not that innocent, are you?"

I glanced down, taking deep breaths. What was I doing here? Had I completely lost my mind?

"Come on, spill it. What's your deepest desire?" he teased.

"I want you to show me... life."

He grinned. "I thought so." And then he hopped off his throne and approached me.

His long strides were measured, each one deliberate, and I didn't know what to say, where to look.

Silently, he motioned for me to stand in front of a large, ornate mirror that hung on the wall.

As I walked towards it, my white dress morphed into a sleek black gown and my reflection in the mirror distorted as he approached behind me. His rough yet gentle hands smoothed out any wrinkles in the dress's fabric, making it fit me perfectly. His gaze swept over me with a slow intensity. I could feel his eyes tracing every curve and line of my body.

The black satin material was adorned with intricate designs, bearing his signature emblem in gold thread. I gasped as I saw the daringly low neckline that hugged my curves, barely grazing my breasts. Turning to examine the back, I couldn't help but admire the plunging cut that revealed the graceful line of my spine down to my tailbone. My heart raced with excitement and admiration for his impeccable taste and skillful design.

I shielded myself with my hands. "What have you done? I want my other dress..."

A throaty chuckle escaped him. "You're in my realm now, and here, we abide by my rules. Clothing you like I want are part of those rules."

Our eyes locked in the mirror.

With a heavy heart, I slowly lowered my trembling hands, giving him full access to see every inch of my exposed skin. His fingers traced along my upper arm and I struggled to breathe.

His breath hot against my ear, he murmurs, "You're spell-binding." He presses his cheek against mine, his grip tightening around my waist. "What if I never want to let you go again?" A possessive glint flickers in his eyes, daring me to resist him.

"Maybe I don't want to leave anymore."

Our eyes met, a charged energy passing between us. Without breaking our gaze, he barked to his court, "We're closed for the night. I've got other things to take care of."

My heart fluttered at his words, but he gripped me in his embrace as we gazed at each other in the mirror's reflection. "Let's go out tonight," he said with a devilish grin. "I'll introduce you to all the forbidden pleasures you've never experienced before."

CHAPTER NINETEEN
ARIA, OLYMPIA 1000 YEARS AGO

He guided me through the dimly lit, labyrinthine alleys of his city, and everywhere he went shadows seemed to dance along the weathered brick walls next to us. Holding my hand, he made me feel like I belonged to him in that moment. His touch was both gentle and possessive.

I pulled my hood over my head, trying to blend in with the shadows.

"What will your people think when they see their king roaming among commoners?" I asked, glancing at him from under my hood.

"Don't worry," he said with a smirk, "my shadows keep us hidden."

Feeling a sudden rush of boldness, I let my long white hair fall out from under my hood. The king's eyes gazed over it, and I couldn't help but feel a flutter in my heart. His eyes held a soft twinkle that made me catch my breath.

"Are you often among the folk like this?" I asked.

"Yes. I enjoy pretending to be a normal passenger now and then. It can be quite entertaining."

He winked at me, and I felt the heat rise to my cheeks.

Quickly averting my gaze, I focused on the darkness ahead of us.

The city, with its worn cobblestone streets, bore the scars of time and echoed with distant whispers of its troubled past. Towering buildings leaned against each other as if sharing secrets, but the further we went, the feeling of being watched, despite the king's shadows, grew stronger. A shiver ran down my spine, and no matter how hard I tried, I couldn't shake off the chilly feeling. We walked past a group of Deadwalkers, their ashen skin and hollow eyes unmistakable signs of their demonic origin. The stench of rot and sulfur filled the air, making me fear what terrors lurked around every corner.

We ventured deeper into the less-traveled quarters, away from the more frequented parts of the city. And then someone screamed.

I halted in my tracks and even pulled Zagrios along with me, as I refused to take another step. I peered into the abyss next to us, a seemingly endless side street that looked like a gaping void. Right before me, a Deadwalker devoured someone *alive*, and I reached out, ready to intervene, but Zagrios' shadows coiled around my fingers, restraining me from employing even a shred of my magic.

"Don't. Everything has its purpose," he said.

"How can you allow all of this?" I asked, anger surging within me while the screams became louder and louder. "Someone in your city is being harmed!"

"In my city, most are sinners. They are here to be punished."

His grip on my arm was tight as he dragged me away from the scene.

The images were seared into my mind, and would probably hunt me for days to come.

Zagrios pulled me forward, and we rushed down some

wobbly stairs while the dim streetlights flickered intermittently, casting fleeting glimpses into the obscured corners of the city's secrets. It seemed like we came into the area where people like to party. The occasional murmur of laughter or the clink of glass emanated from several hidden pubs.

"Where are we going?"

"To the depths of Shadow Court, darling."

As he turned his gaze towards me, I found myself smiling.

"I knew you'd like it. And you know what? I'll assign you a task every night," he declared.

"Every night?" I inquired as we descended a dark spiral staircase.

He halted with a suddenness that left me breathless, a whirlwind of emotions swirling in the depths of his sapphire blue eyes. In that suspended moment, he pinned me against the wall, his presence enveloping me like a heady fragrance, and I caught my breath.

As I looked up at him, air crackled with an unspoken energy, and time seemed to slow to a languid dance. His touch, firm against the wall, sent shivers through me, and the world around us faded into insignificance.

My eyes met his. The air crackled with an unspoken energy.

The sound of our breathing was the only thing that remained constant in the otherwise still street. His hand pressed against the wall, causing the stone to crumble under his grip. I couldn't help but feel a tingling sensation run through my body as he leaned closer. The world around us faded away as we stood in this moment together, lost in each other's gaze and I couldn't tell if it was his charm or my foolishness, but I found myself drawn in by his every move.

Each time he smiled, it caused my knees to weaken beneath me. Was this just part of his power? I tried to calm my racing heartbeat, but it only seemed to quicken with each passing moment.

"My free wish," he whispered, and I felt his hot breath on my lips, "is for you to make me happy."

My eyebrows shot up. "What?"

His nose brushed against mine. "The favor I seek is for you to make me happy."

"A-and how do I do that?"

"If I knew, I wouldn't need you."

I blinked, realizing only now that he was making me his property—and I let him. By demanding that I make him happy without knowing what it entailed, he forced me to do as he wishes. "That's not a real deal."

He shrugged, nudging my nose with his. "That's not my problem, Little Moon. One should never make a deal with a ruler of the Underworld. Didn't your nanny tell you that before bedtime?"

His charming smile lit up his face, and I couldn't help but blush as our eyes met. But the way the light danced on his features and the sheer magnetism of his presence made it impossible for me to hold his gaze for long. I looked away, my heart racing with feelings that I couldn't quite put into words. I've never felt this before...

"What's your first task?" I whispered, realizing that I was a fool.

"Now, I want you to enter and wager for me which Shadowslave should die and which should live."

CHAPTER TWENTY
ARIA, OLYMPIA 1000 YEARS AGO

Entering the Veiled Vortex Inn was like stepping into a shadowy carnival.

As I crossed the ethereal threshold an unsettling tension coiled in the pit of my stomach, like a knot tightening with each passing moment.

Spectral mist draped the entrance, hinting at the whimsical chaos that awaited me within. Nana would drag me out of here. She would sprinkle me with holy water from Athena's bath. And yet, it intrigued me. I know something must be seriously wrong with me because I...liked danger. I liked the thrill. And I desperately wanted to know hat Zagrios did in here and what I have to do.

Make me happy.

My eyes flit over flickering candles in skeletal sconces that cast a dim glow on black circular tables and the animated conversations of various demonic creatures surrounded us. We made our way through countless souls in cloaks. Here and there I saw men and women in loose dresses, sitting on the laps of others. I watched as they held each other firmly, as a woman draped her hand over a man's leg and didn't stop even when she met the middle of his trousers, touching his—my cheeks burned and I looked away. My gaze fell upon another man. He wore a hat with several feathers and on his lap sat a woman; her dress comprised of draped fabric fastened with a golden brooch. I knew men and women with these brooches were paid to sleep with others and I couldn't look away. We called them the Hetairai. The feathered man and her sat at a bar built of obsidian and bone, it showcased potions that emitted an eerie luminescence. Zagrios' hand tightened around mine and we weaved through the eclectic gathering. He drew me toward the heart of the establishment—a colossal boxing ring. I think I heard of this before but seeing it with my own eyes was something else.

Leaning over the railing, I watched as a boxing match unfolded beneath us. Cheers, jeers, and the occasional gasp resonated through the air, while some people behind us were still placing bets with increasing fervor.

My gaze dropped to the souls below us.

Two naked men fought against each other, their blackened eyes revealing that they were already Shadowslaves, and they must have been for so long that they now fought here for their freedom. Typically, Shadow Slaves were formless beings with haunting eyes and a gaping mouth. However, for this occasion, their bodies took on a translucent appearance that resembled flesh whenever light touched their skin.

I glanced at Zagrios. They fought for freedom, for the right to be reincarnated again...something only the Shadow King could grant them—if he desired it.

"Are you here every night, freeing souls?" I asked.

"No, maybe thrice a month."

"And when you're not here? Who grants freedom to the winner, then?"

"No one. Both remain Shadowslaves forever."

My throat tightened. But he could free the souls. Why wouldn't he? Why wouldn't he do good when he had so much power? My fingers clenched around the railing. "But why not come every day? You enjoy causing pain to others, don't you? People come to this place with *hope*, unaware of the truth - that there is none!" He was an awful man. Everyone was right.

He smiled. It was a bitter grin, though. "Well, first, I don't have time to waste every other night, and second, not every soul deserves another chance. The one on the left," he began, nodding towards the blonde Shadowslave whose hair hung loosely like feathers on his decaying flesh. "Raped seven women. The one on the right killed his wife and his own children. Three. Fucking. Kids. They deserve nothing but to rot."

I stared at the two beings as they bit into each other, scratched, and struck. The scent of sweat, blood and adrenaline hung thick in the air as the Shadowslaves faced each other. They hissed like cats.

Suddenly, I realized I didn't want either of them to win.

Zagrios' head turned to me and our gazes collided. "I know you're all quick to form an opinion about me. You see me punishing others and think I enjoy it. Sometimes maybe. Often less. But, well, someone needs to do it, and that someone is me. But instead of letting me do my job, you come with morality. Morality that no one cares about when it comes to justice."

His piercing sapphire eyes bore into mine, revealing a powerful intensity that I couldn't fathom. It was as if the swirling shadows around us held their breath, caught in the magnetic pull of our locked eyes. But when his gaze dropped to my lips, I quickly focused on the Shadowslaves again.

I watched their stomping feet and the clashing of fists that echoed back as the fighters skillfully dodged and countered. The audience became a vibrant part of the spectacle, eagerly expecting every move and expressing their excitement in deafening cheers as black blood spilled on the floor.

"When it's all on you to punish all souls in the Underworld? What about your sisters?" I knew Hades had three children and every single one of them was evil.

He laughed. "They have other tasks. Far less annoying, and the Olympian Gods' focus has always been on me. Nobody has time to check what dirt they have on their hands."

I watched the blonde Shadowslave fall to the ground, barely breathing.

"Which one will you redeem now?" I said.

"The one on the right."

I swallowed.

"It tells me that his soul is ready to be reborn. He has atoned for over 2000 years. The one on the left needs more time. He'd kill again."

He extended his arm, palm facing the man on the ground, and blew a black mist that left a glittering white trail as it slithered towards its target. The mist enveloped the man's body and disappeared with a faint sucking sound, leaving only a pile of ash in its wake.

The one who had actually won staggered back, his mouth gaping and his eyes looking much like the skeletons in the sky... he knew what was coming for him. He won and lost at the same time because it wasn't about strength. It was about their soul and how much they've learned. Zagrios' let him have his victory only to make the downfall even harder. Within a blink of an eye, the man got pulled to the ground as if chains were dragging him down. He screamed, and suddenly, the crowded room fell utterly silent.

"They sense I am here," Zagrios said, his stare still on the chained soul.

Upon his snapping, a shadowy abyss manifested beneath

the soul, engulfing him entirely. It was as though the very ground had indeed devoured him whole.

I noticed how everyone looked around, searching for someone. For Zagrios. "Do you sometimes show yourself to them?"

"When I like someone and need to fuck."

I blinked, suddenly finding the need to distract myself.

My attention wandered, and as I explored further, the secrets of the inn unveiled themselves. Concealed doorways whispered promises of lust, leading to guest rooms that exuded an otherworldly allure. Beds seemed woven from the very shadows of the abyss, their inviting embrace calling out to weary travelers. Mirrors adorned the walls, reflecting glimpses of alternate realms within the accommodations, providing a momentary escape in this strange crossroads of the underworld.

"What's happening in there?"

He chuckled as two other souls were brought in. Another fight started.

"You blush when I say the word fuck, but you want to know what's happening in those rooms over there?"

His low baritone sent shivers down my spine, and I prayed he didn't hear me swallow in embarrassment. I don't know why just the thought of sex made me so giddy. It's just that any contact with the opposite sex was always forbidden to me and it made it so much more interesting. I once noticed that Hecate had a boyfriend. She snuck out and Dad got furious. He hit her until she'd gone unconscious... I saw it as a little kid and maybe it got me so scared that I have had problems with it ever since. And yet here I am, risking everything. Risking my father's wrath. Risking Athena's Wrath, risking—

"Little Moon," he said and all of a sudden all I could hear was his voice. He took my chin between his thumb and index finger, forcing me to look up at him. "Those rooms are for fucking. If you'd like to satisfy a scratch, go in there and wait. Someone will come."

I swallowed. "One of the Hetairai?"

"Could be anyone. The minute you sit on these beds, people get invited. You can turn them away or invite them into your bed."

Something shifted in his gaze and I wanted to look away, but he held my face firm in his fingers.

"Have you ever kissed someone?"

"No."

"Then I'd like you to kiss someone now."

My eyes widened, and I struggled to breathe. "What? No!" I tried to free myself and dug my nails into his hand, but he held me so firm, I had no chance. Not if I didn't want to use my powers, and using powers against the king was anything but wise.

He gave me a lopsided grin. "But it would make me happy."

Oh, he was evil. Pure evil.

"Stop looking at me like that. I told you never make deals with us rulers. It's your fault."

"You saved me. I didn't make a deal voluntarily."

"Life happens."

He finally let me go.

I massaged my aching jaw and shot him a wicked glare.

"You wanted to live, right? Well, in my idea of fun, I ensure you have a good time, too."

"I don't know..."

He nodded toward the locked room behind me as the referee announced the next boxing match, and the crowd erupted into cheers. "Step inside. Just one kiss. You can clearly set the rules."

I didn't know what to do, my eyes darting to the dimly lit rooms. They were all occupied except for one. Something inside me urged me to go for it. To try what was possible. Who was stopping me? My parents? Nana? The gods?

"You want it too," he said, casually wafting his smoke over the boxing area as if it were easy for him to entice me while still going about his business, another Shadowslave defeated.

Then, just as a man was about to enter the vacant room, Zagrios declared loudly, "No."

His voice thundered as if echoing from all sides, and the man turned away as if nothing had happened. I quickly checked the other people, but they seemed oblivious. Everything continued, and new Shadowslaves entered the scene.

"Go inside," he said, and I did.

My heart fluttered, and I struggled to breathe against my erratic breaths.

As I stepped into the room, shadows danced at the entrance. I examined the bed made of shadows. It looked peculiar, like black linen, but when I sat on it, I noticed small holes scattered about and the shadows shifting.

My eyes flicked to him. He didn't take his gaze off me.

Damn it. What was I doing here? I wanted to get up, but suddenly, someone walked in.

A woman.

I blinked, my gaze darting around the dimly lit room as she entered. Shit. Shit. Shit.

She looked beautiful. Brown maroon curls fell down to her hips. Her dress was a simple toga, tied together with a golden brooch. Her smile was all sweet with youth. Zagrios acknowledged her with a silent nod, and the atmosphere shifted. I was suddenly caught between uncertainty and a strange sense of connection. The woman's eyes briefly met mine, a subtle understanding passing between us.

"O-only a kiss," I said.

"I'd love to kiss you." Her voice was velvety, and my cheeks burned.

I never thought about kissing a woman. My parents emphasized to stay away from men so much that I focused on how I could skirt around their rules too much. I just realized I forgot women were beautiful too, that I might liked to kiss them too.

Restless, I fidgeted on the bed, my nerves escalating.

The shadows closed in behind her, leaving us in a dance of shadows. Zagrios maintained his steady focus on us, an unspoken understanding hanging in the air. No one could see us. No one but him and somehow this thought alone made me all shivery. God. I wanted this.

Approaching with an air of confidence, the woman's eyes held mischief. Her fingers lightly brushed against mine as she sat onto my thighs, making me fall backwards on the bed.

"Relax, Little Moon," she whispered, her voice a soothing melody. "We're here to make sure you never forget."

She spread her thighs alongside my hips and her hair hung so low, framing my face. She smelled like roses. But her words did little to ease my nerves. As she leaned in, placing a gentle kiss on my cheek, a mix of anxiety and curiosity flooded through me. The room whirled for a moment, as if the shadows were toying with my senses—or were they playing tricks on me? It felt like they reached out, touched me, touched us, and with each fleeting contact, my breath deepened. Every subtle brush left me gasping for air, as if the shadows themselves had a way of awakening something profound within me.

The woman's lips lingered near mine, and I held my breath. "You're going to like it, I promise."

The anticipation pulsed within me, and I believed her. Believed Zagrios. I wanted to live. I wanted to know what it was like to taste every little bit of what this world offered. And I would.

Finally, her lips met mine in a soft, fleeting kiss. My heart raced, trying to lose itself in the sensation, yet the nervous flutter persisted. Her soft hands cupped my face, and I let my hands feel her hips above mine. Oh, fuck.

She turned her head, and when her tongue slipped past my lips, I struggled to breathe. I couldn't think about anything but that tingling feeling of her mouth on mine.

Just when all of my body tingled, she ended the kiss, and the woman pulled away with a playful gleam in her eyes. "Live, Little Moon, live."

She left the room without another word, and Zagrios stepped in, ushering back the Underworld's chaotic sounds. Left on the shadowy bed, my mind swirled with emotions. The encounter had been brief, but it left an indelible mark, and the nervous excitement lingered in the air, a haunting melody that echoed through the inn. I still lay on my back, and as I pushed myself up on my elbows, I saw Zagrios looking at me. He looked pleased.

"And now what? Are you going to kiss me?"

"Don't be silly." He casually leaned against the wall, his gaze roaming over my body. "You're a child."

"I'm not a child."

"You talk like a baby," he took a step toward me, "you act like a baby," he took another step," and you blush when I say fuck. You are a baby."

When he stopped in the middle of my outstretched feet, his thighs touched my knees. Sighing deeply, I look up at him and all the feelings in me went to war against each other. The desire grew. Even more so than it did with the woman earlier. The way his dark hair tumbled into his face, the gleam of his blue eyes in the dim shadows, and the commanding presence of his body—there was an undeniable magnetism. He was so damn handsome.

A silent voice within me whispered he held the potential to offer far more than the woman ever could. In that charged moment, it was as if an invisible thread connected us, and the unspoken desire between us hung in the air, palpable and tempting. He could tell me what he wanted, but he desired me too. He may be significantly older than me, but maybe that's what intrigues me even more. I know I have a penchant for forbidden things.

"You say all that and act like you have to weigh up whether you don't want to kiss this baby yourself," I said.

He laughed, that dark tone again. "I don't have to weigh anything up. I know exactly what I want to do with you, but I'm old enough to ignore my desires."

"Why would you do that?"

"Because I still have a lot planned for you, Little Moon, and it will not stop today. There's no such thing as love for me. So we better take our time until you're not that innocent baby anymore and you're ready to play with me."

Then, thunderstorms and lightning flashed through my mind, and I think I lost consciousness. Or did I? It was like a dream and a blue feathery bear talked to me. He said a name. A name I never heard off...it sounded otherworldly. Lynne.

Why would a small bear call me Lynne?

CHAPTER TWENTY-ONE
ARIA, OLYMPIA 1000 YEARS AGO

All played out like a surreal dream.

I knew Zagrios, and I had been having a blast last night.

Yet, when I awoke in my Olympian room, the shocking part was that no one had a clue about my nocturnal escapades. My life went on as if nothing had happened.

Iris nudged me awake the next morning, and the routine began again: shower, dress up, attend classes, showcase my skills to Athena, and then, back to my prison and sleep. Or not actually sleep because now I was part of the Underworld during the night and each time I woke up, I had another pomegranate seed in my hand. I used it and visited him.

Night after night after night.

The charade lasted for weeks, and I was as content as ever. With Zagrios, I could explore every fantasy I'd ever harbored. Be it the innocent act of riding astride, both legs on one side of a horse, or dancing in an inn where we had to wear masks and barely a wisp of cloth.

Zagrios and I turned it into our own little game—a voyeuristic exchange.

We watched one another.

How I kissed others, how he kissed others.

But he never kissed me. Not once.

To my embarrassment, the longer I was around him, the more I fixated on his luscious lips, the sculpted bulge of his arms, and his tousled dark hair that always gave off that just-woke-up impression.

During some of our conversations, his gaze lingered on my lips and I thought he might finally kiss me. But he didn't and it almost drove me crazy because I wanted him to finally make a move and kiss me. The fear of rejection consumed me. I pulled back each time even though I longed for his touch, leaving an ache in my heart that I couldn't understand or ignore. I found myself wondering if I was misinterpreting my own feelings. Was I still nothing but a little girl to him, despite the intense way he looked at every inch of my body? I didn't ask because I was afraid of the answer.

One night, we stopped at the base of the Sprawling Hills, also known as the Dragon's Tread, where jagged rocks formed the shape of massive dragons. Sirchas. The Underworld's most formidable dragons.

Zagrios had planned a special picnic for us and and, of course, we didn't choose a flowery field. Instead, we perched on top of the tallest mountain, which provided us with a breath-taking view of the dragons flying overhead.

As we settled onto a dark red blanket, he snapped his fingers and a woven basket appeared, overflowing with ripe fruits and vegetables. The skulls above us glowed with an eerie green light, casting faint shadows across the black grounds below while several silhouettes of rustling animals darted between the mountains.

I couldn't help but laugh at the thought that this was all for me, created by none other than the notoriously ruthless

Shadow King. He could be so sweet and thoughtful. I wondered how many people had actually seen him like this. The way he made me feel so special was truly from another world.

Each time a dragon flew over us, I jerked slightly and he would laugh at me.

I could have killed him with my glance only, but then, his laugh was so sweet and his smile so handsome that I may have jerked even more the next time. Foolish. I know. Sue me.

With each passing moment, I delved deeper into understanding Zagrios—his playful sarcasm, his endearing quirks. It became harder to control my urges to claim him for myself. And I could have sworn that he relished in watching me struggle with my desire for him.

I think he liked the way I looked at him.

But it was both comforting and unsettling to be seen as innocent by him.

On the one hand, it made me feel protected and cared for. But on the other, I couldn't help and feel frustrated he didn't see me the way I wanted him to. I wished to prove him wrong, to show him I wasn't just the sweet, naïve girl.

Yes, he was a sly rogue.

Yes, his decisions were often questionable.

And yes he was an arrogant bastard at times—but he was also the one who liberated tormented souls, especially women in dire straits, the one who lied for his sisters to keep them out of the crossfire, even though they hated him with all they had. The one ready to bear the world's entire burden of hate if necessary. He was so skilled at putting on different masks for people, but I thought that with me, he dropped the act and showed his real self. The kind king who had been hurt so many times that acting tough became his shield.

It was easy to fall for him and over these weeks, amidst all the crazy ideas he had, I fell so hard it hurt.

I even led a dual life for him.

As a goddess from Olympia, everyone expected me to maintain a flawless exterior. And when night fell, and I descended into the Underworld, I shed my perfect facade and reveled in being his playmate. And I loved it.

In his realm, I was free from the expectations and constraints of Athena. The Underworld may not have been perfect, and neither were its inhabitants. But down here, everyone's flaws and secrets were on full display, and no one pretended to be superior to anyone else. It was liberating, and I felt more at home than I ever did in the pristine, golden halls of Olympia. There, we had kept up this front, hoping that once Athena had claimed the throne, things would magically turn around. And yet it was just the same old song and dance, but with a different title.

Tonight, as the moonlight already filtered through the golden window, I waited until I could be sure everyone was asleep, until Nana's shuffling footsteps had long since ceased for the night. It was only at that moment that I took out a pomegranate seed from my pocket. And just as I was about to pop it into my mouth, a deep, soothing voice interrupted me.

"Good evening, Little Moon." There he was, propping himself against the balcony door with an enticing ease.

Startled, I dropped the seed to the ground.

"I just wanted to come to you," I said, sitting straight.

He casually strolled in, glancing at each corner of my room as if he'd never been here before.

I looked down at his long, powerful legs encased in sleek black leather trousers as he confidently advanced towards me, and my heart skipped a beat. I cursed it. My damn heart. It always jumped relentlessly when he was involved. And I knew it shouldn't because there was no way the Shadow King could love me—love anyone.

"You stitch?" he said with a smirk and explored the little flower embroidery I did and left on my bedside table.

I cringed. "No. I have to."

"I figured." He traced the colorful lines and shook his head. "Doesn't it bother you that women in Olympia are only good for crafting useless shit?"

"Of course. That's why I visit you each night."

"Ah, sure, stitching is the reason then. Or is there something more?" His playful grin made my heart skip another beat. Damn it.

That smirk again.

With every breath, I could feel the nervousness building inside of me, threatening to overwhelm my senses. But I pushed it away and mustered up the courage to speak. "What other reason could there possibly be?" My voice was shaky but determined, as if trying to actually beat back the silly butterflies in my stomach.

He chuckled and slammed the embroidery hoop back onto my table, not bothering if he damaged it.

With determined steps, he approached me and came to a halt between my legs.

I leaned my head back, meeting his intense gaze.

When his finger slid under my chin, my breath caught in my throat. "I want to take you out tonight."

"Indeed?" I stupidly said, staring into his piercing eyes as he caressed my chin with his thumb.

"Come on, go get dressed up," he said, glancing at my casual clothes.

I looked down at my simple dress, feeling self-conscious.

With a swift flick of his wrist, he unleashed a flurry of white petals that swirled and twirled in the air. They clustered together into a delicate, lacy gown.

He carefully draped it over my ornate partition, the soft

folds shimmering in the moonlight that filtered through the nearby window.

Gaping, I approached the dress, marveling at the elaborate design of every single flower.

"It's breathtaking," I whispered, letting my fingers dance over the exquisite fabric.

"Yes," he said, but his eyes lingered on me. Not the dress. And I almost fainted.

My cheeks burned and when that gentle shiver of anticipation traced my skin, I quickly sought refuge behind the privacy screen.

With a heavy sigh, I unveiled the layers, slowly shedding my dress.

Fumbling with the delicate lace of my gown, I didn't notice the sudden gust of wind until it was too late. One side of the partition flew open, black shadows swirling around it and revealing Zagrios standing there with a smirk on his face. All I could do was turn around as quickly as I managed. The flush of embarrassment added an unexpected thrill as I inadvertently treated him to an enticing view of my bare back.

Huffing out a nervous laugh, I said, "Well, if you're that enthusiastic, how about you use your magic to help me with the laces on the back?"

"Why use magic and miss out on the fun?"

Despite my best efforts, I sucked in a shaky breath as he closed in on me. His rough hands traced over my back. Oh for the Fates sake. This was going to be one hell of a ride.

"W-where are you taking me?" I stammered, focusing on the wall in front of me.

He took his time, his hot breath tickling my neck.

I gripped the hem of my dress tightly, desperate to maintain some semblance of composure.

He gently brushed away my hair and placed it over my

shoulder. And when his calloused fingers grazed my skin, I couldn't resist leaning into his touch and letting out a breathy sigh.

This tension was unbearable.

"Oh, so curious, my Little Moon. Why don't you wait and see?" he said.

"I don't like surprises."

"Since when?"

Zagrios' fingers continued their exploration, tracing down my neck and making me grip the hem even tighter.

I could feel him expertly tying the laces of my dress until it fit just perfect, leaving us both standing there for a heartbeat. And another. And another.

Without warning, he grabbed me by the shoulders and swiftly turned me around.

My feet slipped on the slick marble, and I stumbled, crashing into his muscular arms. Heat radiated between us as our bodies pressed together, causing my chest to rise and fall rapidly.

"It's rare to meet someone with a mind that's just as beautiful as her face," he breathed.

My head spun as I gazed up at him.

Suddenly, his shadows enveloped me in a caress that felt like he was touching every damn inch of my being—even my very soul.

And we were gone.

CHAPTER TWENTY-TWO
ARIA, OLYMPIA 1000 YEARS AGO

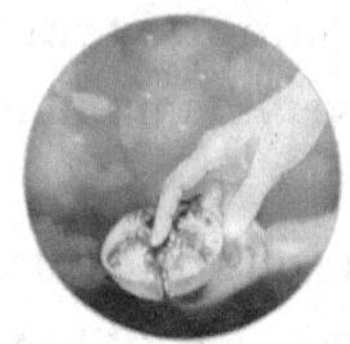

As I opened my eyes, a strong earthy smell filled my nostrils and my feet sank into the soft mud of a riverbank.

Oh no. The banks of the phosphorescent River Styx...

I stopped dead in my tracks and drank in the eerie scene before me.

The inky water lapped against a boat just mere feet in front of us. It was carved from the bones of long-forgotten souls, and shimmered in the unearthly light.

Zagrios must have sensed my unease, because he tightened his grip on my waist. But it didn't stop the fear that crept over me as I remembered what this river represented—the boundary between life and death. This was a holy but dangerous place to be.

"You take me to Styx?" I whispered.

Gods. Nana would scream at me like a banshee.

"Yes, but there's no need to be afraid. I just want to show you something." He stepped onto the boat, one foot touching its ancient surface. As he offered his hand to me, I could tell that he was giving me the choice to either follow him or not.

Despite my fear, I couldn't resist the curiosity pulling me towards him.

Of course, I took his hand and stepped on the boat.

As our fingers intertwined, I glimpsed skulls lining the edges of the river, their hollowed eyes seeming to follow our every move. I exhaled slowly, trying to calm my trembling body.

Oh, I wished I could control my emotions better.

But I couldn't and every damn fiber of my being screamed for me to run.

Instead, he guided me onto the cold, hard seat in the middle of the boat and whispered, "I want to show you there is always a glimmer of light in the darkness and a blossom of beauty in the shadows."

As he spoke, a flicker of recognition sparked within me. He had already said this to me. Hadn't he?

In my mind's eye, I saw him standing beside me in a strange house, our bodies pressed together. But then the image shifted and we were on a flat rooftop, his hair shorter and his clothes unfamiliar. My pulse quickened as another image flashed before me—him sitting on a dragon, holding me in his arms.

I gasped for air, my breath coming out in short, frantic bursts as he gripped my fingers even tighter. "It's okay, you're safe with me," he promised, his voice soothing and I tried to breathe against the rising lump in my throat.

As our boat sliced through the murky waters of the Styx, a fine mist sprayed my face. On either side of the river, leafless trees lined the banks, their bare branches reaching out like skeletal fingers. The distant cries of the tormented echoed through the fog and let me wonder how in the world he wanted to show me anything beautiful down here. It was grotesque.

If I didn't cling to his steady hand like I did now, my heart would race even more and my palms would be sweating. His calm demeanor was the only thing keeping me grounded.

As if he could read my mind, he handed me a goblet, and I noticed him taking a golden flask from under the seat. "Drink up, it will ease you," he said with a knowing look.

I eyed the shimmering nectar warily as he poured it in the goblet. "Trust me, it's good. It's the nectar of the gods."

He winked.

I hesitated.

Zagrios offered me the goblet, carved from pure gold and encrusted with sparkling gems.

"Ambrosia?" I hesitated, knowing only the greater gods were allowed to drink it. But curiosity won over caution again, and I took the goblet from his shaking hands. "What will happen if I drink it?"

"Nothing," he replied with a shrug. "Olympia just hates to share the good things, that's why they keep it hidden. I like to share with special guests." He gave a sheepish smile and gestured for me to take a sip.

Against my better judgement, I brought the golden liquid to my lips and let it touch my tongue. Instantly, a warmth spread through my body, chasing away the surrounding chill. The sweet nectar was unlike anything I had ever tasted before, and I couldn't resist taking another sip. Before I knew it, the goblet was empty and a sense of contentment settled over me.

My gaze rushed to the slightly glowing bottle in his hand and reached out to grab it, but he laughed heartily and put it under the seat again.

"Hmm. Perhaps it was wise to hold off on giving young gods Ambrosia until they were ready. How about we don't drink an entire bottle in under a minute?" he said, smirking.

My hand instinctively reached for the flask again, almost as if controlled by another force. But before I could grasp it, he grabbed my hands and the strange impulse disappeared, leaving me feeling embarrassed and flushed once again.

"My Little Moon, always so eager." His hand caressed mine, and I watched as our fingers intertwined.

"What do you have planned for me tonight?" I asked in a playful tone.

He leaned in closer, his breath igniting a fire in my core. "I thought you'd never ask. I have something special in mind for my naughty little goddess."

I couldn't help but smile. "You won't tell me, huh?"

He shook his head. "Where's the fun in that? I want to see the light dance in your eyes." He nodded forward, and I followed his gaze.

"Come, watch the night with me. In a world full of cruelty, beauty is often hidden like a glimmering gem buried deep beneath layers of dirt and grime."

My gaze swept to the river banks to our sides, where vibrant red hues of lotus flowers surrounded us like a soft blanket. The water glimmered in the greenish light and the bare branches of black willow trees danced in the chilly breeze.

My skin prickled with goosebumps as a chill ran down my spine. But as he wrapped his powerful arm around me, pulling me close to his body, a different kind of shiver ran through me.

"When I was little, my mother would bring us here once a year," he said.

"Isn't it rather frightening for kids?"

He grinned. "Stop with judging this quick. I shit my pants when we came here first, but it turned out to be my favorite place ever since. Mom loved stories, legends and creatures."

I cringed. Creatures didn't sound good. "I slowly but surely believe you calling me beautiful was an insult."

"Oh, you wait, you'll start liking creepy things soon."

I noticed his finger drawing circles on my shoulder and leaned into his touch even more, relieved he didn't pull away. "Zagrios, I—"

"See," he exclaimed, directing his finger straight ahead.

And then, I caught a glimpse of small glowing orbs that emerged from the depths of the water. One by one.

"Will-o'-wisps," I breathed.

My breath caught in my throat as I gazed at the little blue, purple, and green lights dancing and twirling on top of the dark waters. Each one radiated a soft, ethereal glow that reflected off the dark waters in an entrancing waltz.

I turned to Rio, my eyes wide with wonder, and saw the same amazement reflected in his face. It was like we had been transported to another world, a secret realm that only belonged to us.

"Zagrios," I whispered again, feeling his grip tightening around me. "This is..."

"I know," he murmured, his voice full of awe. "It's as if they've come to guide us."

He cupped my chin with one hand and gently turned my face towards the mesmerizing scene before us once again—and all I could do was stare in amazement as more will-o'-wisps joined us. It was a moment I would never forget, as if the Underworld itself had orchestrated this enchanting performance just for us.

As I reached my hand out over the water, the tiny orbs of light swirled around my fingers, tickling them with their gentle touch. They reminded me of a sea of flying dandelions, but upon closer inspection, I saw that each was a luminescent little figure dancing in the breeze. Their skin and hair glowed from within and I smiled.

This was beyond words.

If not for him, I wouldn't have seen it.

No. I wouldn't have lingered here for even a moment longer.

One bold blue wisp danced on the tip of my finger, tempting me to sway my head in unison with it. And as I blinked, more and more of them appeared around us, filling the darkness with their ethereal glow. The blue wisp winked at me and danced away.

The ghostly lights led us deeper into the Underworld, their golden hues illuminating the water, and suddenly there was nothing creepy about it anymore. It was beautiful. Nothing but utterly beautiful. The Stygian waves seemed to shift and undulate with each note of the unearthly song, as if the very river itself were swaying to the Will-o'-wisps tune.

When I lifted my gaze, the gnarled branches of the willow trees caught my attention.

The tips, once resembling bones, now sprouted delicate orbs that glistened like miniature leaves.

"Thank you," he suddenly said.

I turned to him, my heart in my throat. For what? I had to thank him.

"Thank you for remembering me. These nights with you showed me that there was indeed light to my darkness. I forgot about it."

His hand reached up and ran through my hair, resting on my cheek.

I wanted to say something, anything, but the words got stuck in my throat as I struggled to process what I was seeing. The fluorescent lights above cast a faint glow on his skin, making it seem like he was radiating light.

"I want to make my intentions clear," he said calmly as his thumb caressed my cheek.

"T-that's good..."

"I want to kiss you. May I?"

I don't know if I was that nervous, but I actually scoffed. "The ruthless Shadow King asking for a kiss?"

His gaze deepened, a promise twinkling. "I will keep asking

until you bid me otherwise, because you deserve nothing but endless admiration."

I was so perplexed that I just blinked and blinked again.

A small smile appeared on one side of his mouth. "I would appreciate it if you didn't leave me hanging, Little Moon. I'll ask you one last time. May I kiss you?"

"Yes."

Right as I was about to utter the last sound, he leaned in and our lips collided in an intense kiss. The Will-o'-wisps swirled around us, their ethereal light casting us in a searing halo of gold while the softness of his lips ignited a fire I never knew I harbored. My body melded against his, our hearts beat as one as the boat glided onward into the bright painting of swirling lights.

"I've ached for this," he murmured against my lips, his breath hot on my skin. "For so long, I thought my heart was nothing but stone... but with you, I feel..."

"Alive?" I finished for him, kissing like I've never kissed before. His tongue danced over mine, my shaky voice only adding to the intensity of it.

"Yes," he exhaled, his hands tightly holding onto my hips. In one swift motion, he lifted me and placed me on top of his lap. "So fucking alive."

The boat rocked gently as the wind carried us further.

I sighed, my fingers curling into the fabric of his shirt, my body aching with anticipation. He deepened the kiss and his tongue traced the seam of my lips before slipping inside again, tasting me deeply. I moaned and opened up to him. While running my hands along his strong arms, he pulled me closer still.

His grip on me tightened, and I arched into him. One rough hand slid down my back to cup my bottom possessively. I gasped at the contact, my breath hitching as I wound my arms around his neck. Our kisses grew hotter—more fiery, consuming us both as we sank further into the moment.

I could feel the heat between us, the desire that pulsed in time with my own heartbeat. His hand slid up my thigh, tracing the curves of my legs, skimming higher, inching under my dress until he found what he sought. My body jolted at the contact as desire coursed through me. But then I pulled away from the kiss with a pant, looking up at him with hooded eyes.

I couldn't help but ask, "Why all the kisses with different people?"

I immediately regretted my words.

Here we were, in the middle of the best kiss of my life, and I had to go and ruin it.

His response was a wicked smile. And yet, his fingers kept on tracing along my inner thigh—teasing and tantalizing me. "I wanted to be sure you knew exactly what you wanted when I finally asked for the kiss."

The twinkle in his gaze told me he knew it was him alone I desired most.

No need to say it.

It was written all over my face—for everyone to see.

"And why did *you* kiss others?"

"To banish forbidden thoughts of you that haunted me throughout the day."

I twitched slightly, but he saw it. His grip tightened around me.

"It was in vain. No matter how adamantly I tried, I find myself standing here, still wanting you, and I have a feeling it won't ever stop." With a gentleness that made my heart flutter, he reached up and cradled my face in his hands. "Because I would be a fool to let you go again."

When he slowly leaned in, our lips met in a soft kiss.

It was unlike our first one—a fiery explosion of lust and need. This kiss was gentle, deliberate, and started like the brush of butterfly wings, only to grow so intense that I wished we did nothing else but touch and kiss and hold each other forever.

CHAPTER TWENTY-THREE
ARIA, OLYMPIA 1000 YEARS AGO

The inevitable clash between Zagrios and me occurred when he was summoned to the Pantheon, requiring all of us to attend a gathering of gods.

Nana dragged me in, and my father was present too.

I stiffened up when I saw him. He was seated at a table with all the other greater gods. We, the audience, had to stand at the far end of the room. According to the gossip, Zagrios had killed his sister's lover, and Athena was furious about it.

But it was possible. He was with me at the time.

I couldn't wrap my head around when he would have had the chance to commit such a crime, but Zagrios brushed off the accusations. As always. He just let everyone believe what they wanted. But Athena didn't start her speech with Zagrios. She talked about Hecate—my sister.

She had always been known for her strange visions.

However, her latest one, believed by many to be true even by the powerful Fates themselves, brought her instant fame seven years ago. Sadly, the strength of her vision ultimately took her life. I never learned the details because Mom and Dad refused to discuss her after she passed away, and Any was equally cluelessHence, listening to the prophecy for the first time fascinated me, but as soon as I grasped its meaning, I wished I had never learned of it. Discovering that the weeks I spent with Zagrios posed a threat to us all shattered my heart. I was oblivious, but he knew. And now I couldn't stop it. I already loved him. And when love found its way to the Underworld meant the end of worlds...we were already on the verge of destroying everything.

How could he allow us to do this?

Attempting to make eye contact with him during the speech—asserting that my love meant nothing to him—proved futile. He ignored me, as if I were invisible. I couldn't fathom why he consistently played this role, shouldering the world's animosity. I could see the hatred between him and the Blood Queen and the Bone Queen, but the reasons remained elusive for me. They killed each other's lovers for over a decade, and Athena emphasized it must end now. No one should start a relationship until they lifted the curse.

I held my breath, feeling the weight of our forbidden adventures pressing down on me.

Zagrios' eyes darted back and forth, his brow furrowed in deep concentration as my hands fidgeted nervously in my lap. And when our eyes locked, the hint of his smile told me volumes.

We wouldn't stop. He still wanted me to come to him at night.

It might have been all fun and games for him. But not for me.

Was it enough to set the prophecy in motion because I fell for him?

Because by now it was adamantly clear that when I thought of Zagrios, I thought about nothing but kissing his seductive lips, sliding my fingers through his silky black hair over and over again. And I thought of kissing his neck, his torso—hell—even his dick.

I wanted him to sleep with me.

And this was a problem.

This was against the rules.

This was our downfall.

Almost as much as my dreams about another life were. I dreamed of caves. I dreamed of Malachtit, I dreamed of someone called Lynne, Soothie and Bory and at some point, I felt like...it could be true. Maybe all these people and creatures existed.

Or I was going mad.

"WE MUST PUT AN END TO THIS," I whispered to him as he cornered me on the balcony after the assembly. Sensing he intended to talk, I slipped away, praying Nana or my father wouldn't witness our conversation.

"Put an end to what?" he demanded.

"To my visits. You heard Athena and her decree."

"To hell with Athena."

I pushed him farther back. "To hell with Athena? You can't be serious! She's going to kill us."

"She can't kill me. Only Zeus could and he's gone. Plus, you're oblivious to what's happening behind the scenes, Little Moon."

"Then enlighten me."

"I don't want to shatter your idyllic world."

I scoffed. "Oh, please. You shattered it the moment you waltzed into my room." As if my peace of mind was ever a genuine concern for him.

He countered with a bitter smile. "You know what? I'll be generous and let you decide. You've brought me happiness. Your debts are wiped clean. You don't need to come to me anymore."

His words felt like a dismissal, a rejection that somehow cut way too deep. "But—"

"Here," he handed me more pomegranate seeds, and I hastily tucked them into the folds of my dress," If you choose to come with no deals influencing your decision, then you're welcome. My doors are always open for you."

I was at a loss for words.

In that split second of silence, a subtle vulnerability flashed in his eyes.

It was as though a hint of fear lingered there, uncertain of my response. Was he actually afraid I might turn him away? Or was he fearful of the unknown consequences if I took his invitation seriously? If we continued, it was clear enjoying each other's company wasn't because of some silly agreement. No, If I agreed, it was because I genuinely desired to see him. And if he agreed to spend time with me without expecting anything in return, it carried the same weight.

That's when I realized this wasn't a simple decision for either of us.

Finally, I mustered the courage to ask, my voice barely above a whisper, "And if I decide to come? We'll attract the anger of everyone."

"Then we'll both agree to fuck Athena's rules and face whatever consequences may come."

He hesitated, his hand delicately gripping my hip, and when he lowered his head, he kissed me.

"I'd love it if you choose to join me. However, I'll respect your decision. It's going to be perilous, maybe even reckless, but

I want you to know that I'd rather spend my time with you than with anyone else in any world."

As I turned my head, our eyes met and locked in a heated gaze.

The space between us crackled with tension, begging for one of us to make a move. My body leaned towards him, craving the feel of his lips on mine, but he held himself back and took a step away. My heart shattered as I watched him resist the temptation.

"Maybe fate will bring us together tonight," he said and where he had stood just moments before, was now a mere shadow of his former self.

CHAPTER TWENTY-FOUR
ARIA, OLYMPIA 1000 YEARS AGO

As I lay in my bed, debating whether I should risk a visit to Zagrios, my door burst open and Nana stormed in, her face twisted with fury.

"Get up. We need to leave. Now!" she demanded and the door slammed shut behind her with a deafening bang.

I shot up in alarm. "What? Why?"

"Don't you dare ask why," she hissed as she grabbed me by the arm and pulled me up.

I tried to resist, my heart racing with fear. I had never seen Nana like this before. "Nana, you're scaring me."

"You better be scared, foolish kid. Your father...he's livid. He found out about you and...*him*," she whispered, unable to even speak his name as tears started to well up in her eyes. "Iris found one of this hellish seeds under your bed and she hid it for you! The Herald she shared her room with told your father about her betrayal."

My breath catched in my throat. Nana said *shared*. I didn't see Iris today. "Where is Iris?"

"Your father killed her! And now he's coming for you," she pulled me further, "come! We need to hide! We need to run!"

Just when Nana grabbed for the golden handle, the door burst open once more, and the room seemed to shrink, engulfed by an ominous silence. Father's presence filled every corner, his towering figure casting a long, foreboding shadow across the golden marble floor. His eyes, usually warm and arrogant, now blazed with an intensity that sent a cold tremor down my back.

My trembling legs carried me around the bed, desperate to create some semblance of distance between myself and the rod that Father clenched tightly in his iron grip. The seconds stretched out like taffy, each one laden with an unspoken threat. I wasn't going to live through this kind of hatred in his eyes.

"Father," I pleaded, my heart pounding against my ribcage, its rhythm irregular and frantic. "No. Please..."

My words hung in the air, a fragile plea for mercy amidst the storm of his fury.

But the tempest in Father's eyes turned my limbs to jelly. He showed no sign of abating. Instead, he closed the distance between us with large strides and I stumbled backward, my back colliding with the edge of the bed. Fear constricted my chest, choking off any words that might have escaped my trembling lips.

"You slept with the Shadow King?" he said.

"No, please, no," I said holding my hands over my head as he raised the rod high above me, the veins on his temple pulsating. There was a terrifying grace in his movements, as if he were a conductor orchestrating the symphony of pain about to unfold.

"You went to the Underworld. You betrayed us. Disgraced us. Our family is put to shame now and you could have been everything we needed. You could have saved us from the fall and you're stupid enough to think someone like him would care for you. "He let out a snarl and the room seemed to hold its breath, the walls closing in on me, trapping me within this nightmare. "You'll never be more to him than a mere whore!"

I let out a whimper, too scared to even look at Nana. "No, we didn't sleep with each other," I stammered. "I just visited him, that's all...please, father, please—"

"Don't try to deceive me, you disgraceful cunt!" He roared, raising the rod above his head in rage. "You're worthless now. No one will ever want to marry you."

And then he struck me, my screams only adding fuel to his fury.

My body crumpled under the force of the blow, pain searing through my every nerve. I felt the wetness of blood trickle down my face and tasted the metallic tang on my lips. Father's rage was an inferno. He hit me again, and again and again. From afar I heard Nana crying out but she didn't come for me. I saw her from the corners of my eyes, standing there, breaking apart just like me.

My feet gave way under another blow.

I crashed to the ground, spitting blood.

As I lay there, a tangled mess of limbs and shattered dreams, Father stood over me, his breath coming out in harsh pants. He raised his hand once more and struck my back with the rod, leaving red welts on my skin. When he struck my face, the sound rang in my ears before everything went dark for a moment.

But amidst the chaos, a flicker of defiance ignited within me.

And with trembling hands, I pushed myself up from the cold, unforgiving floor.

Every movement sent waves of agony through my battered body, and as Father's temper subsided, so did my fear.

My voice was hoarse but I mustered the strength to speak. "Hit me as much as you want. I don't belong to you anymore. I will not be your pet," I said, my eyesight blurring from the bruising and swelling on my face.

His grip on the rod tightened until his knuckles turned white.

"Oh you will, or I'll end you myself. And then we'll see if you can use your damn magic to come back from the dead."

As my father's final strike landed upon me and I fell head-first to the ground. My teeth banged against the marble.

Trembling, I cracked open one swollen eye, and saw my once-vibrant strands of hair were now matted with crimson. With a cruel smirk, he yanked Nana's long white braid and dragged her out of the room. My heart raced with fear and desperation as I knew what would come next. If I didn't comply, he would repeat tonight over and over again, until I was nothing but a broken weapon for Athena's bidding.

But I refused to be a pawn in their game any longer.

With my last bit of strength, I snatched one of the pomegranate seeds and forced it down my throat. The bitter taste of the pomegranate mixed with my blood burned on my tongue, but I didn't care.

It was my only chance at escape.

There was no one who could take on Athena but the Shadow King.

"Lynne, oh my god..." A faint whisper reached my ears amidst the chaos and I felt soft feathers caressing my forehead as I was whisked away to Zagrios. Relief flooded through me, but I knew this was only the beginning of a treacherous journey towards true freedom.

No story ever began with the Underworld and ended with liberation.

THE SHARP STING of stone against my skin woke me from unconsciousness, and I gasped for air as if I had been holding my breath for eternity. My heart pounded against my chest, and I struggled to push myself up from the cold floor.

All of my body hurt. Each of my damn breaths hurt.

Through bleary eyes, I saw the familiar room—Zagrios' chamber.

He sat at his desk, his magical quill moving across parchment with lightning speed.

Despite my injuries, a wave of relief surged through me. I made it. I was save now. I was with him.

But when he turned, his eyes widened, and just for a fleeting second his usually composed demeanor was suddenly filled with shock.

His voice, usually so calm and collected, now trembled with fear as he knelt down beside me.

"Fuck. Aria."

" Rio..." I blinked back tears as I called out his name, or at least the name I had thought was his. I wasn't sure anymore. "I had nowhere else to go."

But even in my weakened state, I could feel the safety radiating from him just like a protective shield enveloping me. Then, in a fleeting moment, a fracture appeared in his gaze. His jaw ticked, and his hands tightened around my fragile form.

With a voice that was eerily calm yet laced with deadly anger, he uttered, "Who the fuck did this to you?"

"It's of no—"

"Tell. Me. Now. Or I will kill everyone who last saw you."

Summoning all the strength I had left, I forced out the words through gritted teeth. "My father...he—"

The pain was too much to bear and my voice faded into a gurgle as copper filled my mouth.

It felt as if death might be the next destination for me.

Strangely enough, the thought of dying while being held by him didn't seem so bad.

With a tenderness that surprised me, Zagrios lifted me from the ground and carried me to his bed. "You're safe now, Little Moon. He will never hurt you again."

In that moment, the realization washed over me like a gentle tide—I was entirely his. He may not have been something of mine, but I was undeniably his.

As if he could delve into the depths of my thoughts, he spoke with a possessive tone that I found oddly appealing, "You are mine. No one hurts what belongs to me."

I felt the comfortable cushions and blankets below me and for once, I was safe enough to keep my eyes closed.

From a distance, I could hear him giving instructions. "Go get Hecate; she's attending to her, and heaven help her if she's not feeling better when I come back."

"B-but where are you going," I heard a man unfamiliar to me stutter.

"I'll teach the Olympian fuckers that they have drawn my wrath."

"B-but, Milord—"

I heard a gurgling, followed by a wheezing sound, and my eyes closed.

CHAPTER TWENTY-FIVE
ARIA, OLYMPIA 1000 YEARS AGO

Hecate stood before me, her presence bringing back memories of a time long ago.

I fought to keep my eyes open, and I couldn't believe what I saw.

It couldn't be real, could it?

My heart raced as memories flooded back, but they were quickly overshadowed by confusion and fear.

Was she alive?

Was this my mind telling me I was going to die?

Was I dead?

There was another familiar voice. Malachtit? I could have sworn I saw him standing there too, along with that blue bear from my dreams. But how was this possible? Was it some cruel trick or a twisted turn of fate? Did Hecate take the bone Malachtit gave me? Wasn't he called Mal...

As Hecate spoke about me regaining my memories and a high, raspy voice chimed in, my mind spun with questions and doubts. Goddess of rebirth? How could I possibly be worthy of such a title when I couldn't even save myself? And who were these people in front of me—allies or enemies?

Desperate to understand, I tried to speak but my voice failed me once again and I sunk back into the bed. Bory...the name echoed in my mind. Wasn't there a little bear with feathers named Bory? He was my friend, and I once lived in Cave Town.

And...why the heck was I alive? I died. I drank poison... poison that Athena gave me because she wanted me to stop fueling the curse. As my mind drifted to another world, slowly but surely my memories came to me, but it was like a dream. Zagrios took me in and damn. He told me he loved me once Mal healed me. This was how I truly met the God of Healing. Mal hid in Rio's City and we became close friends because I was forced to live down here as well now.

Rio started the fight with Athena, and I was forbidden from entering Olympia again.

Once the world was turning upside down, Athena gave me the poison to kill myself and I did, but Rio bound my soul to his and I turned immortal.

I couldn't kill myself.

I couldn't free myself or anyone from the curse.

But why was Hecate here? She's dead...

CHAPTER TWENTY-SIX
ARIA, OLYMPIA 1000 YEARS AGO

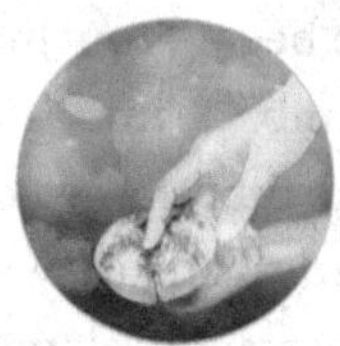

"Good morning, sweetheart," Hecate said as I woke up again.

My head felt like it weighed a ton, but as I slowly sat up and checked my body, I realized everything was healed. I ran my hands over my face, tugged at a strand of hair. It was white, not crimson like before. And to my surprise, my skin was smooth and unmarked by any scars.

I was okay, and there sat Hecate.

Hecate.

She was alive.

Hecate... lived?

"You're alive?" It was like my mind couldn't form words anymore as if it got smashed into tiny, mushy pieces.

"I am and I'm so happy our plan worked and that you're here." Hecate smiled and looking beside her, and my heart nearly jumped out of my chest. Bory. He was alive too!

"Oh god, Bory!" My eyes welled up, and as he hopped onto the bed, I pulled him toward me, squeezing so tightly that he coughed.

"I have... Lynne... you're crushing me. Ugh."

I held him slightly away from me and looked at him. Everything was still there. It was him. My beloved Bory. Nothing happened to him. "God, Bory... I love you so much. But what's happening to me? Everything is so confusing and I don't know what's up...all these memories. I lived three lives and now I have...all of them within me. I feel like...shit."

"It's normal," Hecate began, touching my arm and stroking it slightly with her thumb. "Time travel isn't easy, and not everyone comes out of the timeframe you sent yourself into. But you made it. We just need to ensure we act quickly and that as few people as possible interact with you because every contact changes the future, and we don't want more problems. We already have enough."

"But...how are you here? How can it be? I thought you were dead?"

She grinned, enveloping me in a warm embrace. I melted into the hug, pulling her closer to me. God, she even smelled like back then.

"I faked my death and fled to the Underworld, a place where no one can find us."

"Us?"

"Shhh..." Hecate brushed the hair from my face. "You mustn't get upset; you're still very weak."

"Why upset? Where is Rio?"

"With father," she said, and I was startled.

Of course. It's when he avenged me...It was the beginning of everything.

He tried to kill father, and it didn't work because he's protected by the Blood Queen, so he cursed him instead. From now on, our father could only live for three months in each world....and it was Rio's doing. Never Athena's.

"I'm glad you're well again." Suddenly Mal's voice cut me

off guard. My head turned, and I saw him approach us, handing me some tea. I took a sip and gave him the cup back.

"Your sister called me up with the bone I gave you and briefed me while you were sleeping, and I must say, I'm shocked to have to save my future best friend from death, but they confirmed every perspective I had on things. Athena is evil."

My head throbbed. Damn. It was so difficult.

My former self reconciled with my life on Earth as human Aria, and then there was this whole mess in Olympia.

"I don't remember when things happened anymore..." I closed my eyes and tried to collect myself. There was so much going on, so many lives...so many memories.

Athena was evil, but she tasked me with going back to the past with Zeus' lightning to kill Rio, and she wanted it done before I knew him. That could only mean she didn't know when we would meet. She probably thought it would be on the evening of the great assembly, but we had known each other for months before that...

"Bory, what should I do now? What did you find out while I was away? While I was stuck in my past consciousness..." I said.

Bory cleared his throat. "I honestly think Athena fooled us all, including the Bone and Blood Queen. We were both sent here by the Omphalos Stone, and you immediately merged with your former consciousness. I had to hide to avoid startling you because I knew it wouldn't be good for changing the past. But it was so bad, Lynne. I didn't know you were suffering so much."

My eyes burned. "Any and you," I looked at Hecate, and she still smiled at me kindly. How could she be alive and smiling? "Were all I had, but——" I boxed Hecate's arm, and she winced. Bory gasped. "Why the hell didn't you tell me you were alive?"

Anger rose in me.

I loved my siblings more than anyone else, and they lied to me for all those years? Thousands? And only now came clean?

Hecate wrinkled her nose, her glance stern now, just like when I stole her favorite candies back in the day. "Aria. Maybe take a few minutes to listen to me." She dug her nails into my arm, and I recoiled. My gaze flicked up to Mal, standing behind her now, and to Bory. They were all looking at me.

"Athena lied," Hecate started. "When I had my visions, and all of Olympia found out about it, they locked me away just like they did with you, but I wasn't allowed to see sunlight again. They spun lies because I saw what Athena was really doing. It's all much bigger than you thought. Than we all thought. Back when she conducted the rebellion, she teamed up with Thanatos. They both defeated the gods, and although the change was good, Athena's intention wasn't. She wants to rule over all realms. Water, Olympia, Earth and the Underworld. Olympia alone is not enough for her, so she wants a reboot. It's her that wants to restart the world. Not the Bone or the Blood Queen. We are all just her instruments."

I narrowed my eyes, trying to contemplate everything. "But the Bone Queen is trying to restore Zeus. With the bones—"

"—YES, because she misses the love of her life. The Bone Queen always loved extremely, and Athena knew that if she could sow hatred between the siblings of the Underworld, they would destroy each other, and she could take over. Athena promised the Bone Queen that she'd bring back the love of her life when she teams up with her but Athena lied. The Bone Queen was just a pawn in her game. She tried to bring everyone into her fold with your power, promising that you would bring back the dead." Hecate said.

"I'm the Goddess of Rebirth." I stammered and looked at my hands. "That's why she wanted me... that's why she treated me like her object. She grew desperate and wanted to use me..."

"Losing someone you love is a pain that goes to the core. A commitment to bring them back is a powerful leverage, and

Athena understood that. You ought to have aided her in triumph, and my vision assured me that once love finds its way into the Underworld—once you and Zagrios fall for each other—then she will be vanquished. She twisted my entire vision and wanted everyone here to murder and sow deep hatred, to kill said love before she could be defeated. And it worked until Zagrios caught on to them."

"But how did he do that?"

"I spread rumors about you until all of his court believed them. They talked about you, about the talented goddess entering Olympian Academy and I made him curious, to approach you. I saw that the two of you are our only chance. You will save us."

"You saw all of this? Me... and him?" My cheeks burned hot like fire. Shit.

"Well, I only see what is promised to happen, not whether you will succeed. My visions are divine impulses and come and go as they please. Once someone changes their mind, a vision can change again."

Okay, this doesn't sound like she saw us having sex... "And that's why Mal went to Cave Town? So that he could be close to me?" I said.

Hecate nodded. "He helped you find the tower. We made sure you'd find your way back to Rio. Trying to remember when I first stumbled upon the tower; I recalled wandering aimlessly and spotting Mal in the distance. I followed him until he disappeared, and that's when I noticed the tower. It never occurred to me that I was essentially stalking Mal, as I often did, in my attempts to visit the Blood Queen in secret. Little did I know they were all scheming behind my back, plotting for me to get caught up with Rio once Any was old enough. And then Any passed away, leading to a perfect opportunity for Mal to return to the Underworld. It was like a carefully choreographed dance, but one that was incredibly complex and confusing.

"I went where? I would never live in Cave Town of my own free will. Please tell me that's a lie," Mal said, looking at Hecate in confusion.

"He doesn't know what we know, Aria." She mouthed and pointed at him. "He's the Mal from the past, but yes, he will move to Cave Town."

"You know I'm standing right next to you, right?"

Hecate ignored him and said, "Rio and I will make sure he forgets what we told him. Only I may know the future because I know how to behave, how to change nothing."

"Wow. Just wow..." I saw Mal wandering around and shaking his head.

I looked into my sister's lovely eyes. "And what about Any? Where is he now?"

"Still in Olympia, but he'll be with us soon. Once he learns about what Father did, he'll come, and Nana will come with him. She's no longer willing to work for your father."

I nodded. I remembered. Any was always on my side, which made me even sadder about how mean I was to him. I should never have doubted him. Never. And Nana was there for me, too.

I held Hecate's hand. "Does Any know that you're alive?"

"No, Rio didn't have time to tell him before the resurrection."

"I always felt he was colluding with father."

"Well, in the future, everything looks different. The Blood Queen is doing everything to counteract the curse Rio mentioned today—that our father can only stay three months in one world and then must switch until he's been through them all. After your reincarnation, she joined our side, and we planned how to get you back. Since she collected the energy of your first kiss across the reincarnated forms, she's gathered enough magical essence to make it happen. She put Rio to sleep, and during his slumber, he traversed here."

"Future Rio is here?" My heart pounded even harder. "Since when, and what does he remember?"

"Since yesterday. He should have remembered earlier, and we were afraid his soul wouldn't make it through the dream barrier here. But when he saw you so hurt, he reverted to his old self and looked forward to beating our father's ass again." She smiled. "It was wonderful, and oh... he should be here any moment now."

A tear ran down my cheek. Rio. My Rio. I missed him so much.

"I didn't know if he was on the good or bad side..."

"I don't think there's such a thing as good or evil, Aria," said Hecate.

"Everyone has their ups and downs," Mal added.

I nodded. "I just need to be sure that he'll save the world and not destroy it."

"He will never sacrifice you," Hecate assured, "but he'll find other ways to save the world he loves without destroying it."

"I share the same opinion," Bory said. "We must follow their plan and trust them. They've thought it through while you were away, and now we must fulfill our roles."

"And what would those be?"

"Kill Athena," Bory and Hecate said in unison.

I reached for the necklace around my neck and touched the small lightning bolt. "Athena gave it to me to kill Rio."

"Yes," Hecate said. "She truly believed you were on her side, that you had been convinced he was evil. He's never been. And she just didn't know and stupidly gave us the means to end her once and for all."

"I can't believe it."

"Well, I either can I. All I wanted to do was sell my oils and creams," Mal groaned. "And now I hear I'm going to move to fucking Cave Town soon."

The door burst open, revealing Rio standing in the doorway like a god of fury.

His dark hair was tousled, and his eyes were wild with emotion as they fell upon me.

He entered the room and our eyes irresistibly drew to him like moths to a flame.

It was like we were frozen in time.

Neither of us moved a single muscle.

As Rio stood in the doorway, I watched his body tremble with exhaustion. The stench of death clung to him like a thick fog, and every labored breath he took echoed the fierce struggle he had just faced. I remembered this was the night he slaughtered my father's soldiers, killed everyone who stood in his way to get to him only to find out his sister protected him from being killed, because he was her lover and all love in the Underworld was to be destroyed. He later protected me with that very same spell.

I watched the blood dripping from his face in a steady stream, tracing a glistening path down his chiseled features.

"Aria," he said, and my heart did a double take.

That was the man I loved.

He was mine. I was his.

And he was alive.

He was here. In full conscience.

My man was here.

Zagrios sauntered into the room, his movements oozing with a raw, primal energy.

The dim candlelight flickered upon his massive body, accentuating every curve and crevice. With my heart racing in a mix of excitement and nervousness, I quickly scrambled off the bed and ran up to him.

He sped up his steps and in that very moment, it was as if time itself had ceased to exist, leaving only the two of us suspended in our own universe. I crashed into him and swung my arms around his body, my head leaning into his chest.

When I glanced up at him, the intensity of his sapphire gaze sent shivers down my spine, as if he possessed the power to unravel me with a single look. I believe he did, as my knees now felt as though they were made of butter.

Oh, I missed him so much, and it felt like I hadn't seen him for years.

Well, I didn't.

Not him with all his memories and all my memories.

With all the hundreds of hundreds of kisses we had. And every single one was perfect.

When his hands, all rough and calloused, reached out to cradle my face, he looked deeply into my eyes. As if to check if it was me or one of my other personalities.

But it was me.

And It was him.

It was us. Finally.

"Rio," I whispered, my voice barely audible. "I love you. I love you so fucking much."

Without saying a word, he scooped me up, his muscular arms wrapped around my waist, pulling me close. The warmth of his skin against mine sparked a fire inside of me—the mingling scents of sweat and leather adding to the primal energy between us. Our hearts beat together, lost in the blend of candlelight and desire.

"Out," he said towards the others, his gaze never leaving mine.

I didn't look, but I heard the scurrying of every single soul in the room—even Hecate and Mal—practically running out in haste.

"I've always loved you and I'll never stop falling for you, Little Moon."

When the door fell shut behind us, his lips crashed onto mine and my legs wound around his hips even tighter.

I knew this was where I wanted to be—in his arms.

Forever.

And when his tongue slipped into mine, each single kiss we ever had whisked past me, as if a tiny tv screen from Earth pressed play and showed me how many times he undressed me.

How many times we flirted with our eyes only. How many times he bit his tongue because he couldn't kiss me in a situation where he wasn't allowed to kiss me. How we fucked relentlessly.

As teenagers on Earth. As Lynne and Rio. As Aria and Zagrios in shady inns or when he held court.

No one could ever come between us. Not even death.

As all of him claimed all of mine, his shadows danced sensuously around us, a familiar and intoxicating embrace. With a swift, effortless move, my dress unveiled itself, slipping over my shoulders. But he wasn't leading me to the bed, not this time. No, he craved the thrill of showcasing our love to the world. He guided me straight to the balcony.

Amidst everything, there was this moment. When we needed to merge again, transcending the pain of losing each other repeatedly.

He positioned me on the balcony rail, shadows swirling around us, veiling our bodies from prying eyes. In a passionate frenzy, he tore the rest of my dress away, and I willingly spread my legs, inviting him in. The friction between us intensified as he pressed me against the middle of his desire. "God, you're—" I just couldn't finish my sentence.

"—perfect I know."

I chuckled, kissing his neck, knowing all too well that there's blood on him, but I just didn't care. I needed him in whatever shape he was because we never knew how long we'd have each other. We needed to cherish every second we had together.

CHAPTER TWENTY-SEVEN
ARIA, OLYMPIA 1000 YEARS AGO

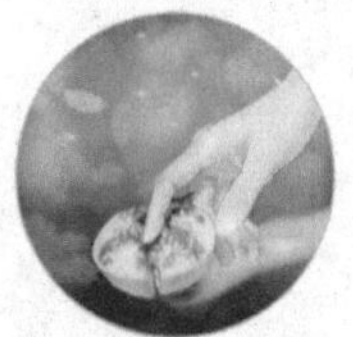

His shadows seemed to have a mind of their own, moving and gliding over my body with expert precision.

When he pulled me closer, his eyes turned dark with desire, and I watched as his shadows danced around us, wrapping us in their cool embrace. His hands slid down my body, removing each piece of clothing with practiced ease.

Tilting my head back, I let out a contented breath and allowed myself to truly feel his touch. Fuck. It felt amazing.

The room was shrouded in darkness as his shadowy hands roamed over my body, as his teeth grazed my neck, leaving a trail of fiery desire in their wake. I frantically stripped off his metal armor, revealing the toned muscles and scars underneath.

My hands trembled, and I felt the cool metal against my skin before revealing the warmth of his body underneath. His skin was smooth but firm, and I couldn't resist running my hands over the scars, tracing them with my fingers. I placed a kiss on each scar I uncovered, tasting the salty tang and the lingering bitterness of past wounds. Mine. All this was mine.

"I never thought I'd have you in my arms again," he murmured, tracing circles on my bare back while I let out a shaky sigh. The clanging of discarded metal echoed around us—finally—our naked bodies melted into each other's embrace.

I reached behind me, gripping the cold metal of the railing for support.

He positioned himself between my legs, his hands gripping my thighs as he pressed his erection against my entrance. We both gasped and he pushed into me, our thighs slick with sweat already.

His fingers dug into the soft flesh of my thighs, creating red marks that would surely bruise. Sighing deeply, I wrapped my arms around his neck, pulling him closer.

His thrusts became more urgent and his cock reached deeper inside me.

"Gods, I've missed this," I whispered.

His lips trailed down my neck, planting kisses across my collarbone, down my chest, and finally the swells of my breasts, where he took my nipples in his mouth and sucked them hungrily, leaving them pink and swollen with pleasure. He cupped my breast, squeezed tightly and sucked stronger, and I couldn't help but moan loudly.

My back arched off the railing as he picked up the pace, thrusting harder and faster into me. Every movement sent waves of pleasure coursing through my body, and I could feel myself getting closer to the edge.

"Remember how you made me scream each time we fucked out here?" I leaned in close and whispered in his ear, feeling the vibrations of his deep chuckle against my chest.

He spun me around and playfully smacked my exposed ass.

Then, he pressed his body against me, I arched my back and felt his hands firmly gripping my hips. The shadows surrounding us seemed to come alive as they intertwined with my skin, teasing and tantalizing my sensitive areas just like tendrils of smoke should. I smiled. Yes. This. Exactly this.

A shiver ran down my spine and another of his shadows traced delicate circles around each of my nipples. Another snaked down my stomach to my pulsing clit. Oh, my. Every touch felt like he was worshiping me with his shadows, bringing me almost to the edge with just their gentle caresses.

"God, yes," I moaned.

"Damn, you smell good enough to eat..." He let out a low, guttural growl and sank his teeth into my neck, the sharp points piercing my skin.

"I want to take all my time to explore you, darling," Zagrios said. "Tonight. We may only have this one night and we'll make it count."

With a sudden burst of force, he grabbed my chin from behind and forced me to look up at the skulls in the sky. His thrusts were relentless, in and out, in and out, as I my fingers clung desperately to the railing as if it were my only lifeline. Each fierce movement sent shockwaves through my body, blurring the line between pleasure and pain. And hatred filled me while I gazed upon the sky. This was the balcony I almost killed myself if it weren't for Rio.

"I love you," he whispered next to my ear, still holding my chin as we both stared up and fucked like there was no tomorrow and maybe it wasn't. But it was clear. Athena lied to me, lied to us. I believed her, and she threatened everyone I loved. Wanted to manipulate me into killing my love, fed me lies about saving the world while secretly preparing to bring it to its downfall.

"Tomorrow," he rasped. His voice was like gravel, rough and irresistible. I couldn't help but let out a gentle moan. "We'll make them pay for fucking with us."

His words were filled with venom as he thrust into me violently, his grip tightening around my body until I felt like I was being crushed. All my emotions came up, all my love for him, the hate for all these gods playing with us for over a millennium. I felt like exploding. "We'll show them who the Shadow King and Queen are."

I gasped and moaned in agreement. "Yes...we're giving them that fucking curse back."

"That's my wife." He said it with such ferocity that it made my body burn. He took his hand from my chin and trailed his blood-stained fingers down my breasts, my hips to my clit. I watched how he smeared a fresh crimson trail on my white skin. It's a testament to the violence he was capable of. That we were capable of and, oh, I knew then, without a doubt, that we would kill everyone who stood against us.

I pushed him out of me, spun on my heels, and he grabbed me back into his embrace.

With an insatiable hunger, I pushed him against the wall and crashed into his lips once more. Something shattered behind him, and I heard glass shattering to the ground, but I didn't care. He didn't care. Our tongues tangled in a passionate dance as my hands roamed over every inch of his insanely sculpted body. God, he was hard. Everything about him was so hard. "No one will part us ever again," I said, pulling him towards the bedroom with an intense desire burning inside me, never leaving his lips once.

I pushed him onto the bed, eagerly straddling his body like a predator on its prey, and a devious smirk played on my lips as I took in his masculine form beneath me. "Oh, how you've missed me," he growled. "Come on, crawl to me. Show me exactly how much."

Like a seductive feline, I slowly made my way up his body, crawling and savoring every inch until I reached his captivating face. His muscles tensed beneath me and I sighed, making him smile and pulling me in so that my clit touched his shredded stomach.

He reached out and ran his fingers through my hair, tugging me closer until our lips met. "Ride me. Ride me as if you wanted to kill me with it," he said.

There was a pregnant pause.

Only a single blink passed as we locked eyes.

But instead of pleasing him the way he wanted, I wrapped my hand around his dick, stroking it once. Twice.

"Soon," I said, watching him come undone. He grabbed the bedsheets as I worked his cock. My hand wrapped around his hard length that felt like silk against my skin. He gripped the bed sheets even tighter as I straddled him, taking all the control over my king. The head of his cock was hot and rigid against my entrance, demanding to be pushed inside. I sat on him and the ridges and veins along the shaft stretched me to my limits, filled me completely.

"You're mine," he groaned through gritted teeth, fully succumbing to the feeling of all of me around all of his.

"Yours," I breathed and circled my hips.

While I rode him, I watched every detail of his body—the way his muscles tensed, how his veins in his arms bulged, the sweat on his forehead glistened... He closed his eyes, but I saw the intense pleasure on his face. Lifting my hips up and down and up and down, I glimpsed the thick shaft of his cock, glistening with my slick juices. I could feel every inch of him inside me, filling me entirely.

My walls clenched tightly around his thick length, feeling every vein and ridge. And then, in one swift, commanding movement, he flipped me over and hurled me onto the bed beneath us.

My body jolted against the soft mattress when he pinned me down with his strong frame.

My breathing was ragged and I looked up at him.

His tousled dark hair hung into his face while those glorious eyes of his—this otherworldly myriad of shimmering blues—were filled with desire.

As he pressed his body against mine, all I felt was the weight of his body on top of me. Damn. I reveled in the sensation of being trapped under him.

My breath caught in my throat as his tongue expertly explored every crevice.

I ran my hands along his strong, defined arms, gripping onto them as he devoured me with a hunger that matched my own. And when he slid into me, my back arched off the bed.

With a smug grin on his face and without hesitation, I dug my nails into his back until I was sure It would hurt him and he plunged into me in answer. With no mercy. His hips thrust against mine as he slid in and out again, not caring about me anymore, just doing what pleased him, and I loved it. I fucking loved it when he was unhinged. I clawed at his back, urging him to go harder, faster. He obeyed, his hips slamming against mine with a primal force as we moaned simultaneously.

I could feel the pressure building within me once again, my muscles clenching around him relentlessly. God. The way his hot skin moved against mine, the weight of his body pressing me into the mattress, and the way his hips met mine with each thrust...I was seconds away from coming.

"Come for me, Little Moon," he demanded.

And with those words, I exploded into ecstasy, crying out his name. He followed soon after, releasing himself inside me with a low growl. He continued to thrust into me as I rode out my release, prolonging the intensity until I collapsed back onto the bed in a state of blissful exhaustion. We stayed like that for a few moments, our bodies still intertwined as we caught our breaths. His fingers traced lazy circles on my skin while I ran my hands through his hair.

I turned my head towards him and saw that same smug grin on his face that always drove me crazy. But this time, instead of wanting to punch it off of him, I smiled back at him.

"God," I said with a laugh. "You really know how to push my buttons."

"I live for it," he replied.

CHAPTER TWENTY-EIGHT
RIO, OLYMPIA 1000 YEARS AGO

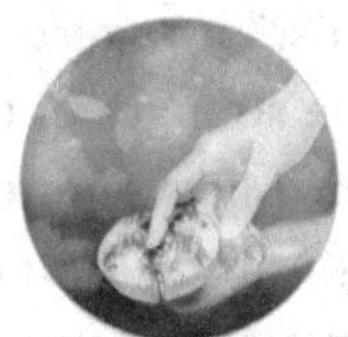

The assembly hall door groaned under the pressure of my push, its solemn echo reverberating against the towering stone walls. It was good being back. Although it's strange to go from living as a human to liberating souls again, deciding if they were ready to cross over to the soul river.

Hell. At first, I didn't believe in Macaria's plan. The thought of leaving the big picture and letting Aria take on Athena seemed too risky for me, but I knew what my wife was capable of and I had to let go so we could win together. And since Athena had a gift for detecting lies, and Aria wore her heart on her sleeve, making her doubt me was all we needed to convince Athena. We made her believe she had another pawn in her game. But my wife would never be anyone's pawn ever again. I was going to make sure of it.

She followed close behind, her hand in mine, and I held on tight. I promised myself that I would never let go of her from now on, no matter what challenges lay ahead. There was no dividing us ever again.

As we entered, our footsteps echoed loudly on the cold

stone floor, the only sound in my vast castle. It was odd to be back since I neglected it for hundreds of years.

We fucked all night long and if it weren't for the shit consuming the world above us, I would have never stopped.

I gave Aria's hand a gentle squeeze as we walked into the strategy room.

"Are you ready for this?" my voice was low, barely above a whisper, yet it carried the strength of thunder. I would love to kick her father's ass again. My memories came back the minute I had Aria bleeding in my arms all over again. I needed a couple of minutes to gather my composure. This was my fucking nightmare.

When I saw her beautiful face bleeding, bruised... the sight made me lose control all over again, my body shaking with rage. It took all of my willpower to compose myself, to just head over to her father and not Athena, too. But this damn curse was a living hell that I couldn't escape from. So, I kept to the script. The rush of adrenaline had surged through me as I had landed the final blow on her father's face, relishing the satisfying crack of bone beneath my knuckles. There was not much left of his house and I cursed him. Thanks to me he would be stuck between realms forever and even though I promised Macaria to free him for her help, I wasn't so sure about that now. Not after watching him hurt the love of my life again.

"As ready as we can ever be," she replied, her gaze flitting across the faces of Hecate, Mal, and Bory.

They slumped on the red satin couch, their bodies sinking into the plush in a dramatic ballet of boredom. Each face sported a masterpiece of indifference, a symphony of subtle frowns and eyes playing hooky with enthusiasm.

I couldn't help but chuckle at their dramatic display. "Looks like we've kept them waiting for a while," I said with a smirk.

Aria smiled, a seductive glint in her eyes. "Luckily, they're playing for our team. Although, I can practically feel them eyeing the fridge. Maybe we should whip up some enticing snacks to keep their minds off the wait next time."

Bory giggled but no one else cracked a laugh, so I sat next to them on the couch, placing Aria on my thigh. If I could, I would straddle her against me. If someone so much as looked at her in a wrong way, I was at the point of killing them straight away. Her face in that pool of blood brought the worst of me back.

"Let's get to the heart of it, then," I said, nodding to Hecate, whose eyes flickered with otherworldly fire.

She motioned toward the table, and they all sat up, the wood groaning under the weight.

"Killing Athena is no small feat," Mal started, his voice trailing off into the silence that hung heavy in the air.

"Indeed, but I think my sister has an idea," Aria mused, her fingers tracing the intricate carvings on the table's edge, each groove a testament to countless strategies laid bare on this very surface. Hecate was prepared.

"We need Athena away from the court. We can't kill her in Olympia. It's amazing you brought us Zeus' lightning bolt, but we need to find a suitable moment to distract her." Hecate said. "Then we can pierce her with Zeus' bolt and be done with it."

"She's not as protected now as she is in the future," Bory added, sitting on Hecate's lap and melting upon her little caresses. "This is good since we could never get as close as we can in this period."

"Part of the plan," I said, more than pleased that everything worked out.

"Don't humble yourself," Hecate said, rolling her eyes and Aria fell into laughter with her.

"He can get all lovey dovey about himself," she said, and I bit her shoulder, which made her squeal a little, but in a good way.

"God, you guys are gross," Bory sighed while Mal looked like he didn't know whatever he got himself into.

"What I wanted to say," Bory started again, "was, that we can actually lure her away, bring her here... because we need to meet her without raising suspicion."

"Or altering the course of time," Mal added.

"I think I know when," Aria said, looking up at Hecate and she smiled, knowing already what she wants to get at. "The first night she met me to manipulate me drinking poison."

I breathed out. This was something I never knew of and if I had, I'd have torn Athena's head off right then and there. It would grow again, but well, it was something I dreamed of anyway. She was the spitting image of Zeus. In and out.

"She came by a few times, gave me a small brooch, and told me to reach out whenever I felt ready. But it wasn't until we secretly got married, after the war against the Olympians, that I finally decided to take her advice and open up," Aria said, checking my eyes, probably seeing my dark shadows swirling in there while I fantasized about biting Athena's limbs off one after another.

She suddenly grew silent, and I held her tight, laying my neck on her shoulder as I gripped her from behind. "And I'll kill her for it."

"No. I will. Don't you dare take this away from me," she snapped, and I smiled.

"Your wish, my command, darling."

The fireplace crackled, casting shadows on Hecate's sharp features. She stared into the flames, her pale eyes gleaming, and I wondered what she saw in there.

"So, little prince, what's this plan of yours after defeating Athena?" Hecate's mocking tone grated, but I refused to rise to the bait.

"Then we reshape Olympia into what it should have always

been," I said firmly. "A realm of equality and justice for all. And the two of us—"

"God no, please, no, no," Bory chimed in with a frantic wave of his tiny arms, "No need for further elaborations. We get it. Loud and clear."

Mal's smile sharpened. "I do enjoy a good coup, though. Consider me in."

Hecate tilted her head, then bowed. "As am I."

Now, we had everything we needed to launch a revolution." It's not going to be easy, as she will come with soldiers. You need to tell us how she approached you, where and what shields she may have on," I said to Hecate. "I'll summon my Horsemen and we'll get this straight. Malachtit, we need you for healing and we need to get your brother," I glanced at Aria.

"You know how we can convince him," Aria said and then suddenly widened her eyes. "Oh, but Mal, you can't be here when my brother's here."

"Why?"

"You two are going to fall for each other in the future."

Mal tore his eyes up. "What the fuck?"

As Bory attempted to describe Any's personality and backstory to Mal, Aria leaned in closer to me, speaking in a hushed tone. "There's something else... While we wait for Athena to show up, I need to do something for Ebony."

She didn't have to elaborate on it. "She's not in my team yet, but will soon be. If you want to stop something from happening, we might never meet her in the future though."

She nodded. "I know. I promised her."

I looked to Hecate. "Can you help us save a friend?"

CHAPTER THIRTY
ARIA, OLYMPIA 1000 YEARS AGO

The Shadow Castle's garden, draped in moss, seemed all quiet as I made my way down the twisty staircase to find Hecate waiting on a weathered stone bench. She had her green eyes fixed on the waterfall, lost in thought. I couldn't help but remember the nights Rio and I used to hang here, shooting the breeze. Now, it was my sister sitting there—the one I thought was six feet under but ...was not.

I stood there just watching her, feeling my heart go all wild, beating against my ribs.

The hope bubbling up inside me was intense. I couldn't bring myself to ask if she's alive in the future. No, couldn't do it. I was scared her eyes would spill the truth and wreck my heart. I've lost her once, I couldn't lose her again.

She looked up at the skulls in the sky, and it felt like I was thrown back in time.

She always did that—staring into nowhere, and I remembered the days when she'd weave cryptic tales and speak in riddles. As children, her insights guided us—she'd let us know if our plans were a go, if we could snag some cookies without getting caught, or if we could sneak into the flower gardens past midnight. But just as abruptly as she had started with her visions, she stopped laughing like she used to. She used to toss her head back and laugh freely, even teasing us that this would happen if we did that. But then, without warning, her joy vanished, and she sank into a deep sadness. I couldn't understand it at the time, but looking back now, I realize what was in store for us. I can only imagine how much it must have pained her to see it all unfold before her eyes.

"I know you're there, silly." Her laughter, a melody that danced through the air, cracked the midnight air.

She patted the worn stone bench next to her, inviting me to join.

I took an extra minute, wanting to imprint that image in my mind, to ensure I'd never forget it. The way she sat there, her expression resembling Any's so much. We all shared the same green eyes with a yellow circle in the middle. Her hair, unlike ours, wasn't white but rather blonde, almost golden. Her facial features were a bit more slender, yet within seconds, anyone could see the unmistakable family resemblance. Same height, same posture.

"Come on," she said with a warm smile.

I gave in and sat down beside her.

Seeking comfort, I wrapped my arms around her neck and held on tightly, feeling the warmth of her embrace ease some of the hurt inside of me. That familiar scent, a comforting blend of jasmine and thunderstorms, enveloped me like a warm shroud.

"Tell me," I said, pulling back just enough to see her face. "Why? Why for skull's sake would you let us believe you were dead? I just can't believe you. Do you know how hurt I've been? How hurt Any was?"

Hecate looked into my eyes, a mess of feelings swirling in that gaze. "I saw it, Aria. But it had to happen, no matter how much it broke my heart. They would have hunted me down and killed me, killed you, and Any. Zagrios would have done everything he could, but Athena is too strong. Playing ghost among the living was the only choice I had until she gave you the weapon to kill Zagrios. She realized her mistake, and wanted to create a strong desire for revenge within you in order to want to kill Zagrios for her. It's amazing how hatred can cloud our judgment. That's what became clear to me, and it was the foundation of our plan. That's why we couldn't disclose anything to you, Aria. You had to play your part accordingly. Otherwise, there was the risk of Athena sensing the deception."

A shiver rolled through me, not from the cool night settling in the grove... Doubt nibbled at my thoughts, but I held onto trust in her wisdom. She'd always been our guide, the one with visions shaping our journey, but it hurt, nevertheless. It felt like I fell into a trap. But tricking a goddess as strong as Athena was not easy. It needed a good plan. It's just not easy to know I couldn't be trusted more, and it was then I realized that I always wore my heart on my sleeve and they simply had to work around me in order to get my stubborn self to act. Maybe I should have listened to them once...but then this was me. I was reckless and stubborn. "So there was no other way to save us all from this misery..."

"No," Hecate shook her head. "Athena's curse was too strong. You had to fight it first. Find your way back to Zagrios even though she wanted you dead. You had to fight back with no one telling you why. You needed to trust in love because sometimes love will save it all."

Trust. This is the most essential aspect of love.

Without trusting each other, we couldn't love, and Hecate was right: no matter what Rio did, I stood by him, and he stood by me. No matter how many times they told me he was bad, that he was wrong, I didn't want to believe it.

But we got together tonight for another reason.

Hecate had a feeling that Ebony would be coming out of the waters soon, so she suggested scrying to figure out how we could save her.

"There's someone... someone dear who may be in danger. Could you—would you scry for me?" My plea hung in the air, mingling with the scent of night-blooming jasmine that crept along the edges of the grove.

"Shall we begin the search for your friend, or do you still want to scold me?" Hecate's voice was a gentle whisper, yet it carried the weight of mountains.

I smiled.

I might scold her again, but not now. "Let's start."

She outstretched her palms, and the surrounding air thickened.

I watched, a silent sentinel, as she summoned her power.

Hecate's fingers danced an intricate ballet, weaving invisible, shimmering threads of magic. The ground beneath us hummed, resonating with energies old as time, and I could feel the pulse of the earth sync with my heartbeat.

"Show me Ebony," Hecate intoned, her focus narrowing on her hands.

The atmosphere churned, coalescing into a mirror-like surface within her grasp—a window into realms beyond our sight. Through the scrying glass, a vision coalesced. Waves lapped gently at the silhouette of a figure poised between sea foam and shore.

I gasped.

It was Ebony, her raven hair catching the glint of starlight, her posture one of resolve tinged with trepidation. She stood amidst the Nereids, creatures of beauty and caprice, their songs weaving around her like chains of melody.

"She's still part of the sea," I whispered, my voice barely a thread of sound. "But she looks... ready to step onto land." That's when she got captured.

"Tonight," Hecate confirmed, her eyes reflecting the unfolding scene. "She will seek the sands under the cloak of dusk."

A shiver raced up my spine, though the night was warm.

Why now? What called her to the world of man and dry earth? "How can I save her?"

"Kill the man."

I hesitated, and Hecate's brow furrowed slightly, her expression mirroring my concern. "Be wary, sister. The future is a river with many currents."

I understood her, even though she had a habit of expressing herself in peculiar sentences. That's just how my sister communicated.

"You mean killing him could sever the bond Ebony and I share, shatter the memories, right?"

"Sometimes, Aria," Hecate replied with a gentle firmness, "to save the bloom, one must prune the thorns. Even if those thorns are laced with precious remembrances."

I paced the mossy ground, feeling the pulse of the earth beneath my boots. The whispering leaves seemed to echo the tempest of my thoughts. I could feel Ebony's essence, like a beacon in the darkness of my mind, guiding me, calling out for salvation—my salvation entwined with hers.

"Would you do it?" I asked, seeking something, anything in her gaze. "If you stood where I stand?"

"Without hesitation."

"Then how can I handle it?" I asked, a plea breaking through the tough exterior I put on to hide my feelings. "How can I risk never seeing a friend again?"

"Because, sister," she said, coming closer, her hand on my shoulder, "you're braver than you think. Love isn't just about holding on; it's also about letting go, too. You'd be willing to forget, just to make sure she's safe. That's the real deal in love."

I turned away, unable to bear the truth in her words.

My heart pounded against my ribcage, each beat an echo of Ebony's name.

"Promise me," I implored, feeling the sting of tears begging for release, "that if I no longer remember her smile, her voice, her touch—promise me you'll tell me our story one day."

"Every chapter," she vowed. "Every word."

"Tonight, then," I said.

CHAPTER THIRTY-ONE
RIO, OLYMPIA 1000 YEARS AGO

"That reminds me of something," I said as I put on my old armor.

Aria came up to me, adjusting the leather cuffs and pulling on my gloves.

I glanced down at her and brushed a long strand of hair from her face. "Do you remember our wedding night?"

She smiled, turning away, her cheeks tinted pink, but she nodded. "I finally remember everything, Rio."

I kissed her. "Even when..."

"Yes," she laughed, throwing her cloak over her shoulders.

Like back then, we snuck away. Our wedding was spontaneous, wild.

We got married in a tavern. The entire bar celebrated with us, not knowing who we were. We loved to play, to slip into other roles. Little did we know soon we would involuntarily slip into several lives and almost never come back to our own again. As news of our union spread, the people of Olympia grew angry and hostile towards us. The Bone Queen declared war for Athena, unleashing destruction upon the lands. Aria's heart ached as she saw the consequences of our love causing pain to those around us. And just as Hecate found me with a solution to all our troubles, Aria came up with her own plan.

I knew one thing for certain: I would do anything to save her.

She tied her hair into a long, silver braid, and I couldn't stop devouring her with my glances. She wore long black leather pants, a leather shir and a black cloak.

My little warrior.

My thief.

My assassin.

My queen.

I pulled her close, and she leaned into my touch. I needed to make something very clear to her. She was not only smart but also damn stubborn. "No matter what happens tonight, we don't put ourselves in danger, okay?" She looked at me as if she understood, but we both knew it wasn't that simple. "Is this clear?"

She rolled her eyes. "Crystal."

"When I say we leave, you go with me. No matter. What. Happens."

She nodded, but I knew it wasn't as clear-cut as it seemed... after all, it was Aria. "If there's a risk that we can't save Ebony, then so be it." My wife opened her mouth, but I immediately cut her off. "We have a bigger agenda here, in case you've forgotten."

"But, I—"

"Are we late?" Mal asked, entering with Hecate, carrying Rory in her arms. That guy always found a pretty woman to cling to.

"You're coming?" Aria asked.

"Not me," said Hecate, and I noticed a sad glint in her eyes.

I always admired her. I could never dedicate my life to a noble cause like she did. She had her visions since she was a child. Witnessing Athena stealing everyone's trust and climbing the ranks, and eventually seize everything. She spoke of democracy, freedom, the end of oppression, and in the end, our new leader was worse than her father. We all thought she had ushered in a new era, but as always, with power came addiction. No matter the field. Whether as a mafia boss, as a god, or even just as the head of the family. Once you have power over something, there's always the risk of abusing that power.

And Athena couldn't handle it.

"Of course I'm coming," said Mal. "I never had a purpose before and I think this may be it."

"I'm coming too," shouted Bory, but Aria shook her head.

"No," she said. "You stay with Hecate."

"Lynne! I'll certainly come along because you know I'm always useful."

She looked at me as if I would help her, but I just shrugged. "Your call."

"Lynne. How many times did I save your ass?" Bory folded his puffy arms. "Don't act like I'm useless."

Aria didn't say a word to him and the both of them stared each other down until Aria sighed. "Damn it. You mean everything to me, Bory. I'm so afraid that something could happen to you!"

"IT won't. And I feel the same about you!"

"Fine. But you stay in the pouch!"

Bory grinned, jumped out of Hecate's arms, and climbed up Aria's cloak before hopping into the pouch.

"So, who are we meeting again?" Mal asked.

"We're meeting a soul trafficker who slipped under my radar. He didn't really make himself noticeable, but he catches creatures and makes money selling them for sex," I said.

"A friend in the future," Aria added, "will be captured by

him today, and I promised her I would do something about it if I could."

"And now we can," I said, nodding to Mal, a signal for him to come closer to me.

He stepped forward, and I conjured my shadows.

"Make sure everything stays the same," I said to Hecate, stretching out my hands and everyone touched them at the same time. "And greet Any from me."

"It won't stay the same if it has to be," she simply replied.

"You could, for once, not speak in riddles. You sound crazy," Aria snapped as my shadows circled around us, writhing with power.

"It is what it is," she said.

Aria sighed, and I conjured us to the edge of Catterville.

BEHIND THE CITY, where houses jutted into the night sky like mushrooms, the sea tossed high waves. In those turbulent waters lived the Nereids. Sea nymphs are said to surface when the sea is restless, often engaging in playful antics with sailors. Yet, from what I observed, they seemed to reserve their games for those who sought solace, those who had nothing else.

"Hecate didn't say when the guy is coming, did she?" Mal said, staring at the sea.

I could see he wasn't thrilled to be so close to the water. In all the stories everyone knew, the Nereids liked to pull men into their realm with their beauty, their songs.

He clenched one hand into a fist, and I took Aria's hand in mine.

"No, she never gives clear times. We'll have to wait," I said.

"What exactly for?" Bory asked, his head popping up from the pouch.

"Ebony is about to make the mistake of her life. She's running away from her family to explore the world on land and then gets abducted and held captive by the Ravenman. We'll prevent that moment," Aria said.

"But... but then you risk never getting to know Ebony," Bory said, his little eyes all glittery in the faint light.

"Yes... there's the risk that we'll never get to know her," Aria said and bit her lip.

I wrapped an arm around her waist, stroking her with my thumb.

"But, I promised her. She belongs in the sea," she said, her voice suddenly much softer. "Yes, Ebony belongs to them."

And so we waited.

Behind Catterville, demonic exchanges took place, and I saw a few shady souls that I would have had to punish immediately, but there was no time for that. I wasn't entirely back in my position as Shadow King yet. I just pretended until I woke up in the present again, hopefully without Athena and her fucking power play.

Mal questioned Aria, asking how he would land in Cave Town and stay there, and I had to laugh. We all swore together, met with my sister Macaria, and she asked us for help when I brought back Cyril and lifted the curse. So, we formed a rebellion against Athena, not realizing that Aria was looking for a way out. Like she always did. She thought she could somehow solve it without us. It's her risky nature. She's always been like that, never wanting to put us in danger and thought that if she died, everything would end. But she forgot Athena was a bitch. She wanted her to die forever, and that only became clear to Aria when she was dead in my arms.

I had to act, and within minutes, we made our plan.

It was far from perfect, but it was all we got.

I hid everything necessary on Earth, drank the rest of the magical poison, and tried to keep my soul from entering the river for as long as possible while connecting Aria's soul and mine. A spell as old as time itself, one I only knew because of my father.

He bound my mother to him the same way, and in a desperate moment, I managed it, handed the scepter to my sister, and asked her to plan everything while we're gone, which is why Mal worked with her. They led Aria to me as Lynne, and we made it back just in time to finally defeat Athena.

But my other sister, Mel, came between us. She desperately wanted to get her former love back and Athena promised her that if she helped with bringing back Zeus, he would help her find her soul. That's why she was on Athena's side, trying to set us back as often as she could, and when I conjured her up on Earth, it couldn't have been any better for her. She used me and had enough time to collect all of Zeus' bones. In our original plan, Macaria should have brought me back with the book we stole for her from the auction...but she had no magic and needed time to get Aria to transfer her magic again. Yes, it was risky. Yes, it almost failed, but in the end, my wife was back with me again. And that was all that mattered.

"There," Aria said, and we all stared expectantly at the waves.

They twisted until they transformed into powerful, galloping horses.

The sea spray splashed against their hooves as they raced along the shore.

Ebony's coat glistened in the sunlight, but she was falling behind the other Nereids and her movements became sluggish.

She let out a whinny of frustration, determined to catch up to the others.

Aria wanted to rush off immediately, but I held her back. "Wait until she gets ashore. If we hinder her too early, she'll try again, and he'll catch her at another time. We have to kill him tonight. There's no coming back ever again."

Aria nodded, never taking her eyes off the water.

And then we saw the crowd of horses ride by, the waves begged, and the water became calm. Slowly, one wave approached and washed over. The bubbles mingled with the sand, and suddenly we saw a woman rise from the water. Her skin was dark, the delicate light shining from the skulls above, reflecting off her skin.

Her fins turned into arms and legs.

With a wide grin on her face, Ebony emerged from the water and stumbled onto the shore. She tried to take a few steps, but her legs probably felt like jelly underneath her. As she fell to the ground, she kept her smile on. She was determined to experience everything this new place had to offer, no matter how difficult it may be for her aquatic body to adjust to land.

And yet, without warning, a sturdy net flew out from the shadows and wrapped tightly around her, causing her to let out an ear-piercing scream. She struggled against the strong cords, but it only caused them to tighten around her limbs. Several men approached her, their expressions sinister and determined.

Aria recoiled, but I held her back, my hands trembling with the effort to restrain her.

"We have to get her out of here," she growled between clenched teeth.

"No, we need *him*," I whispered urgently. "But wait and see."

We scanned the area, and suddenly our eyes locked onto the Ravenman.

He advanced towards Ebony while six burly men surrounded Ebony, their hands gripping her arms tightly as she kicked and hissed like an angry feline.

"Rio," Aria hissed.

I knew Aria wanted to storm toward them but I wanted to wait until the Ravenman was with her, until Ebony saw his face, until she realized it was dangerous here. This rescue mission wouldn't do us any good if she ran off at the next opportunity. She had to know this wasn't her place, that it would break her forever if she ran away from her family.

"Wait." I put a hand on Aria's shoulder, my voice barely above a whisper.

She shuddered and I could feel her heart pounding against my chest.

The Ravenman's deep, gravelly voice broke the tense silence as he addressed Ebony.

His hat was adorned with feathers, his pants a faded black, and a jagged scar ran down his face. When he adjusted his blood-red gloves, the light caught on his fiery hair.

They talked, and when the Ravenman hit her, Aria broke free and rushed forward.

"Fuck," Mal said, and we trudged after her.

"What did I say—" I started, but she interrupted me as she ran, her hand already directed at the Ravenman.

"I won't let my friends be beaten by a dirty bastard," she snapped, and when I wanted to say something again, she turned around and looked at me with eyes glowing white, and I knew I had nothing more to say.

I killed thousands of men, stood in countless wars, but one glance of this woman brought me to my knees. I grumbled and reluctantly followed her, reminding myself that killing my wife would make over a thousand years useless.

The wind blew around our heads, and when Aria's hood flew back, her white braid fluttered in the wind.

She raised her hand and shouted, "Stop whatever you're doing, and I may let your men live."

And what I hoped wouldn't happen did.

The men next to him turned out to be demons, their black eyes saturated with blood. They all simultaneously turned their heads to Aria, hissing, showing their rotten teeth. The Ravenman grinned at us, and I could have waited longer, but they dared to threaten Aria, so I concentrated my shadows around me.

Mal swore under his breath, suddenly wielding a long sword, and Aria being Aria shot a beam of light at the demons without thinking first, triggering a god's damn chain reaction.

"Fuck," I swore and my shadows whirled around her like a protective barrier as she prepared for another attack.

The demons rushed toward us, and with a quick gesture, I unleashed a whirlwind that shot towards them like a wall. The trafficker hesitated when he recognized the supernatural forces conspiring against him. Everyone knew only I ruled over the shadows.

Magic awakened in a crescendo around us.

Aria's dazzling light danced around him like a holy shield, blinding the demons. Her power was like a weapon of its own in the Underworld, for no one was accustomed to light.

She smiled and sent another beam at the demons. Their terrible screams mixed with the howling of the storm, and I could feel the elements themselves resisting their corrupt exis-tence. The demons tried to resist our powers, but they had no chance against the mighty alliance we formed.

They wavered, their repulsive bodies struck by the forces of magic. Aria unleashed a final dazzling explosion, and I drew the surrounding shadows, the storm I controlled sweeping them away like dust. However, driven by anger, the demons began to regenerate and gather in a malicious counteroffensive. Their eyes glowed with a dark intensity as they lunged at us. Aria and I defended against their attacks, but the demons seemed to comprise of impenetrable shadow, ready to drag us into a dark abysses.

The air filled with the putrid stench of their corrupted existence as the Ravenman anxiously sought my gaze. His red-rimmed eyes reflected concern for me. In that moment, I realized that not only did the demons pose a threat, but the darkness in which we fought demanded a high price.

The storm forces I unleashed were repelled by the demons as they rushed towards us. Aria tried to break through their attacks with dazzling light, but the darkness seemed to amplify her power. A demon attacked me from the side, and my shadow form couldn't deflect it quickly enough. I would have sent them straight to Tartarus, but since I was only mentally present, I couldn't unleash my full powers.

I swallowed, but suddenly the number of enemies increased.

I felt Aria's concern. Her light orbs trying to protect me.

Amidst the battle, we lost control of the darkness, which condensed around us into an impenetrable mist. I tried to call back my shadows, but the demons surrounded us, their malicious claws reaching out to us. Mal, usually so unshakable, looked desperate as our eyes met. He beheaded one after another while my dark power pulsed.

In a desperate attempt to regain control, we united our powers. Aria unleashed a dazzling beam that pushed back the demons, while I condensed the shadows around us and released one final powerful whirlwind. The darkness gave way, and the demons screamed in pain and anger. Exhausted but victorious, we found ourselves in a moment of relative silence.

Mal beheaded another, and Aria shattered a demon with a beam of light as I let my shadows consume another. When the Ravenman stood alone, I approached him and was about to smash his skull when Aria held me back.

"No, she should kill him," she said, nodding towards Ebony.

"It's dangerous to free her—it's not Ebony we know. She's a Nereid."

"Rio, I take my promises seriously."

"Aria," I said, but then she simply shook her head and approached the two.

"Touch her, and I'll send you to Tartarus forever."

The Ravenman fell to his knees. "I didn't know it was you; I—"

I raised a hand. "Everything you say now is pointless. You're a dead man. The question is if you're allowed to atone for your sins or not."

I fought to control my shaking fingers, eager to unleash my magic as I watched Aria slowly and carefully cut the net. Ebony hissed in protest, and for a moment, I thought I might have to intervene. But then Aria spoke to her in a low voice, soothing her with words I couldn't make out.

My hand curled into a fist, ready to strike, but my shadows pulsed with agitation, wanting to lash out at Aria for her foolish actions. She handed Ebony the knife, and I fought the urge to strangle my wife. This was so fucking risky. Ebony was deadly. Did she not understand the danger of Nereids?

My shadows lunged and then retreated, my powerful feelings for Aria preventing me from attacking Ebony in that instant. "Damn it, Aria," I muttered through gritted teeth.

"Oh shit," said Mal, and my head snapped to Ebony.

She crawled towards us with the knife in her mouth.

Dark strands of hair fell in front of her face as I sprinted towards my wife, grabbing her hand and pulling her away. As we watched from afar, Ebony let out a fierce hiss and leaped onto the Ravenman, overpowering him with deadly grace.

When she was done, I expected her to come towards us, but instead, she threw the fucking knife at us.

I pushed Aria out of the way just in time, and the knife buried itself in the sand right before my feet.

Despite her actions, this wasn't the Ebony we knew. Her hair was wild and unkempt, her eyes were glazed over, and there was a ferocity in her movements that was animalistic.

"You must go," I told her firmly, trying to push my stubborn wife behind my back but she rammed her nails in my hand instead and I did all I could to stiffen my anger. "This is not where you belong."

"Stay in the water, Eb," Aria said, stepping before me. "The souls out here are cruel and will harm you. Stay in the water with your family, live happily."

Ebony hissed at us once more before retreating into the waves, and once her knees were submerged, she dove into the sea with a somersault, disappearing beneath the foam.

I took a deep breath and glared at Aria. "This wasn't what we agreed on."

She pulled her ellbow away from my grasp. "I never promised you anything."

"Here we go again..." Bory chimed in, but I resisted the urge to silence him with shadows.

"Perhaps we should--" Mal began, watching us with concern as our anger sparked between us.

Raising my hand, a wall of shadows emerged right before them, blocking their voices and us from their sight.

My fists clenched and unclenched at my sides as I glared at her.

"You just don't understand the danger you put yourself in, right?" I yelled, shadows exploding to all my sides.

But she wasn't afraid. No, her eyes blazed with defiance, daring me to keep talking.

I closed the space between us. "You could have been killed and that we've done so far would have been for nothing!"

My voice rose and rose, shaking with emotion.

But then I noticed the little tremble of her shoulders.

Despite the anger in her eyes, she'd been scared too. She knew this was a step too far.

And she'd done it all for her. For Ebony. Who was a friend of mine too. She saved my friend.

It was a sobering thought that made my anger dissipate slightly and I took a deep breath.

I reached out and cupped her face firmly.

"I just had to try," she whispered, looking up at me, her glance softening as well. "I had to try, Rio."

"You're the most stubborn, reckless, and risky woman I know." I pulled her into my arms, and we stood there, our hearts pounding against each other's chests. Her fingers tangled in my hair as I leaned down to kiss her forehead, my lips grazing the soft skin tenderly. "And I love you so fucking much for it but stop risking your life. It's the death of me."

"I'm sorry," she murmured against my chest.

When she looked up at me again, I kissed her.

Only it wasn't a gentle kiss of apology or gratitude.

It was fierce, almost violent.

Our tongues danced against each other's lips as our hands roamed restlessly over exposed flesh. My palms burned where they touched her back, and she gripped me tighter around the waist as if she would never let go. Our bodies were flush against each other now, and I could feel her heart racing against my chest.

"I'm sorry," she said again.

"I'm here," I breathed against her mouth, a hand slipping

under her leather jacket. I traced circles on her bare back, reveling in the silken feel of her skin against mx fingers. "I'm with you."

She moaned softly into the kiss, encouraging me.

My other hand found its way to the small of her back, pulling her even closer as she deepened the kiss. Her lips parted, inviting me in, and I took full advantage, thrusting my tongue inside her mouth hungrily. We tasted each other, desperately devouring one another.

As our breathing slowed, we broke apart, gulping for air.

We stood there, panting, staring into each other's eyes.

I brushed a strand of hair from her face, my fingers grazing her cheek softly. "I'm sorry, too. I hate yelling at you," I said, "but please, for fuck's sake, don't risk your life ever again. There are different ways to help others."

BACK AT THE PALACE, we waited until Hecate informed us that Athena planned to come and ambush Aria in three nights.

Meanwhile, war raged on in Olympia, and several gods visited us, trying to persuade me to return Aria.

Her father called for war, and I was surprised that I had almost forgotten we were on the brink of another war at this point already. However, Athena wasn't foolish. They wouldn't stand a chance down here—that's why she focused on my sisters. The Underworld belonged to us, which only fueled her desire to annihilate us all. She hated not having control everywhere.

Our plan was straightforward. We had to kill Athena, and that could only happen if we killed her in the past while Aria would go back into the present. All at the same time.

We couldn't risk Athena dying in the past because we didn't know how many lives were connected to her, and, most importantly, whether Aria and I would have come together if she didn't exist. I didn't want to jeopardize that, so we'd kill her in the present, and since she was heavily guarded there, we took her past form with us.

Easy? No.

But we had no other choice.

CHAPTER THIRTY-TWO
ARIA, OLYMPIA 1000 YEARS AGO

I knew exactly where she was lurking in wait for me.

While Zagrios negotiated with the gods because they threatened to come into the Underworld and take me by force, Athena sent me a message.

A small gold brooch with a minor note.

Probably placed on my balcony by Hermes himself. He was one of the few gods who had access to the Underworld, the messenger of all gods, seemingly on Athena's side.

Zagrios could determine who had access down here and who didn't, and it was diminishing as more gods opposed him. I had realized back then that only the Underworld could provide me with enough security. No one down here was stronger than Rio. While his sisters had their own realms, they had lost their magic and had to draw power from other magical sources, making him by far the strongest.

However, that didn't stop Athena from sneaking into my mind with manipulative sentences.

I remembered everything, but this conversation felt like it happened even longer ago than everything else. It was blurry, and I wondered why.

Somehow, it didn't give me the security I expected, and I had a bad feeling.

"That's probably because you're excited," Bory said as he sat with me on the bed.

I held the brooch in my hand, inspecting the tiny golden bird.

Athena's letter instructed that if I allowed her to speak with me, I should rub it, granting her an hour in the Underworld. I remember waiting for weeks before I finally called her. I was reluctant to speak with her, not until more and more deities were perishing after invading the Underworld. Not until thousands of souls became enslaved shadows while defending the castle against Athena's attack. It wasn't until the guilt consumed me that I made the decision to end it all.

"I don't know. It just feels strange. I just can't remember this conversation. Something's not right, Bory."

"A lot of things aren't. I still can't believe you met Athena behind Rio's back then."

I sighed.

Yes, it was one of my hundreds of mistakes, and I would never do it again, but back then, I wasn't like I am now. I was uncertain. Young. Naïve. "I wasn't the person you know today. I was scared, and it was the first time I was away from home. Away from Any... away from everyone, and suddenly, a war was declared because of me. I didn't want anyone to get hurt, and Athena wrote me so many letters after that meeting, reminding me we triggered the curse, that we were bringing about the apocalypse by staying together. She wanted me to come back. No I now why, because she needed me and because she'd lost her greatest weapon."

"But to be honest, it makes little sense for her to persuade you to kill yourself..."

"Yeah, I know. Everything feels strange. I was under Rio's

protection, and no magic could take me away, transport me to Olympia. But Athena tried everything, listing all of Rio's evil deeds. We both know there were quite a few. I knew he wasn't perfect, yet I believed people could change. I saw the good in him, and much was just projected onto him. But the fear that all humans would die, that Olympia would be destroyed, that Any would die too, ...just like Hecate did... made me consider to just doing what Athena wanted, hoping that everything would be better after. But as we know, it naturally wasn't. It was an act of desperation, hoping to find an easy way out."

Bory hopped onto my thighs and hugged me. "I love you, Lynne."

"I love you too. So, shall we call Athena?"

"Yes, let's get it over with."

Bory hid in my pocket and as I took a deep breath, I reluctantly went to the balcony and rubbed the little bird. It chirped and blinked. And suddenly, a small, living gold bird was in my hand. It stretched its feathers as if it needed to revive the dormant muscles first, then flapped its wings and flew until it disappeared behind the skulls in the sky.

My hands turned sweaty, and I tapped on the spot.

I waited and waited. But she didn't come.

"Bory, do you think she knows anything?" I asked softly, staring into the dark city below us. Nothing but shadows.

"Patience, Lynne..."

That was something I didn't have. I couldn't wait. It was terrible.

I bit my lip and knead my fingers. What If she knew what we were planning? I grabbed the small lightning bolt around my neck.

What if she knew that Rio, Mal, and Hecate were waiting in ambush, ready to support me at any moment if something went wrong?

I reached into my free coat pocket with one hand. There was the piece of the o she had given me. I had to touch it and wish to come back. With her. Like with Bory... I could.

"Thank you for letting me in," I heard Athena's delicate voice, and my heart almost stopped in my throat.

Oh, something was off. Something was——

"How are you down here? Did he hurt you?" She approached, throwing back her blue cloak in motion, and the long brown waves emerged. Her face was as beautiful as it was malicious. She wore a light golden armor over her dress and reached a hand towards me.

I flinched. Something was off.

"No need to fear me, child. I'm sorry we couldn't save you, that he took you into his terrible world. You should have listened to Nana and not taken the pomegranate."

I tried to respond as I did back then, but I just couldn't remember. I only knew that I was very polite to her and agreed with her. So, I tried to keep to the script. "I'm sorry." I lowered my head, hoping she didn't see my excitement. "I thought he loved me..."

Athena laughed, a bitter sound. "HE cannot love. He only wants to show his sisters that he holds the power and can have a lover, even though I forbade it from everyone. They prioritize their well-being, their desire for power and prestige over the common good. But we have a responsibility to humans, and we must first break this curse."

I nodded. "I noticed he wishes us no good, so I called you."

Athena smiled, taking my hands in hers and clasping them. "Look, I was right, but I have a solution to solve everything. It will take courage, though. Can you muster the courage for our land, for our worlds, like I did back then when I freed us from Zeus?"

"Yes," I said, and Athena smiled again, as if all the puzzle pieces were falling into the right order. "Good. You must kill him then."

I blinked. What? Not me?

She gripped my hands. "Only if he dies, we are redeemed. I'll give you poison, and you must give it to him. It can kill an immortal god. There's only one dose of this poison, so take good care of it. We have to fetch it from the Detekei Caves first, but when you give it to him—maybe pour it in his wine—he'll take anything from you. He trusts you."

I still couldn't believe it.

She wanted to commission me to give *him* the poison?

The more I thought about it, the scenes came back like a slap in my face.

She wanted me to kill *him* to end the curse—but I couldn't do it.

From her explanations, I understood that one of us had to die.

So, I chose myself over Rio. I never did as she said.

And then it hit me. She wanted me and would never want to kill me. Athena desired me to kill Rio for her, because she needed me to resurrect Zeus. She would never kill me. And this meant—she tricked us.

I couldn't breathe anymore.

My heart seemed to stand still.

The whiteness in the Omphalos Stone was a bone.

"No..."

I staggered back and crashed into the balcony railing.

I glanced into the bedroom, searching for Rio. But he didn't appear. I couldn't say anything, for fear that Athena would use her magical powers and fly away, and we would never get the chance to kill her again.

But I know what she did now.

Unconsciously, I had touched a bone, and my touch revived

things. It revived bones, and I had revived all the bones of the Bone Queen, and Athena made me touch the last bone of Zeus. She must have found it...

Zeus had been brought back to life while I was occupied here!

Athena knew I might not kill him; she speculated on that because I couldn't do it. Still, her primary concern was to distract us while resurrecting Zeus and, in the meantime, destroying the world. Her only goal.

"Oh, I know how you feel. Being afraid is a normal reaction." Athena approached me, probably sensing that something was amiss.

When she halted, I knew I had little time before she could detect my lies.

We had to act now.

Desperately, I touched the shard of the Omphalos Stone in my pocket and pulled her towards me. "Bory. Now."

Bory shot out, tore the chain off my neck, and at the same moment as I wished us back to Earth, Bory thrust the lightning bolt into Athena's heart.

In an instant, a powerful force yanked us apart, sending Athena's cry of pain in all directions.

She shattered into tiny fragments that glittered like stardust in the sunlight. We were surrounded by a swarm of intense light, and everything else around us became a blur.

We might have killed her, but the worlds were already on the brink of destruction.

The curse had taken effect because love found no entrance to the Underworld.

Athena did everything to keep us apart.

But we were betrayed nevertheless.

Somebody must have tipped her off that we'd request her

help to return and alter the past. She only permitted it to distract us from our true mission.

But who would have betrayed us? The Blood Queen?

As it brought me back to the present, my heart broke because I didn't know if I would ever see Rio again. If that kiss his sister stole from us years ago was the end of us.

CHAPTER THIRTY-THREE
ARIA, PRESENT DAY

My eyes fluttered open to the sound of crackling energy and my bones trembled with its force.

As I blinked, the rough-hewn stone ceiling of the bunker greeted me, a familiar sight that brought both relief and panic. This was Earth. My chest tightened as I took in the faces of Any, Jamie, and Bory huddled next to me, their expressions mirroring my fear.

The air on Earth always carried a green scent, reminiscent of fresh leaves after rain. But now, it was acrid and biting, filled with smoke and ruin. My heart raced as I scanned the room, taking in the familiar surroundings of my cot. Mal sat on the free one next to mine, his presence bringing a sense of safety amidst the chaos. But as my eyes fell upon the empty cot, a sinking feeling settled in my stomach.

Something was missing, but I couldn't place what.

Then, there was a deafening boom that shook the walls around us and sent my heart into overdrive. Damn. It sounded like an explosion, and my mind immediately went to Rio, my husband. Whispering his name like a prayer on my lips, I begged for his safety.

Was he still alive out there?

With a sigh of relief, Any's tense muscles softened as he embraced me. "You made it."

I could smell the lingering scent of gun powder on his clothes, and when he pulled away, I noticed the faint bruise on his cheekbone and the split lip.

"What happened?" My voice cracked from disuse or screaming—it was hard to tell which one. "Weren't we in Olympia? I... I think I went back in time, but everything is so confusing."

Any brushed a strand of my hair out of my face, and I sat up, feeling dizzy. "I brought you back once you materialized. You've been asleep for a little while. We changed your clothes and put some battle gear on you. But good job, you killed Athena."

"No, she tricked us."

"She did," Any said, squeezing my arm.

"The headaches and disorientation are normal, though," Mal chimed in. "Time travel takes a toll on the body."

As I tried to calm my spinning head, my hand brushed against something sharp in my pocket.

I reached in and pulled out a fragment of the Omphalos Stone—the same one that transported me back here.

"It's still intact?" I said.

"I don't think it's of any use, but keep it just in case," Mal advised. "We'll check it later."

Later. In case we're still alive...

I nodded and returned the shard to my pocket. "And what's happening outside?"

"The Bone God," Jamie spat, her knuckles white as she gripped doorframe. "He's unleashing hell out there."

Damn. So I was right.

"Everyone's out there fighting," Bory added grimly, his cute face set in a determined scowl that seemed out of place among his feathers. He didn't change back in his human form then. "They're trying to keep those creatures away from the bunker."

"What kind of creatures?" I asked, pushing myself up to my feet despite the swaying room.

"Deadwalkers, wraiths…you name it," Any said.

"And where's Ash?" I asked.

"He's leading the eastern flank out there."

My heart swelled with the need to assist, to fight against the overwhelming sense of helplessness that threatened to consume me.

"Then we have to join him," I said.

With a commanding presence, Any rose from his seat at the head of the long oak table. His once calm demeanor had shifted, and his voice now carried an urgent tone. "Prepare yourselves," he bellowed, causing everyone to stand up straighter. "If this is truly our last stand, let it be one that will be remembered."

As he spoke, I could feel my heart race with adrenaline and my fingers tingle with power. My magic surged beneath my skin, ready to be unleashed in defense. Outside these walls, a battle raged on, and we were determined to come out victorious, no matter the cost.

My legs shook with every step as I mustered the courage to ascend the stairs and leave the safety of indoors. Every creak of the steps seemed to reverberate through the bunker, reminding me of the danger that awaited above.

The bunker's stale air was thick with dread, and the walls seemed to press in around us, echoing with distant roars and the unsettling clatter of bones.

"Did you hear anything about Rio?" My voice came out as a croak.

"He's not here, that's all I know," Any replied, his eyes avoiding mine, dark circles beneath them like bruises on his soul.

Panic clawed its way up my throat, a wild thing desperate for release. "But he's alive, isn't he? Tell me he's alive."

"We heard nothing... I'm sorry"

The weight of Any's words settled on my chest, crushing the breath out of me as we came to a halt in the common space.

"No," I whispered, shaking my head in denial. "He has to be alive."

"We'll find him," Mal promised, placing a comforting hand on my shoulder. "He can't die easily."

"Yes, maybe he still sleeps and after this fight we go wake him up?" Bory said, his eyes big like a child.

My mind raced with possibilities, each one more terrifying than the last.

"Athena wanted me to kill him, it was never me because she needed me," I stressed and noticed Cherry coming to us. She hugged Jamie and gave her a brief peck on the forehead. "Athena let me go back in time, because she needed me to wake the Bone God. What if the Blood Queen betrayed us, what if—"

"No," Any said. "She didn't. We can trust her."

"Yes, we totally can," Mal chimed in.

"But someone told Athena where the bones are and—"

"We need to focus on the present," Any interjected, breaking through my thoughts. "We have a battle to win, Aria. I know you worry about Rio, but if we don't act now, we all die."

He was right. I couldn't let myself get lost in despair when there were still people fighting for their lives above ground.

I forced myself to take a deep breath, trying to hold back the flood of tears that threatened to escape. But I just couldn't ignore the gnawing pain in my chest. My thoughts were consumed with finding Rio, but a part of me wondered if it was selfish to put my own feelings first.

Yet, I knew I couldn't just give up and go find him, as much as my heart was breaking.

I had to push through this internal battle and keep fighting.

I had to believe in him, his powers, his strength, that he was alive.

He had to be alive.

He was Hades' only son.

He was the Shadow King.

No one but me could break him and I would never.

"Oh, hi there, Bory!" Cherry's gentle voice broke through my reverie, and she crouched down to look at Bory peeking out of my jacket's pocket.

His small face wore a mixture of embarrassment and frustration, knowing he couldn't take on a human form for Cherry again.

"Is this how you usually appear? You're so cute!" she cooed, reaching in to give him a kiss on the cheek.

Bory grunted in response, his sense of self-worth visibly struggling with being called cute. But when Cherry declared him her "strong warrior," he beamed with happiness and determination.

"I will fight for you," he vowed with a nod.

"And you'll be the bravest," she said.

"Okay, let's go," I said, determination filling my voice once again. We'll give it our all. For everyone.

Cherry hugged us and gave us some weapons to fight with. She stood behind with the wounded. Before we ascended the stairs, she made a cross sign on Jamie's forehead, and prayed for us.

"Do we have a plan?" I asked, making my way up the stairs. My fists clenched as I glanced up at Any and Mal, waiting for their response.

"Just one and it might be bad," Mal said.

"Better a bad one than none," Any said, clearing his voice. "You have power—actual power. Maybe it's time to use it."

I stopped dead in my tracks. "*I'm* your plan? Against the Bone God? Are you kidding me?"

I felt my breath catch, the weight of what he suggested anchoring me in place.

"I already said it *could* be a bad one," Mal said, and my gaze shot daggers at him.

"It makes sense, though. You're the Lifebringer. But you're also the Deathbringer, so turn his bones back," Any said. "It falls and stands with you. That's why you've always been so valuable to Athena. You were the only one that could stop her and you did. I think you can stop him, too. We all fought for your life, Aria because you are the key."

I grunted. I didn't want to be the damn key.

But as much as I hated it to be true, life and death were two sides of the same coin.

All added all up.

"Gods damn it," I muttered, feeling the stirrings of my magic respond to his words.

It was a risky idea, a desperate gambit, but it sparked something within me—a defiant hope that refused to be extinguished. Maybe it could work. It was skulling Zeus but it could work.

"Can you do it? Taking life from bones?" Bory asked, his eyes searching mine with a fierce intensity.

"I don't know. But I'll try."

"Then we'll buy you the time you need," Jamie said behind me. "We'll fight our way to him, together."

"Let's make it count," Any added, opening the door for us.

I looked at each of them, their faces etched with the resolve of warriors who had seen too much and yet still stood ready to face the abyss.

"Thank you," I whispered, my voice steadier now, my mind

clear. There was no room for doubt, only the certainty that this might be our last stand.

"Whatever happens," Bory said, his tiny hand on my arm, "we're with you."

"Then let's bring an end to this nightmare," I said and left the bunker behind me.

THE AIR OUTSIDE was a tempest of swirling ash and chaos, the sky a bruised canvas that bled crimson at its fringes. While the horizon seemed on fire, it cast an eerie glow over the land. But amidst the turmoil, something far more sinister emerged—the Deadwalkers. Thousands of Deadwalkers.

Their limping gaits were deceptive as they lurched forward with ravenous intent, their grotesque features contorted into hungry snarls. The stench of decay wafted from their decaying bodies, filling the air with a putrid odor. As they closed in on us, I could see the glint of hunger in their lifeless eyes, ready to tear us apart. It was a scene straight out of a nightmare, and I knew we needed to act fast if we wanted to survive.

"Stay close!" Any's voice pierced through the deafening chaos, his sword gleaming like a silver star as it sliced through flesh and bone.

In response, I unleashed a spell from my trembling hands, weaving intricate patterns that burst with dazzling white light. The energy crackled and surged, consuming the nearest undead monstrosity in a blinding inferno.

My heart raced with each beat, every thump a battle cry that fueled my magic.

Soothie landed next to me, as if summoned by my thoughts.

I couldn't resist hugging him, grateful for his presence in this dangerous battle.

"He's been invaluable in protecting our bunker from all those beasts. He incinerates Deadwalkers like a pro," Jamie commented as I gently stroked Soothie's scales.

"Good boy!" I said, and he purred contentedly under my touch.

"Keep moving!" Any yelled over his shoulder, taking down another monster with a fierce swipe of his dagger. His eyes reflected the blazing destruction that surrounded us. "We must reach the Bone God! He's at the cemetery, concentrating on his magic. If we can't get to him in time, he'll wipe the world away."

"Watch out!" Jamie's warning rang out just as a decayed hand reached for me, its fetid fingers exuding death itself. But before it could make contact, the hand crumbled to dust—burst by a shot from Jamie's gun, loaded with silver bullets.

And as the cries of tormented souls echoed around us, we trudged onward into the abyss and all I could see were dozens of Deadwalkers rising from their graves, their skeletal hands reaching out for us.

It was time to fight.

CHAPTER THIRTY-FOUR
RIO

I opened my eyes and a curtain of fiery red hair fell over my face.

I reached up to push the hair away, and stared into the intense blue eyes of my sister Macaria. The fucking Blood Queen. Startled, I pulled away and sat up, trying to understand why she was here in my bedroom. "Mac? What's going on?" I asked, still half-asleep and disoriented.

"Sorry," she said, sitting back and casually brushing something off her dress.

She said on the chair beside my bed.

"Were you here the whole time?"

"Don't flatter yourself. I sensed you coming back and dragged myself over. Sleeping beauty must've had the nap of the century, huh?"

I grinned, not the friendly kind. "Aria looked so startled at the last moment; I think something's wrong."

"Your hunch is right, little brother."

"Fuck." I jumped out of bed, feeling oddly exposed without my armor. Pacing around my room, I searched for my metal, but it wasn't there. "My armor!" I roared, hurling the

278

door open with my shadows. "Bring me my armor immediately!"

Mac laughed. "Ow. Sweet. They're like overexcited puppies, aren't they?"

I wasn't in the mood for humor. Something was definitely amiss with Aria.

"What did Athena say to her? What happened?" I pondered aloud, tapping my foot impatiently as I waited for my servants.

"Hmm," my sister mused, giving me a sideways glance.

I raised an eyebrow. That woman and her fucking plays.

Just then, Brix and Isix entered the room.

My Horsemen approached, heavy with fatigue and carrying my armor on their outstretched arms. I grabbed the familiar weight of it and hastily strapped it on, eager to be fully armed for battle once again.

"Nice of you to join us," Isix teased while I struggled to latch my breastplate. Her eyes flickered with a mixture of amusement and worry.

"Yeah, yeah, skip the pleasantries and give me all the intel you have."

"Athena fucked us over and found Zeus' last bone. The Bone God is alive now."

I nearly choked on my own breath. "What? Why didn't you tell me sooner?" I turned to Mac with an accusing tone. "Or were you too busy enjoying my struggle?"

She some blood from under her nails, smearing it on a ragged shirt hanging above my bedpost, which had definitely seen better days.

"Cyril, that son of a bitch," she hissed. "He sold us out to Athena. And now Mel has unleashed the Bone God's wrath upon Earth. See, I told you."

Rage boiled in my veins at the betrayal. "Damn it." I turned to Brix and Isix. "We have to find my wife."

I turned to put on my other armor, nodding at my horsemen to approach me.

"Athena is gone, just vanished," my sister said, still focused on her nails as I summoned the shadows to transport us to Earth. "Looks like you did your job well."

"Stop talking," I snapped.

"I don't think you want me to," she retorted.

My gaze narrowed on her.

"I'm going to Olympia to get help from the other gods. We'll all need them if we're going to stop this, but I need something from you first."

"What?" I said.

"Make me a promise. Promise me you won't harm Mel."

"Mac, we have little time—"

"No. Now you listen to me for once!" She stood up, her face all stern and serious. "I know she helped Athena, but I ruined her life by killing her lover long before that. We've all made mistakes. I trusted Cyril and acted impulsively. But that ends now. Give me your word. That after we make it out of here alive, we will follow our father's wishes and rule the Underworld equally without resorting to violence against each other. That means you won't punish Mel."

"What about punishing both of you?" I said through gritted teeth. All the gods know I had more than one reason to just end them.

She stood with her arms crossed, determination in her eyes.

I"You and Mel deceived me for centuries behind my back," I said.

Mac raised her hand with an expressionless face. "Zaggy... people are dying."

I grunted at that stupid nickname and took her hand when she offered it with a sly smile. Reluctantly, I shook it. "Fine, we have a deal. I won't hurt Mel—or you. Bring everyone. Anyone who doesn't fight is considered a traitor and will face consequences."

"As you wish, brother."

CHAPTER THIRTY-FIVE
ARIA

We battled through the thick underbrush, our feet stumbling over roots and fallen branches as we made our way to the cemetery. In the distance, a strange light flickered, casting an eerie glow over the darkened landscape and my vision blurred, overwhelmed by shades of gray and black.

We cautiously stepped over the decaying bodies of Deadwalkers and other unidentifiable creatures, their bones gnarled and bent in disturbing positions on the scorched earth. Our backs pressed together, we scanned the desolate landscape for any signs of danger.

As soon as I heard another shrieking of Deadwalkers, I let a lightning arrow fly. It struck the skull of a creature with a satisfying crunch before I quickly took down two more in rapid succession. Stones littered the surrounding ground, and I grabbed a handful, hurling them at the oncoming monsters with deadly precision. Beside me, Mal's sword cleaved through their spindly frames with ease, while Jamie's pistol fired off rounds into their empty eye sockets.

The sweat poured down my face, and my arms burned from drawing back so many light arrows. But we kept moving forward, our weapons never missing a beat. But for every Deadwalker we took down, it seemed like two more appeared. I took a moment to catch my breath after sending another creature to its demise. Mal let out a fierce yell as his sword sliced through multiple monsters at once, while Jamie dodged and fired off shots with expert aim.

But despite our best efforts, the number of Deadwalkers was overwhelming. I reloaded my power and took aim once again, hoping to buy us some time. And then one of their bony hands grazed my cheek, and I instinctively pulled Jamie behind me. The ground shook beneath us as we fought together, our combined strength barely enough to hold them back. How long could we keep this up?

I sent another lightning flying through the air with a soft whistle, piercing straight through a Deadwalker's eye socket and into its brain. I cursed under my breath when one grabbed Jamie from behind, but she spun out of its grip easily, drawing her dagger. She sliced its throat before it could take another step.

I sighed in relief.

Any cackled madly, his sword dancing through the air in a flurry of steel and bone dust. He was a whirlwind of death, cutting a path through the horde that seemed endless. But I noticed he was moving slower than usual, favoring one leg.

"Any, are you alright?" I ask worriedly, reaching out to touch his armor.

He shrugged me off with a grunt. "I'll be fine. Keep moving!"

The smell of rotting flesh and decay surrounded us, mixed with the metallic tang of blood and the sound of clashing weapons echoed in my ears as we fought on, our breaths coming out in ragged gasps. Sweat dripped into my eyes, stinging like fire, but I didn't have time to wipe it away.

Mal leaped into the fray, his sword singing as he swung it with deadly precision. He almost didn't notice when a Deadwalker bit down on his armor, but Any saw it and sprinted over to him. He plunged his dagger into its skull just as it released its grip on Mal, yanking it free with a sickening sucking sound.

"Thanks," Mal muttered.

As I spun around, my eyes locked onto Punchy, his silver sword firmly lodged in the chest of a massive bone beast. His once confident face now twisted with terror as he desperately struggled to free himself from the jaws of another Deadwalker.

That's when I saw it.

I jerked up, coming to a sudden halt as my stomach dropped.

Blood poured out from his leg where its sharp teeth had pierced through, and he howled in agony as he frantically tried to break free. My hand instinctively created an arrow, but I knew it could cause even more harm to Punchy.

Praying for him, I sprinted towards him. All that mattered in that moment was reaching Punchy. With all my strength, I plunged my sword into the Deadwalker's eye socket, shattering its head into pieces. As Punchy fell back, gasping for breath, an eerie silence descended upon us, and we collapsed against each other, panting heavily.

But amidst the chaos and carnage, something else bloomed between us. With our eyes meeting in understanding and unspoken words passing between us, I realized that Punchy was leaving me.

"No," I cried out, searching frantically for where the Deadwalker bit him. "No, Punchy."

"Lynne..." Bory's voice broke through my panic as he tore at my shirt.

I saw Jamie and Any closing in on us, shielding us from the advancing Deadwalkers.

Suddenly, time stood still. Minutes dragged by slowly.

Punchy coughed, blood spilling over his lips.

"Punchy…"

He took my hand weakly. "My name…is Christopher."

And I understood why he was telling me this now. In our gang, revealing your true name was a death sentence.

"No, Punch," I choked out through tears welling up in my eyes. "It's…it's okay."

"Lynne," Any's voice joined in this time as she sliced down another Deadwalker.

"Wait!" I snapped, turning to face him. "He's our friend. I won't…I won't let him die alone." The words caught in my throat, and I took a deep breath, trying to hold back the sobs threatening to escape. "I will never abandon a friend when they need me."

But deep down, we both knew what needed to be done before Punchy turned into one of them.

"So…" he croaked, his voice hoarse and strained from the loss of blood. I gripped his hand tightly. "You'll…be my…queen soon?" He tried to smile through the fear in his eyes. "Is that better than cheesecake?"

I tried to laugh, but it came out as a sob as tears streamed down my face. "Yes, Punchy," I choked out. "Because I will give you all the cheesecakes you want."

He attempted to laugh again, but his voice caught, and he let out a pained groan. "Thank you for everything, Barbie," he whispered, tears welling up in his own eyes.

"No, thank you, Christopher."

A lump formed in my throat as I struggled to keep back the tears. "I will never forget you," I promised.

With unspoken understanding between us, Punchy tried to

say something else but couldn't find the words. As he looked at me with pleading eyes, I sobbed even harder, trying to maintain a brave front for him until the end.

"Close your eyes now, Christopher," I whispered softly. "Think of the people you love."

Bory knelt beside me, resting his head against my leg as I gently closed Punchy's eyes. And in that moment, as his face relaxed in peaceful slumber, I launched an arrow straight into his forehead with a heart-wrenching cry. "Goodbye, my friend," I whispered through the tears. "We will meet again."

"We need to get to the Bone God," Any whispered after letting me breathe for a few heartbeats.

I nodded, my heart pounding. He was right; we had to end this before more innocents died. With a heavy heart, I made my way to the cemetery. The once vibrant street was nothing but charred earth now. Everything was destroyed, not a single house was standing. There were mountains of dead bodies and I was so sick of it.

As we approached, a strange sensation prickled across my skin, like tiny insects scurrying beneath the surface.

It grew stronger with each step until I could barely stand it.

Any looked pale as we entered the cemetery gates, and when I followed his line of sight, my stomach dropped. The Bone God loomed before us, a towering figure made entirely of bones that once floated in the sky in the Underworld. As we watched, he moved, stretching his skeletal arms out like he was embracing the world.

As he tilted his skull-like head back, a chilling sight met my eyes. Bones of all shapes and sizes rained down from the sky above like a deadly hailstorm. It was only upon closer inspection that I realized it was not the actual sky raining these bones, but the towering figure before me. He seemed to be made entirely of bones - each joint, every appendage, and they cascaded from him in an eerie dance. My heart raced as I took in the sheer size of him, feeling small and insignificant in comparison.

"It's like he's collecting all the magic... all the power," Mal whispered.

I noticed Jamie trembling and wrapped an arm around her waist. "You can go, if you like," I said. "Wait with your mom... This isn't a battle you have to take."

Although I could see the fear in her eyes, she said: "We came here to kill him—I won't back out now."

I took a deep breath. "No. We can't."

Mal raised his sword as he spoke, but I could see the fear in his eyes. We embraced, and I could smell the lingering smoke on his clothes. In this moment, everything was uncertain, and we all knew that the odds were against us.

"Let's try our best," he said. "I'll be by your side, trying to heal you if something goes wrong." I tried to laugh, but it came out more like a desperate huff. We both knew that things would most likely go wrong.

"Thank you," I said, my voice trembling with emotion. "Guys, I love you and—"

"We're not saying goodbye," Mal interrupted firmly, stepping back from me. "No, we're going to make it."

But then Any spoke up, his eyes flickering to the Bone God beside us. "Actually, we only have a minute left. It's most likely that we'll die." My heart raced as I looked at him, the realization sinking in that he was saying goodbye for real.

"You're going to be an amazing queen," he said, his words filled with admiration and sadness. "Please make sure our father gets what he deserves."

Tears welled up in my eyes as I saw the piece of leather hanging from Any's leg, evidence of a bite from one of the Deadwalkers. He wasn't immortal like us. He had been bitten.

Any turned to Mal, their gazes locking in a bittersweet moment. "Mal," he whispered, moving towards him. "I'm sorry you fell for me."

"What is this?" Mal asked, backing away as Any followed him with determination despite his limp.

"For this second, it's just me and you," Any replied before kissing Mal deeply. The tears that dried up earlier now flowed freely down my cheeks as I watched them say goodbye through their kiss.

When they broke apart, Any turned to me, his face pale and his movements slow. "Go save this world, Aria," he said, his voice shaking with pain. "Keep my sister alive, will you?"

I wanted to scream, to run to him and pull him away from the impending battle before it was too late. But I couldn't move. I felt paralyzed with fear and sadness.

Mal desperately tried to heal Any, but it was too late. Any refused his help, knowing that it would use up precious magic that we needed for the upcoming fight. He accepted his fate and told us to run.

As more Deadwalkers closed in behind us, Any limped towards me one last time. "It's okay," he said as he reached out to touch my collarbone. "I'll always be with you, right where your heart is."

He then turned me around and pushed me towards Jamie and the others. "Run!" he yelled, his voice breaking with emotion.

I wanted to stay, to fight alongside him and not leave him alone in his last moments. But I knew he was right. I had a role to play, and I needed every ounce of magic I had left for the coming battle.

"Save the world," he whispered one last time before kissing my forehead. I shook my head, not wanting to leave him behind.

"It's okay," he said with a sad smile on his face. "I'll always be with you."

With those words, Any gave me one final push forward before turning back towards the approaching Deadwalkers. I couldn't bear to watch as they surrounded him, but I could hear his brave cries echoing behind me as we ran towards our destiny: saving the world from darkness.

Tears stream down my face like a raging river as I ran straight towards the Bone God, fueled by adrenaline and fury. A Deadwalker lunged at me with bared teeth, but I effortlessly parried its attack and drove my dagger into its chest with a powerful grunt. It continued to snap at me, but I was consumed by pure rage. Nothing mattered except for taking down this giant in front of us. My body spinned away from another bite, narrowly avoiding it. Mal's blade came down just in time, slicing off the Deadwalker's head with ease. "Thanks," I mutter before unleashing a barrage of arrows at the creatures closing in on us.

I stole a glance at Jamie, her gun firing relentlessly at a wall of Deadwalkers. She looked exhausted—so very tired. "I've got this," she breathed, her voice hoarse.

"Just keep shooting," I replied, silently praying that she won't be the next one to fall.

Turning back to face the onslaught of enemies, I stumbled forward until I was close enough to feel the pull of the Bone God. It was as if he was drawing everything towards him— bushes, life, Deadwalkers, and bodies—as he grew larger and more menacing. Standing firm, I summoned all of my strength and shot a lightning arrow straight into his massive face. It appeared as nothing more than a tiny line against his enormous body, but I poured every ounce of power from within me into that shot. To my dismay, it had no effect except for causing one small bone to glow—the same kind that I had stolen from the Underworld.

"I think it works!" Mal screamed beside me as he fights off an impossible wall of Deadwalkers.

I saw more allies join our side, with Ash leading them, but we are still vastly outnumbered—only a dozen against thousands. "It worked, Lynne!" Mal shouts again, but I could barely hear him over the deafening screams of our people being slaughtered.

"Focus!" Bory's voice rang out, and I fired another arrow towards Zeus, aiming for a different bone. One by one, I hit each glowing bone with all of my might. "I think you need to hit every single one..." Bory's words trailed off as he is cut down by a swarm of Deadwalkers.

Gritting my teeth in determination, I continued to fire and fire, knowing that the fate of our world rests on this one desperate attempt. But the screams and deaths around me only grew louder, and I was forced to shut them out as I solely focused on Zeus. If he completed his conjuring, we were all doomed. "This is going to take forever," I muttered through clenched teeth.

"It's our only chance," Mal replied, grunting as a Deadwalker nearly bites him.

With renewed determination, I unleashed arrow after arrow at Zeus, each one hitting a bone and causing it to glow. It felt like an eternity, but finally, every bone on his massive body was aglow.

"Now what?!" Jamie cried out beside me.

"Now...we hope and pray our idea was good at last," I said, sweat dripping down my face as I continue to hold my bow steady.

But as I fired with all my might, a laughter emerged and I noticed Thanatos. The God of Death.

My heartbeat sped up. "Thanatos," I said, firing another arrow, "can you help us?"

"Help you?" he laughed and walked around me, only to stand in between me and Zeus. "I always hated your spoiled ass, bitch. I'm going to stop you."

"Why?"

Mal cried out and Jamie ran up to him.

"Jamie!" I said, but she was gone. "Bory, please watch over her."

"Lynne..."

Black liquid splattered on the ground where I had just been standing, and I felt my heart race in fear.

I dodged another attack and desperately tried to think of a plan while I shot a lightning arrow at Thanatos, which he easily dodged.

Shit. I couldn't let Thanatos kill me, but I also couldn't let Zeus finish his conjuring.

But how?

Before I could wrap my head around it, a powerful force knocked me off balance and sent me flying to the ground.

I groaned as I struggled to get up, only to find myself face-to-face with Thanatos.

I fucking refused to let him defeat me. With determination and a fierce sense of purpose, I got up and pointed my finger at him once again.

"You dare defy me?" he snarled, his eyes blazing with fury.

"I do," I replied firmly, my voice steady despite the trembling in my hands. "I'm immortal. You can't kill me."

Thanatos laughed mockingly. "You think you can stop me? I don't intend to kill you, stupid girl. I'll buy time for Zeus to absorb all the magic in all three worlds and bring about a new order. And we will be there to help create a better one without humans, just gods."

My heart skipped a beat.

And Thanatos raised his hands, firing burning hot liquid at me. I could barely dodge. I fired another arrow, but Thanatos quickly stepped away, smirking.

"Enough playing around," Thanatos growled as he raised his hand again for another attack. I spun around, but he fired again. When Mal cried out in pain, I made a mistake. I looked and Thanatos hit me.

Pain seared through my chest as I fell to the ground, clutching at the wound. I could feel my blood soaking through my clothes and a sense of panic flooded over me.

"Lynne!" Jamie cried out, rushing to my side. "Are you okay?"

"I'll be fine," I grunted through gritted teeth, trying to push myself up. But the pain was too much and my vision blurred.

"Stay down," Bory said firmly, frantically standing on Jamie's shoulder.

"No," I protested weakly. "I have to stop Thanatos."

"You can't do anything in your current state," Bory argued. "But we will handle it."

I reluctantly nodded, knowing that they were right. I needed Mal to heal me before I could face Thanatos again.

But before I could crawl to Mal, an unexpected figure appeared behind Thanatos—and my heart froze.

"Step away from her," Rio's voice was calm yet utterly lethal as he stood between me and Thanatos.

CHAPTER THIRTY-SIX
RIO

The wind whipped strands of my hair across my face, stinging my eyes as I squared off against Thanatos. His dark robes billowed around him like a storm cloud, his shadowed face twisted into a sneer.

"Give up, Zagrios," he taunted, his voice dripping with disdain. "You may overcome me, but before then, Zeus will be back, and you cannot defeat him."

I gritted my teeth, my anger flaring at his arrogance. My breath came in quick puffs, fogging the air in the chill night. As we stared each other down, I glimpsed Jamie helping Aria limp to Mal out of the corner of my eye. Their pain fueled my determination; I couldn't let Thanatos win.

"Watch me," I spat.

My muscles tensed as I gathered the power of my shadow magic, drawing it close to my chest like a protective shield. My heart throbbed with a dangerous excitement as I prepared to unleash it on Thanatos, the dark tendrils seeping into every crevice of my being. With a fierce roar, I directed the shadows from my fingertips towards him, the sharp flicks slicing through the air like deadly whips.

He narrowly dodged the flick, and I felt a charge brush past my cheek. Adrenaline coursed through my body, heightening my senses.

"Is that all you've got?" I taunted, grinning at him. It might have been foolish to provoke him, but I couldn't resist the urge.

"Far from it," Thanatos replied, smirking. He raised his hands, summoning a torrent of black ink that raced towards me. I barely countered with a gust of shadows, propelling myself out of harm's way.

As we continued to exchange blows, I noticed Aria watching from a safe distance while Mal was healing her, her eyes darting between us. I could tell she was worried about me, but I couldn't let that distract me from the fight.

Focus. I had to fucking focus.

But Thanatos' attacks grew more powerful and precise, while my own defenses weakened. A sharp pain shot through my arm as one of his spells grazed me, leaving a searing burn.

"You're slipping, Zagrios," Thanatos taunted, sensing my growing fatigue. "It shows you spent too many years in the human realm, Shadow King."

"Shut up," I snapped, my frustration mounting. I knew my skills were rusty, but against him, they were more than enough.

"Make me," he challenged, his eyes gleaming with mischief. "Or should I go fuck your wife? I longed to get that face crying for me for eons."

In that moment, something inside me snapped. A bestial fury surged through my veins, fueling my every move as I unleashed a savage wave of dark shadow tendrils at him. They slithered and twisted with malicious intent, thrice the size of him and seemingly unstoppable in their ferocity. His eyes widened in shock as he realized the true extent of my power, his body tensing as he braced for impact. My heart raced with primal adrenaline as I fought for control, refusing to give into the savage urges that threatened to consume me. But as I felt myself growing stronger with each passing moment, I couldn't hold back any longer. With a feral roar that echoed through the air, I launched myself at him.

His eyes widened with shock as the shadows entwined around his body, binding him.

"Listen to me, Thanatos." I bared my teeth, channeling all of my rage into the shadows that pulsated under my fingertips. The pressure I exerted on him was suffocating, every nerve in my hand trembling with the force as I held it. One wrong move and he would crumble to dust, a mere speck in the wake of my power. "You should never have dared to challenge me." My heart thundered in my chest, but my words were steady and confident, even as my insides churned with uncertainty, yearned to check on Aria and Jamie.

"Arrogant fool, it's better to start over. This world and all its inhabitants are a waste of creation," he spat, struggling against my magic. But I could see the fear lurking behind his eyes, and it fueled my power. I tightened the shadows' grip on him, forcing him to his knees.

"Remember this moment," I whispered, my voice cold and deadly. "Remember that you were brought down by Zagrios, the Shadow King. And remember what brought death upon you. Talking bad about his wife." My breath hitched as I stared down at him.

"Release me!" Thanatos snarled, his voice dripping with venom as he realized I would make him suffer. But I held my ground, relishing in his agony. I would make him pay for what he did, and he knew it. Sometimes, I still reveled in others pain, a malevolent grin spreading across my face.

"Too late for that," I said, my eyes locked onto his.

"Make him hurt," Aria's voice came up next to me. I didn't

need to look to see she was fine. "Make this fucking bastard suffer."

"Oh, darling, I like when you're talking dirty."

I closed my eyes and allowed the shadows to envelop me, a dark cloak that had become ingrained in my very being. With a wicked grin, I plunged into his mind, delving deep into his memories and fears. A cruel satisfaction filled me as I twisted his thoughts and emotions, creating a labyrinth of terror and despair within him. His screams were like music to my ears, a symphony of agony that I conducted with precision. He begged for mercy, but I only laughed, relishing in the searing pain that emanated from him.

"You thought you could destroy us," I spat, my voice laced with hatred. "But now you will suffer for eternity."

I unleashed the full force of my power upon him, filling his mind with nightmarish visions and torturous illusions. His body writhed in agony as he screamed and thrashed against the shadows that bound him. "Enjoy your first thousand years as a shadow slave, Thanatos. I can't kill you, but I can make you pay."

Aria's slender fingers linked with mine, her powers pulsing and enhancing my own.

We were like opposites, constantly at odds - day and night, light and darkness. If angry, we were an unstoppable force of chaos and destruction. And fuck, were we angry.

As soon as I spoke the incantation, "Skut atea a," Thanatos's body changed.

His skin grew cold and clammy, his muscles tensed as if in pain, and darkness engulfed him—swallowing his form whole. His eyes widened with horror as he felt himself transforming against his will, but there was nothing he could do to stop it. The graveyard grew eerily silent save for the sound of his anguish-filled cries that echoed off the walls. A low, menacing growl rumbled through my chest as I watched my enemy twist and contort into a shadowy version of himself. His once-noble form now reduced to little more than a slave, a slave who would obey any command I gave him. I couldn't help but feel a twisted sense of satisfaction at seeing him like this—helpless and at my mercy.

Thanatos tried to resist, but it was futile. The shadow magic wrapped tighter around him, weaving itself into his very being until he was no longer recognizable as the God he once was. His features honed into a gray blur, and the anguish etched on his face was unmistakable as he emitted a piercing cry that sent chills down my spine. It was delightful... witnessing his torment in such vivid detail.

With a wave of my hand, I sent the new Shadowslave away. He disappeared in a puff of smoke, sent straight to Tartarus to serve the gods who ruled that realm. My heart raced with anticipation, knowing I had won this round—at least for now.

"I would marry you now if I hadn't already," Aria said next to me and I pulled her into a quick kiss. "Go kill that ugly beast in front of us. I got your back."

She nodded, faced Zeus and raised her hands, palms facing outwards, and concentrated with all her might. Two brilliant beams of light shot forth from her fingertips and struck that fucker head on. He stumbled a bit, his bones beginning to glow with an otherworldly power. It would take a while but we could make it. We could.

I whipped around to see Jamie's shocked expression as I summoned black tendrils to take down the Deadwalkers behind us. With my free hand, I pulled my daughter into a tight embrace, grateful for her safety amidst the chaos.

"Dad..." she whispered, her tiny frame of a body shaking under my grip.

"Baby girl, I'm so happy you're alive."

I held her tightly and gazed into her sparkling eyes, my heart overflowing with love and joy. Despite the chaos of fighting off the Deadwalkers, I couldn't help but smile as I saw she was safe and sound in my arms.

I pulled her into another hug, holding on tightly as if I never wanted to let go again. She buried her face in my chest, sobbing uncontrollably, and I felt a pang of guilt for not being there to protect her when the Deadwalkers attacked. For not being there when she grew up.

"It's okay, it's okay. We'll get through this," I reassured her, stroking her hair gently.

"But...mom..." she choked out between sobs.

I closed my eyes briefly and took a deep breath.

"She's strong, Cherry will last until we got this," I said fiercely and flicked my wrist, sending another shadow wave at the Deadwalkers—they were like little ants, crawling toward us and eager to get some fresh flesh.

"But first we need to get to safety," I said, glad to have fought off most of the Deadwalkers. "There are more coming and we need to help Aria."

I looked around at the destruction that surrounded us—a once beautiful city now reduced to rubble and fire. Bodies littered the streets and screams echoed in the distance. The sky was dark with ash and smoke.

"How?" Jamie said, and I felt so much love when I looked at her eyes, her father's eyes.

"I'm going to burst everything I've got into that fucker. This means you need to seek shelter.

"No," she said, and I was surprised at the ferocity of her voice. This somehow reminded me of myself.

I huffed out a surprise laugh. "What, no?" The girl just saw what I could do, and she held her chin so high I was about to bow.

"I didn't come all this way just to hide," she declared boldly. "I left my mother behind to protect herself while I came here to fight."

And that's when my heart filled with such pride that I believed her. Yes, she was ready to fight. She can do it.

"Okay, I'll help Aria and you watch over the Deadwalkers and keep Mal safe?" I nodded at him in the back of the cemetery, fighting against Deadwalkers right behind the entrance.

Jamie nodded, and I put a kiss on her cheek, saying, "I'm so proud of you. I'm sorry I wasn't there for you."

"I'm sorry I hated you."

I chuckled, relieved that she was speaking in the past tense. I turned to face my wife, our legs touching as we stood side by side. Her hand gently rested on my thigh, a reassuring reminder we were in this together. She urged me to give it my all, her brow glistening with sweat as she struggled to lift every bone off the ground. The once muscular body now resembled a dalmatian, covered in hundreds of white spots that glimmered under the dim lighting. I saw him rise to one foot, signaling his final move, and my heart pounded against my chest. He was not just any god; he was the Bone God - stronger than Zeus himself and the most powerful being in all three realms.

"We won't make it," Aria whispered, her hand trembling.

I shot tendrils of smoke at him, trying to destroy the bones as she turned back.

"No," I said. "But we will give it our all. We will try until we can't anymore."

"I love you," she said.

"I love you, too, darling."

CHAPTER THIRTY-SEVEN
ARIA

As we stood beneath the towering Bone God, I felt my legs trembling under my magic's immense weight.

My body strained, and I tried to keep on channeling, but my concentration wavered. Some bones creaked above us, a deafening sound that only added to my sense of fear and helplessness.

Rio's knuckles turned white as she clenched his teeth. "Come on, keep holding up."

We were flinging bursts of dark and light sorcery as if it were the rhythm of a staccato symphony. The air crackled with energy as our powers clashed. I felt like fainting any moment but pushed through it.

"More Deadwalkers," Jamie said behind us.

"You got this," Rio said and notices his hoarse voice.

The sound of Jamie's shots rang loud in my ears while Rio summoned massive tendrils from his hands and hurled them towards Zeus, the god-like figure before us. Each strike made Zeus' bones glow brighter, but it seemed like there were endless layers to break through.

Despite my best efforts, I couldn't maintain control over my magic.The pain in my arms was excruciating, causing my hand to spasm and lose its grip. But thank the gods, Rio's hold on me remained strong and steady.

"Should I go get Mal?"

"No, he can't help me with magic exhaustion." My eyelids drooped, and every muscle in my body ached. I wanted nothing more than to collapse into bed and sleep for days, but I knew that was not an option. The looming deadline hung over me like a dark cloud and I forced myself to stay awake, determined to finish—no matter what it took.

Rio grabbed me by the wrist, saying, "Come on. We need to get closer."

I nodded, and with fierce roars on our lips; we ran towards Zeus.

Bolts of white and black electricity burst from our fingertips, striking his powerful legs and leaving deep cracks in their wake. Chunks of bone crashed to the ground as we continued our attack, but as we pushed forward, it became clear this fight was far from over.

One massive shadowy whip sliced through the thick bones of The Bone God's massive legs, but the creature barely seemed to flinch. Rio's muscles strained as he continued to hack away, his face contorted in determination and fear. I joined in, my lightning arrows clashing against its tough exterior.

The skeletal creature let out a thunderous roar that shook the ground beneath us. Its hollow sockets burned with malice as it towered over us, its massive form covered in ancient markings.

"Oh, my fucking... god," Jamie stammered behind us, her voice trembling with fear.

I couldn't believe what I was seeing, too. This creature was unlike anything I had ever encountered before. It was bigger than anything I'd known.

"We need to keep fighting," Rio panted, his hands shaking now too. "There's no telling what this thing is capable of."

He was right. We couldn't afford to back down now. All our lives were on the line.

With gritted teeth and a fierce glint in his eyes, Rio extended his arms and thick, writhing waves of shadows shot forth from his hands, dark energy swirling around him. I cried and sent a giant cone of light towards Zeus. But even as we poured our combined powers into the attack, it seemed to have little effect on the indomitable creature before us. Some more bones glowed, though.

"We're not enough, Rio," I shouted over the chaos.

As we huddled together, frantically trying to come up with a plan, the massive Bone God let out another deafening roar. It swung its massive arm towards us. Rio and I narrowly dodged the shock wave, but Jamie was surprised. The force of impact sent her flying like a rag-doll, her body crashing onto the ground with a sickening thud.

"Jamie!" I cried out, rushing towards her as Rio continued to hold off the Bone God's attacks.

I checked for any injuries, but thankfully she seemed to be just winded from the impact.

"Aria," Rio growled.

"Right back," I shouted and helped her up to her feet and we both turned towards Rio, who was now standing in front of us protectively.

A sudden realization hit me, and I shouted over to Rio, "Focus on the markings on its body!"

He nodded, his eyes gleaming with determination as he signaled for us to huddle together.

But deep down, as we stood amidst the carnage and ruin, I

couldn't help but feel that our efforts had been in vain. The Bone God was too powerful, and we were nothing more than two rusted gods standing against a force beyond our comprehension. We fought against him and when Rio had struck all the markings but one, I realized that last one was at the top of his head—seemingly miles away from us.

Every time Rio attempted to reach it with his shadow magic, he missed. We were too far away.

"I need to get up there; maybe I can climb him..." he suggested, but I snatched his arm, trying to anchor him with me. I needed him; he couldn't leave.

Turning to confront the god, I declared with enthusiasm, "Over my dead body. We'll fly. Soothie and I can do it." I aimed another beam of light towards him and whistled for my loyal companion. Soothie couldn't be too far from me, especially with occasional bursts of fire emanating from behind the cemetery walls.

"No, you can't stop fighting him. You need to keep on shooting. Leave the markings to me. I'll fly," Rio said.

"You need to shoot at him. You can't stop," I said.

If Rio stopped, Zeus may walk again and we wouldn't live through that.

Amid our despair, Bory hopped from my shoulder, his eyes filled with determination.

"Aria, Rio, I'll fly and ram the dagger in him," he said, his voice trembling slightly as he held up a dagger he stole from my sheath.

"Wait, what are you doing?" I asked, my heart hammering in my chest as I looked at him. I could barely hold on to sending the lightning streaks towards Zeus.

"Buy you time. I bet destroying the markings will slow him down." Bory stood resolutely.

"I said no." I grabbed onto his arm, trying to pull him back, but he shook me off gently.

"This is my fight," he said firmly. "I've always known I'll be of use to you one day."

Tears welled up in my eyes as I watched him take a deep breath. "Bory, what do you mean? I would have been dead like a hundred times without you! You've always been useful. always useful. Bory—"

Rio's face was grim as well, but he nodded and stepped back, giving Bory the room he needed.

Behind us, wings flapped, and I shivered. No, he could not leave me as well. No. "Bory, I mean it."

I reached out for him, but he eluded me quicker than I've ever witnessed before.

"Sorry, Lynne, but we all have to fight to survive. You've been the best friend I could have wished for."

With a loud battle cry, Bory charged towards Soothie and as I let out a cry, he hopped onto the Sircha and both flew up to the sky.

And my heart broke.

"Focus on the markings!" Bory shouted to us.

"Believe in him," Rio said, taking my hand and aiming it at Zeus. I came back to my senses, and crying and shaking, I struck at the glowing bones in his body again. But even as we fought with everything we had, the Bone God was still too powerful for us to defeat.

I gasped as one of its massive hands came crashing down towards Soothie. He barely managed to dodge out of the way before it could crush him.

„NO!" I screamed as I saw its other hand glow with dark energy.

Without hesitation, Rio and I leaped forward just as a

powerful blast hit us head-on. The force sent us flying backwards and slammed us into a nearby tree. Pain shot through my body as I struggled to get up from the rubble. Slowly piecing myself together, I looked around frantically searching for Rio, Soothie and Bory.

Relief washed over me when I saw Rio lying a few feet away, groaning.

As I glanced at Soothie, I witnessed a tiny blue orb leaping onto the Bone God's head. And my stomach dropped into a void of emptiness.

Bory's dagger glinted menacingly in the dim moonlight as he struck with fierce determination. Just as my little best friend destroyed the last marking, and just when a glimmer of joy began to stir within me, a faint, hesitant smile creeping across my face—another explosion sent us hurtling to the ground, the earth quaking beneath us.

I wailed, a primal scream erupting from the depths of my being, while Rio held me tight. I screamed Bory's name into the chaos and through swirling mist and debris, I caught a glimpse of Soothie fleeing.

Panic surged through me as I desperately searched for Bory aboard him—only to find he wasn't there.

"Bory," I whispered as Rio helped me up again.

A torrent of tears streamed down my cheeks, each droplet a testament to the overwhelming sorrow engulfing me. Time itself seemed to grind to a halt and crumble into a pit of desolation.

My heart shattered into a million pieces as I watched Soothie dragging himself towards Bory's lifeless body. There he was. My best friend. My savior. My little brave hero. Form one second to the other he was nothing but a tiny blue ball lying a mere distance away from us and the Bone God.

There were no coherent thoughts, no words capable of expressing the pain gripping my soul. It was as if I was watching someone else's life. I knew what just had happened but I suddenly felt so numb.

There was so much pain.

I just couldn't breathe past it anymore.

Soothie extended one trembling wing over Bory's tiny body and he let out a mournful wail that pierced the darkness.

And that's when my legs gave out, the breath escaping my lungs as if they had been punctured straight through my flesh.

Rio held me up as I wept uncontrollably.

This couldn't be true.

It just couldn't be.

Everyone I loved died.

I was losing everyone. This can't—They had taken all from me.

My life.

Bory's life.

Any's life.

Everyone's life.

Then, something shifted inside of me. Through gritted teeth, I clawed desperately at Rio's skin, using his support to pull myself upright. Anguish surged through me like a raging river, fueling my screams of pure wrath. And that's when I unleashed it all—the fury, the pain, the sheer injustice of it all—I directed it at the Bone God, at Athena, at every deity who deemed themselves superior.

With a primal roar, I bellowed, "I will fucking kill you!"

„Shit," Rio cursed beside me, but his words felt distant, drowned out by the haze of my anguish.

With trembling hands, I thrust them forward, channeling every ounce of wrath into blinding white blasts and shot all of my power at the Bone God.

The blast tore through my very soul, but I pushed through the searing pain, fueled by an unyielding determination to avenge the loss of my beloved friends.

I might have continued doing this until my dying breath, but in the midst of the chaos, a deafening roar suddenly echoed through the carnage.

The very earth shook in terror beneath the unrelenting onslaught of thundering hooves and the clashing of weapons echoed like a cacophony of death. But even in my terror, my fear, my sorrow—I tilted my head and behold the sight before me.

"Rio," I gasped, my voice trembling. "Look."

There was an army coming to our aid and right behind us two queens rode at the forefront. One with fiery red hair that billowed behind her like a banner of war, the other with skin as white as bleached bone—leading an unstoppable army of gods from Olympia.

As soon as I saw their silhouettes on the horizon, my heart dared to feel something like relief. They galloped towards our enemy, weapons raised and determination etched on their faces.

"NOW!" the Blood Queen's voice rang out like thunder, and a symphony of power wove through the air in response.

"Everyone focuses on him!" The Bone Queen's cried out.

Behind them surged a host of familiar faces—Iris, Hecate, Hermes, even my father—each wielding their power in unison. They came to help us. They came.

Rio grabbed my hand and pulled me closer to the fray, our joined hands reaching out towards Zeus once more. I kept my power concentrated on him and just like that—an explosive burst of raw energy erupted from within us, surging forth, striking the Bone God with an unparalleled force. Rio and I shared a glance, our hope renewed as we saw everyone fighting fiercely by our side.

"Let's finish this monster," I said, my fingers tightening around Rios.

"Agreed," Rio replied.

I gritted my teeth as we channeled every ounce of our strength into the joined attack, feeling the searing heat of Rio's own power intertwining with mine.

A cacophony of divine forces collided in a dazzling display of light and raw energy, engulfing us in an awe-inspiring spectacle. We stood amidst a mass of powerful gods unleashing their attacks upon the colossal figure before us. The intensity was blinding— forcing me to squint as I struggled to keep my footing.

But with one final, united effort, we struck the Bone God with the force of a thousand suns, causing him to shatter into countless fragments. As his bones rained down upon the battlefield like a macabre storm, a deafening silence fell over us all.

We did it.

A mixture of relief and triumph washed over me.

The deafening silence was almost suffocating.

My heart raced with adrenaline, my breaths coming in short gasps as I tried to make sense of what had just happened.

But before I could even begin to comprehend it all, Rio's voice shattered the silence.

"It's done, love," he murmured, his breaths uneven with both weariness and elation.

I turned to him, gazing into his blue eyes through my own swollen and tear-filled ones.

„I-is it truly... over?" I whispered, my voice quivering with disbelief.

I just couldn't bring myself to fully embrace the moment,

fearing that it might be snatched away from me once more. What if this was just another fleeting dream? Another illusion?

"Yes," Rio replied softly, his gaze sweeping across the remnants of our foe as my legs gave way once more. He scooped me up in a swift move. "We did it. You did it."

As the tears streamed down my face, Rio held me tightly. I crashed against his chest, finally releasing all the pain.

CHAPTER THIRTY-EIGHT
ARIA

Think of life as a big, intricate tapestry where joy and sorrow mix.

Losing is like the falling leaves in autumn, each one a memory or experience gently drifting away. It's part of the cycle, making room for new.

And it hurts.

Life fucking hurts.

CHAPTER THIRTY-NINE
RIO

After the battle, we tried to bring everyone back, but Aria could only revive those who died naturally, without magic. If touched by a Deathwalker, it meant death for lesser gods and humans alike. Of course, we tried desperately to bring Bory back, too, but when his heart gave out, he disappeared from our world. The Bone Queen had made him, and since he wasn't born in either world, Aria couldn't bring him back even if she wished with all her heart

So, we decided to give it a few weeks to let the wounds heal a bit. During that time, Aria kept to herself, only talking to me, and even then, her words were brief and curt. The sweet sparkle in her eyes all gone.

Soothie slept on the balcony beside us, crying as much as Aria.

Hecate was there, taking care of them; she already knew what would happen, who died, and what she needed to say to ease their hearts even a bit.

I, along with Mal and a few other gods, took care of restoring earth.

Without Any, we couldn't fix their memories anymore, but

we made them believe that a major environmental disaster had struck Earth. We helped them rebuild, letting them handle a part of it themselves. I showed Cherry and Jamie how to get back on their feet, giving them a couple of pomegranate seeds—just in case.

Now it was easier for me to wander between worlds since there was no Athena anymore. However, it was crucial that we soon regulated our coexistence, creating new rules for how the gods treated each other, how we organized ourselves.

My sisters and I restored balance in the Underworld, closing the gates with the Book of Silva so that souls could find their redemption normally again. I immediately took the book away from them after—better safe than sorry. Helen stored it in Olympia.

What was harder, though, was going back to my wife in the evening and seeing her broken heart. But there was nothing I wanted more than to hold her in my arms. We slept entwined, and the days passed until I felt she was strong enough to meet with the gods again. The ball was in our court since the world still stood, thanks to us, and so I invited everyone to the Underworld.

It was time to talk.

TAKING A SHAKY BREATH, I saw the final rays of light bolt from the castle's grand hall, devoured by the shadows that were keen to reclaim their territory. The cold from the massive, stone-filled rooms seeped into my bones as I stood next to Aria on the balcony outside our room.

The air held the scent of burning cedarwood from the

hearths, a faint reminder that warmth still existed in this place despite the shadows that clung to its corners.

"Easy there, Soothie," Aria whispered tenderly, her hand caressing the dragon that had become more phantom than beast since Bory's death.

Drawing a deep breath, my hands found the soft fabric of the scarf I'd been clutching—a weave of blue sprinkled with golden threads, like the night sky captured in cloth. It fit perfectly with her golden dress. As I draped it over her shoulders, she leaned back into me.

"You're sure you're ready for this?" My lips brushed against her ear.

She tilted her head up, her hollow eyes meeting mine, glistening with an unshed storm. "I have to be," she said, her voice steady even as it betrayed the tremors of her inner turmoil. "The gods are on their way, and we can't send them home again."

"Of course we can."

"Don't be ridiculous. I may be hurt, but I'm not fragile."

"Okay fine, but if you need help, just say the word and I'll get you out of there."

She rolled her eyes at my overprotectiveness, refusing to give me a full answer.

Our shoes echoed in unison as we strode down the marble hallway.

Ahead, the door to the throne room loomed, and we approached with determined strides.

Hecate fell into step alongside us. And Mal, ever the pillar of strength, moved with a grace that belied his warrior's build, his keen eyes scanning the corridor with an alertness that spoke volumes of his protective instincts. I convinced him to join me as my advisor, knowing it wouldn't fully ease his pain over Any's passing. However, he was a valuable asset and I couldn't afford to let him slip away and return to my sister's court. And Aria needed her friends. Losing Bory shattered her. He was not only her best friend but also her anchor in the darkest of times. When I couldn't be by her side, Bory was there.

Anyone and anything that made her smile had to be around.

As we approached the grand doors of the throne room, I felt Aria's resolve bolster my own.

And with a shared look that conveyed our unbreakable bond, we entered the throne room.

It was a chessboard, and we were all players, whether we acknowledged it or not. The air was thick with the scent of wine. The mighty gods sprawled upon their gilded seats, radiating an unspoken dominance that seemed to reverberate through every inch of the black marble floor. Aria's fingers dug into mine with a fierce intensity, and I knew she felt it too—the weight of countless eons pressing down upon us and the overwhelming might of these assholes.

We walked confidently towards my shadow throne, our heads held high with pride as the clamor rose around us like the tide. Courtiers clinked glasses. The gods told tales of the battle, and during it all, the Bone Queen stared at us. Mel's green eyes, sharp and calculating, followed our progress with interest that bordered on hunger.

"Did you forget to tell me something?" Aria's voice was a low murmur, barely audible above the din.

I followed her gaze across the vaulted room, where Ash leaned against one of a dozen marble columns. His eyes were veiled, but the corners of his lip quirked upwards in response to something unseen. My attention shifted, and I caught Hecate's glance—once, twice, thrice.

Her smiles were fleeting, secretive, meant for him alone.

"Interesting," I muttered under my breath, storing away the oddity for later contemplation.

"I wouldn't have thought she was his type," Aria responded.

"You mean all this wisdom and words?"

"Exactly."

"Ah, the royal minds at work," chuckled a voice rich with mirth. "Ever so busy, even amidst a feast."

I looked at Mac and there it was, the Blood Queen's sardonic grin framed by a crimson veil. Oh, she was always a pain in the ass. She raised a goblet in mock salute before turning back to her courtiers, who fawned over her every word like moths to a flame.

"Zagrios, Aria," Mel's voice cut through the cacophony, clear and commanding. "Join us. There is much to discuss, and time waits for no one—not even for you."

Without giving my sister's response a second thought, I smiled and continued on our way up to the dais. Aria waited for me to take the throne, but I gestured for her to sit instead. Everyone should know she was my queen. Their queen.

The shadows that made up my throne seemed to dance with joy as she took her seat. A hushed whisper rippled through the hall, and I beamed with pride as I stood next to her, placing a hand on her shoulder.

Hecate remained in our midst, still sharing smiles with Ash. And while I watched our guests under us, Mal positioned himself behind Aria.

The gods' eyes—some as deep as the ocean's abyss, others flickering with the fires of creation—were all fixed upon us. They sat on long , dark tables, each of which had rich food and wine on it. To our sides stood soldiers of all courts and kingdoms and some courtiers enjoyed being mere spectators. Some gods always needed someone to cheer at them.

I stared at every face, nodding at some and hesitating as I saw Erebus, or Cyril. Whatever he likes to call himself nowadays. However, Aria's father didn't sit with the Blood Queen—not anymore—since she dumped his fucking ass.

But he still had the nerve to come here.

I balled my fingers into fists. That fucking traitor.

"Later," Aria whispered and I gripped her shoulder tightly.

"Let the discussions begin," I proclaimed, my voice ringing out.

The Bone Queen tilted her head, an elegant spire of ivory amidst her stoic warriors, while the Blood Queen, draped in crimson silks, lounged upon her seat with the ease of someone who had commanded legions.

"Deities of our realm, let's talk plainly," I began. "I propose democracy—a council where each of us, deities of great power, sits as equals. No single ruler lording overall, but a collective, ensuring fairness and balance."

A murmur rippled through the assembly like a stone cast into still waters, causing even the shadows to stir. Aria glanced up at me and I smiled back at her. Of course, everyone thought I wanted to claim ruler of all realms now, but I had no interest in this. I had a kingdom, and that's enough to rule properly for me.

"Democracy?" Helen mused, her laughter rich as fertile soil. "You speak of human methods for immortal beings?"

"Even immortals can learn from mortals," I countered, feeling Aria's hand touch mine in silent support.

"Meetings once a month," Aria pressed on, "to discuss the matters that shape our realms. Every voice heard, every concern weighed."

"An interesting notion," the Bone Queen intoned, her skeletal fingers tapping against her armrest. "Yet how do you ensure the lesser gods will not be trampled by the greater? Or us by you and your *wife*?"

I couldn't ignore the frosty look she threw Aria's way.

Oh, she must be longing for the days when she gathered

bones for her. Seeing the bones protruding from her skin now, she must miss the magic to regain her beauty. What a shame. Some people truly reflect what lies within.

"By giving them an equal seat at the table," I answered, my resolve hardening like cooled lava. "Everyone's insight is invaluable. It is the essence of our new order."

"Chaos would ensue," the Bone Queen warned, her gaze sharp enough to draw blood. "You underestimate the hunger for power."

"Then let us temper that hunger with unity," I said, locking eyes with each deity in turn. "Let us show we can evolve beyond conquest and tyranny. Can we dare to dream of such a world?"

"Can we dare not to?" Aria said, her voice a rallying cry that seemed to ignite a spark in the hearts of those present.

There was another murmur, and I saw the gods talking to each other.

"They'll say yes," Hecate said behind us. "Don't worry."

I could feel the tension in the air.

Some of the gods looked at us with hopeful eyes, eager for change and progress. Others glared at us with suspicion and fear, not wanting to give up their power. At first, many were skeptical and dismissive. But as they delved deeper into the benefits and fairness of this new system, they could see the wheels turning in the minds of the deities. One by one, they nodded in agreement, and soon enough, the majority had been won over.

"Tonight, we will agree to bring balance and fairness to our realm," I declared. "Each of us will contribute a drop of blood into this jug, and Aria will use it to give life to our collective decision."

A servant walked among the rows of tables, offering the jug to each deity.

Apollo, always a proponent of equality, was one of the first to support the idea. He calmly took a dagger and pricked his finger, allowing three drops of blood to fall into the jug.

But not all agreed.

Agerion's red eyes glared fiercely as he slammed his fist on the table, rattling the delicate goblets and causing Macaria to raise an eyebrow.

"Democracy is a foolish notion," he roared, slamming down his mug of ale. "Order can only be maintained by a powerful ruler."

But Aria and I stood united, our voices ringing out confidently as we argued for a democratic system. The council was split, with heated debates raging between those in favor and those against it. But slowly, with the help of my logical arguments and Aria's unwavering support, we swayed the majority towards our side. It was the only solution.

With each god or goddess adding their contribution of blood to the jug, the tension in the room dissipated and was replaced with a sense of unity and hope for our future together. And as I turned to see Agerion's expression soften ever so slightly, I knew we had made the right decision.

"So be it," Mel said and held her bleeding finger in the jug.

We observed as the other gods also made their contributions, and when everyone lifted their goblets, we joined in and raised ours to make a toast.

"To the council and democracy," I said, and everyone chimed in.

"Then how about we cast our first vote?" I said and held my breath, knowing what was to come, feeling the sharp edge of betrayal like a thorn in my side.

"A traitor walks amongst us," Aria said, her gaze sweeping across the silent deities, each one poised like statues carved from the essence of the earth. "My father, Erebos, had conspired with Athena to destroy our worlds, the very reason we had to fight in such a hard battle."

A murmur rippled through the hall, each god and goddess exchanging furtive glances, the tension palpable. I could almost taste the bitter tang of suspicion in the air.

"How can this be?" Apollo questioned, his harp forgotten in his hands, the strings silent.

"Proof has been laid bare before us," I continued, my voice steely, unwavering. "Evidence of their plot to sow destruction, to end the balance we strive to uphold."

"Such treachery cannot go unpunished," Mac stated, rising from her throne, the embodiment of regal wrath.

"Indeed," Helen agreed, her gaze now an impenetrable storm. "But first, we must understand the full scope of Erebos' intentions."

"His intentions matter not," I said, clenching my fists at my sides. "The damage he sought to inflict is all that matters." The sting of betrayal burned within me, a fire that no amount of divine intervention could quell.

"Let us vote then," Mel's voice boomed, her eyes flickering with the lightning of decision. "All in favor of sentencing Erebos to Tartarus for his crimes and betrayal, say 'aye'."

"*Aye*," the chorus rang out, a storm surge that echoed through the marbled halls of my castle.

"Opposed?" Aria said and my gaze swept across the assembly, but there was only silence, a heavy blanket smothering any dissent.

I signaled to the guards and observed Erebos as he attempted to resist them.

However, when a few gods stood up, facing him with their formidable powers, he fell silent.

He allowed my guards to handcuff him with silver shackles, ready to inhibit any of his abilities.

But when my eyes met his, I searched for some semblance of remorse and found none.

Only the cold reflection of ambition gone awry.

"Any last words, Erebos or shall I call you Cyril now?" I asked, my tone hard and unforgiving.

His lips curled into a smirk, his gaze defiant even in the face of certain defeat. "Even the darkest night will end and the sun will rise," he replied, his words cryptic and taunting.

"Oh, please." I heard Hecate scoff behind me. "Leave the cryptic sentences to me, jerk."

At that, he was startled for a brief moment, realizing that his daughter was alive.

He stopped dead in his tracks, his gaze wide-eyed as he took in Aria and Hecate. He shook his head, but when I nodded just once, my guards pushed him out, and Hecate took a deep breath.

"He's never been bright, why try now," she said, but I could see her hands shaking.

Aria's other hand slid into hers, and I caught a glimpse of her eyes shimmering in the dim candle light.

"It had to be done," I whispered, my thumb brushing over the back of Aria's hand in a small comfort.

"I know," she murmured back. "But why does knowing it was right not ease the weight?"

"Because your heart is pure," I said. "And purity feels the cut of betrayal deeply."

"Zagrios, Aria," Apollo's voice thundered across the expanse, echoing off the columns that stretched toward eternity. "Your valor has not gone unnoticed. You've saved not only Olympia, but all realms from the brink of chaos. What reward would you claim for such heroism?"

I glanced at Aria, her profile etched with the soft light now. I gave her hand a reassuring squeeze, silent permission to voice her yearning that fluttered in her chest like a caged sparrow eager for the sky.

"Thank you, Apollo," she said, standing up. Her voice was steady despite the tempest of emotions whirling within. "There is but one thing that I desire."

My heart hammered against my ribcage, each beat a drumroll to the words poised on her lips.

"Name it, sister," Hecate encouraged, her eyes reflecting the wisdom of ages, and perhaps a knowing glint that suggested she already expected her plea.

I took a breath, sensing Aria's anticipation matching my own. "I want to utilize the final fragment of the Omphalo Stone. It was supposed to be completely destroyed, but like a miracle, one tiny piece survived," she said, the words rushing out, "I want to use it to live one life with Rio. As a human."

A murmur rippled through the hall, like wind whispering through leaves. Aria turned to me, her eyes wide with shock and something deeper, more vulnerable.

"Yes," I interrupted, my voice fierce, as fierce as the love that burned within me for this woman—this goddes—who had stood by me through trials that would have broken lesser beings. "Yes, we do wish to use the last piece of the Omphalo Stone. I want to feel the sun on my skin, the age in my bones, the precious weight of years passing. With her. Just once."

Her fingers curled tighter around mine, the divine strength in them belying the tremor that ran through her touch.

"But to be mortal means pain, loss," Mel said.

"Life," Aria interjected, her eyes still locked onto mine. "It means life. A life that is raw and real—one we can share, truly share, without someone having us end it before we can enjoy it."

"Is this your heart's deepest wish?" Apollo asked.

"It is," I affirmed, my resolve steeling. "More than power,

more than eternal youth, we crave the mundane miracles of mortality. To wake beside my wife each morning, to grow old together, to learn what it means to live and love as humans do."

"And if your paths diverge, if human frailty leads you astray? What if your life won't be as happy as you wish for it now?" the Mac said, her voice laced with curiosity.

"Then let it be so," I whispered, staring into Aria's green eyes. "For a single lifetime with you is worth an eternity apart."

"Very well," Mel decreed, her voice resonating with the finality of fate itself. "If that is your shared desire, then let the us seal your bond to humanity."

As the gods murmured their assent, a golden warmth enveloped us, the blood in my grasp pulsing with ancient power. I looked at Aria, her face alight with love and fear, hope and sorrow—a tapestry of emotions.

And in that moment the Blood Queen stood up, saying, "There's just one more thing I have to do before you go."

She flipped her wrist and Bory materialized in front of Aria and it took her two split seconds to realize her friend was back.

She crashed to her knees while hugging her little bear and whispering a soft *thank you.*

"Bory, you're... you're okay..." she croaked, and I nodded proudly to my sister, meeting a faint smile.

I never saw her doing something nice. There's always time for change, isn't it? She grinned back as if to say there's always time for a second chance.

Bory's tiny arms hold on to her stomach as she hugged. "Lynne, I'm so happy you're alive!"

She laughed through her tears. "That I'm alive? You were dead!"

She pushed him away from her, checking every inch of his body.

"Thank you so much," my wife whispered once more, smiling as she hadn't done for days.

"Thank *you* for saving the worlds," Mel said, and a tear slid down my wife's cheek.

"Thank you for creating him again." I said. "This means the world to us."

And in that moment, everything felt right again.

WE PARTIED with the gods all night long and the next day, hand in hand, hearts entwined, we went, into a future where gods walked as mortals, where love was the greatest adventure, and where every fleeting moment was a treasure beyond compare.

CHAPTER FORTY
ARIA, NOW

I rush into the classroom, making a beeline for my usual seat.

In frustration, I fling my school bag onto the cold marble floor.

Tina is already sitting in her spot, her eyes fixed on me. It's almost as if she has never seen me before, taking in my short uniform skirt and neatly tucked in white shirt. I give her a puzzled look, wondering what's going on with her. She simply shrugs in response, the rays of the setting sun streaming through the large Victorian windows casting a warm glow on her red hair as she smirks at me. It's really getting on my nerves how she's constantly asking me about Any's favorite things because she's going on a date with him—my brother.

She seems nice though, so why not.

"Good morning," Mr. Callaghan says, leaving the door open behind him, much to my amazement. I glance at the door and realize a shadow behind the gap. Someone is waiting outside. Did we have an expert lecture today? Have I missed something?

"I heard we're getting a new student," Tina whispers.

Mr. Callaghan puts his bag on the table, runs his hands

through his hair, and smooths out his suit. "Yes, indeed, we have a new student." Mr. Callaghan nods towards the doorway as a tall boy slowly walks in. My breath catches in my throat as I take in his appearance. He is older than us and undeniably attractive. And then he does the unthinkable—he looks directly at me.

With. Piercing. Blue eyes.

My cheeks flush with heat as I fight to maintain composure.

"Class, this is Rio Rènero. He won a scholarship to our school, and—"

Mr. Callaghan's words fade into background noise as Rio's gaze locks onto mine once again.

"God. He's so hot," Tina whispers excitedly beside me.

"Dibs," I blurt out, nervously tucking a blonde strand of hair behind my ear.

She is right — he is incredibly hot. Boiling.

And he is mine.

Undeniably mine.

HAVE YOU HEARD OF MY KICKSTARTER YET?

Thank you for reading all three books!

I love you from the bottom of my heart! In case you love fancy books, swag and discounted special editions as well, check out my new Kickstarter project! It features a special hardcover print run with all three books of The Bone Thief Saga.

The project is not live yet, but in case you'd like to get notified once it does, please follow me here.

WHAT IS KICKSTARTER YOU ASK?

Kickstarter is a funding platform for creative projects. It's is full of ambitious, innovative, and imaginative projects that are brought to life through the direct support of the costumers.

This way you have the chance to get affordable, very pretty special editions from many authors!

PRE-ORDER MY NEXT BOOK!

My next series is called: OF GILD AND BLOOD

It's a new adult dark academia for everyone who loved the romance between Cole and Phoebe in *Charmed* and the brutal academic setting in *Fourth Wing*! The story is set in a magical prison college for troubled (very naughty) magical beings. It's spicy, angsty and with a *who done it* to solve! More infos are to come, keep an eye to my Instagram or newsletter!

Pre-order OF BLOOD AND GUILD for a discount here!

THANK YOU FOR READING!

If you enjoyed The Bone Thief Saga, please leave a review/or rating on Amazon and/or Goodreads and don't forget to follow me on Amazon, Instagram and TikTok so you'll be notified for every new release, giveaway or preorder!

Want to be a beta reader for me?

I have a new series coming up, and in case you'd like to know more about it, you'll find a little description in the next chapter! And in case you'd like to become a beta reader for my new series, sign up and I'll contact you! You'll get a free paperback edition for each book you betaread for me <3 Here's the sign up link!

Want to Find Out How Mal and Any met?

Then Join my newsletter and get your free story now! Meet the Blood Queen at the Dance of the Dead! Just click on the picture:

ALSO BY HELEEN DAVIES

The Bone Thief Saga

The Bone Thief's Tale

The Bone Weaver's Curse

The Bone God's Wrath

SOMETIMES LOVE CHANGES EVERYTHING
The Bone God's Wrath
HELEEN DAVIES

ACKNOWLEDGMENTS

I still can't quite wrap my head around it but I actually wrote a whole trilogy! I'm drawn to writing about morally ambiguous characters, and Rio and Lynne fit that bill perfectly, at least in my eyes. Lynne's innocence and naivety provided such rich material to explore—watching her stumble and then pick herself back up again was a joy to write. After all, don't we all make mistakes? In the book, I wanted to emphasize that we're all capable of second chances, and sometimes even thirds. It's a reminder that people are often quick to judge, but sometimes it's best to reserve judgment and see how things play out.

This story has been a rollercoaster of emotions, and I couldn't have done it without a lot of help from some amazing people.

First off, let me just say that writing in a language that's not your native tongue is like trying to juggle flaming swords while riding a unicycle on a tightrope. Seriously, it's tough. So, to all the grammar police out there who might've chuckled at my linguistic acrobatics, thanks for keeping me on my toes. Your critiques were like boot camp for my writing skills.

But you know what truly made this journey worthwhile? The amazing Bookstagram Community and readers. From the very beginning, I was blessed with the support of so many wonderful people, and I'll always hold that close to my heart. It's one thing to root for the big names, but taking a chance on a small author like me? That means the world. To every reader, bookstagrammer, blogger etc. who shared my work, left reviews, or simply dropped a little heart emoji, you've made a huge impact on my life. And mark my words, as my name starts to gain traction, I'll never forget that you were there for me when I was just starting out.

And to my fellow writers who've been in the trenches with me, swapping war stories and offering pep talks when the going got tough, you're my heroes. Whether it was brainstorming plot twists over late-night chats or commiserating over rejection letters, I'm forever grateful for your camaraderie. Karen, thank you so much.

Of course, none of this would've been possible without my amazing family. From putting up with my late-night writing binges to cheering me on at every milestone, you've been my rock. Mom, Dad, sis—you're the real superheroes in this story.

Thanks a million to my beta readers, Karen, Gretchen, Saya and Sarah and Christina. So, to everyone who's been a part of this wild journey, whether you've been with me from the beginning or just stumbled upon this book today, thank you. Your support means the world to me, and I couldn't have done it without you. Here's to many more adventures together!

Love

Heleen

About the Author

Heleen Davies is a German and History teacher with a passion for writing and creating different worlds. She lives in Europe and writes Fantasy Romance, set in magical worlds with fierce heroines and broody, morally gray heroes you'll fall in love with. Heleen is a mother to a little girl and a Golden Retriever, lives in the mountains and usually sticks her nose in all kinds of books. Find her on TikTok, Instagram, Twitter and Facebook!

For updates about upcoming releases, giveaways and Kickstarter announcements, please visit her website and sign up for the newsletter to get access to free short stories within the Bone Thief Saga universe and upcoming novels!

9 783950 534610